CHICAGO MAY

CHICAGO MAY

By

Harry Duffin

Chicago May

Spiderwize
3 The Causeway
Kennoway
Kingdom of Fife
KY8 5JU
Scotland UK

www.spiderwize.com

This is a work of fiction. Names, characters and incidents are products of the author's imagination. Any resemblance to persons living or dead is entirely coincidental.

The views expressed in this work are solely those of the author and do not necessarily reflect the views of the publisher, and the publisher hereby disclaims any responsibility for them.

ISBN: 978-1-907294-61-7

For all the feisty women of the world;
past, present and future

To Helen,

With very best wishes,

Harry.

PROLOGUE

Her new life had started with a crime, but she had not expected to end her life as a criminal. On the steamship bound for America, when the other passengers had taken to their bunks with sea-sickness, she had clung to the rail, white-knuckled, reveling in the awesome black waves crashing against the prow, feeling the icy spray sting her cheeks till they were raw. On calmer days, when the ocean was a miraculous mirror, she had stood watching the shoals of fish, leaping out of the waves around the ship like playful children round their mother. Finally, she had marveled at the drifting seabirds effortlessly riding the wind, and felt the excitement rising in her chest knowing that she was nearing the New Land, her new home. On those balmy days she gazed out to the horizon and dreamed of her future. Of becoming a lady. Refined. Respected. Respectable. But today, under the prurient eyes of the crowded public gallery, she knew that she had failed.

With the court adjourned until the morning, when the defense would begin its futile presentation, May spent the night alone in her bleak cell preparing for her suicide. For despair had replaced her fiery defiance. The infamous, once proud, Irish beauty had only one defiant act left in her.

Her lawyer had been dismayed when she told him, at the end of the day, that she wouldn't speak in her own defense from the witness box. It was pointless, she said. The evidence couldn't be refuted. The judge had a personal grudge against her. Her case was hopeless, and she wouldn't give the sensation-seeking gallery the satisfaction of hearing her try to justify herself, or beg for mercy. May Sharpe was not a beggar. She was a thief and, not so long ago, back in her own country, she would have been hanged for what she had done. So be it.

CHAPTER ONE

May Sharpe was sixteen years and one month old, and she was all alone in the world. Except for Mick. Standing by the white, rust-flecked rail of the steamship, she gazed across the grey rolling waves towards the horizon, watching a tall, mysterious shape emerge from the early morning mist.

'What on earth d'you think that queer object is, Mick?'

The small, wiry ginger-haired terrier in her arms barked in reply.

'A statue, is it?' May said, pressing her cold cheek to Mick's warm coat. Despite the biting wind and sudden snow flurries in the air, she was determined to catch the first glimpse of her new home. 'Sure, it's mighty big.'

Below her the ship's engines slowed. Out of the snowy mist, which shrouded the approaching land, boats of all shapes and sizes were appearing and disappearing, busily crossing the sea lanes of the wide outer harbour. May watched, transfixed, as the towering, green statue became clearer.

'Is it a woman? Yes, it is! A woman with a crown. My, doesn't she look grand, standing up there, all proud and the like?'

'That's Old Liberty herself.' May turned at the soft-spoken voice behind her. It was the young soldier, Henry Rawl, who had befriended her on the long voyage, bringing scraps of food to her cabin for Mick and telling May stories of the horror of the Great War, from which he was returning mercifully unscathed, in body, if not in mind.

'Old Liberty? Is she a queen?'

1

Henry gave a little laugh and came to stand beside May at the rail, dumping his large canvas kitbag on the deck at his feet. He patted the little dog nestled in her arms, affectionately. During the crossing he had fallen for this beautiful young Irish girl, with her slender, but shapely body, her tumbling, strawberry-blonde curls and lively wit, and now they would soon be parted. His parents were waiting for him in Connecticut and, she had told him, her uncle was expecting her in Kentucky, though she had seemed a little shaky about the details of that side of her family.

'No, she's not a queen.'

'Sure, she has a crown.'

'Ain't you never heard of the Statue of Liberty? That's what she supposed to be, freedom. She's the gateway to America. Land of the Free,' he said proudly. 'She was given to us by some Frenchies. There's an inscription underneath it. Know what it says on it?'

May shook her head. She didn't know what an inscription was, but guessed it was to do with words. Words were something she had no knowledge of.

'It says, "Give me your tired, your poor.."' He grinned. 'Guess that's me. But not for long, no sir.'

As if to block out memories of the slaughter of his friends and companions in the trenches, over the past ten days Henry had regaled May with his plans for a shining future. She had listened, bright-eyed, as he told her how he would take over the little farm from his ailing father and make it the most prosperous in the state. Maybe the whole of America. He had almost given his life for his country, he said, and now it owed him something in return. A chance to make something of his life, to rise above the poverty his parents had endured all their lives. A chance to help build a brave new world for all to share.

May gazed at the statue, every moment becoming clearer through the mist, and felt the excitement rising in her breast, like a fluttering bird trying to break free. She was free. She had escaped and she could hardly believe it. 'Are we nearly there?'

'You are. Ellis Island is right by Old Liberty.'

'What's Ellis Island? Is it America?'

'Well, it is and it isn't. It's the place all new folks go to get checked out.'

'How d'you mean checked out?' There was a slight catch in her lilting Irish brogue.

'They need to check out your identity and stuff,' he explained. 'They'll most probably get in touch with your uncle to vouch for you before they let you in. Everybody stays there 'til they check you're not a criminal or something.'

An icy gust of wind caught them. Henry sensed the young girl stiffen beside him. 'A criminal?' she repeated.

'Like a thief or a murderer.' He smiled reassuringly. 'It won't be a problem. I don't see you as any of those.'

May looked away at the gigantic statue, then at the hazy red-brick buildings beyond on Ellis Island. The place she would be held until they checked her out, as Henry put it. There was definite concern in her young voice now. 'And...if they find out you're...well...I mean..?' Despite the cold her cheeks were suddenly burning.

Henry turned to look into her emerald-green eyes. 'Are you in some kinda trouble, May Sharpe?'

The white-coated steward made his way busily along the wood-paneled internal corridor of the ship, knocking on each door to make sure that all the passenger cabins had been vacated. He stopped at a cabin door and knocked. The pretty young Irish girl who had occupied the cabin with her little dog had a touch of mystery about her, arriving, as she had, out of the blue and at the last minute, breathlessly clutching her steamship ticket in her hand like a talisman. It wasn't until they were several days out at sea before he saw the tension ease from her young face and was treated to a first glimpse of her radiant smile.

He entered the cabin and stopped in surprise. Strewn on top of the single narrow bed, which almost filled the small space, were a pile of clothes and personal items which had been hastily dumped there. Even at a first glance he could see they were the contents of a soldier's kitbag, down to a spare pair of well-worn boots. The steward shook his head, puzzled. Whatever mystery the Irish girl had arrived with she had left another one, equally puzzling, in its place.

In their heavy army boots the platoon clattered noisily down the wooden gangplank in single file, their kitbags slung over their shoulders. At the barked orders of their sergeant they formed ranks on the dockside, warming the cold winter air around them with their intense relief and excitement at being home again. Against all the odds they had each survived. Pretty soon they would be going their separate ways, out of the army, back to their old lives or into new ones. Bringing up the rear Henry Rawl swayed down the plank, struggling under the weight of his bulging kitbag. Mick, yapping at his heels, almost sent him sprawling headlong to the dock below. At the foot of the plank Mick jumped up at his kitbag barking excitedly. The young soldier kicked out at the dog and chased it behind a stack of bales waiting to be loaded onto the ship.

Once out of sight of the platoon, he lowered the bag gently and hurriedly unfastened the drawstring at the top. May struggled up out of the bag, clutching her little cardboard case, gasping for air. Mick jumped up at her happily as she stumbled to her feet, straightening her crumpled clothes.

'Are you okay?' said Henry, a little out of breath from the exertion and the excitement.

'I am, now I can breathe.'

Beyond the stack of bales the sergeant barked orders to his platoon. 'I gotta go,' said Henry reluctantly.

'Here!' May pulled a purse from the pretty tapestry bag that she had bought from the first shop she had come across in Cork. She fumbled inside and held out a handful of coins and notes to Henry. 'It's Irish, I'm afraid.'

Henry waved the gesture away. 'Hey, just say 'Hi' to your uncle for me...and,' he added bashfully, 'if you're ever in Connecticut, you got my address.'

'Where's Rawl?!' The sergeant's bellow echoed over the chilly dockside.

'I gotta go!'

May took hold of his sleeve and planted a kiss on his flushed cheek. 'God bless you, Henry Rawl.'

With a shy smile, Henry hurried away, his boots rasping on the icy ground. After taking a moment to regain her composure, May walked slowly around the bales to see the platoon marching away across the bleak concrete dock. She looked around her. The tall imposing skyline of the city loomed in the distance, big and alien. She had never seen buildings so tall and wondered how on earth they didn't fall down? Standing in the freezing air of the quayside, May suddenly felt very alone and lost, but at the same time elated. Thanks to Henry, she had escaped the interrogation on Ellis Island, which would have sent her packing, all the way back to Ireland to face her punishment, which would be hard and brutal. Mick jumped up at her and barked once. May bent down and picked him up in her arms. 'Yes, Mick. We made it!'

Hunching her coat around them both against the arctic wind, she walked briskly towards the exit of the dockyard, mingling with the throng of passengers disembarking from the ship. The uniformed guard, huddled in his tiny wooden hut, barely glanced at her as she walked by and out through the tall wrought iron gates. Once outside she stopped, bewildered by the sight and sound of more vehicles than she had ever seen in her life. She looked both ways, uncertain. She had no idea which way to go.

A shiny limousine, longer than she had ever dreamt was possible, was parked by the gates with a man in a peaked cap and uniform behind the wheel. As she watched, a suave middle-aged man, with an immaculate grey double-breasted suit and silver hair, stepped from the back of the limousine and hurried to meet an elegant young woman in furs, walking through the dock gates. He planted a chaste kiss on her pink, powdered cheek and escorted her to the car, where the uniformed driver was opening the rear door. Holding the woman's hand, her companion helped the woman into the plush interior and got in beside her. The chauffeur resumed his seat and drove smoothly away. Wistfully May watched the limousine glide into the traffic, deeply conscious of her own cheap, crumpled suit and tiny cardboard suitcase.

'A dollar she's his mistress or a whore.'

May turned to see the speaker, with the broad New Yorker accent, lounging nonchalantly against the door of a sleek roadster. He was in his late twenties, showily dressed in a black overcoat, with white silk scarf and matching bowtie, holding white Saks gloves in his hand, the whole ensemble topped by a shiny black homburg. He smiled at her, revealing gleaming white teeth. May's heart skipped a beat. He was the living image of the magazine illustrations she had pinned on her bedroom wall back in the croft. Handsome, sophisticated, assured, and he was talking to her!

He nodded in the direction of the departing limousine. 'You want that, you can have it.' As he strolled over to May, touching his hat, Mick growled in May's arms. The man took a step back.

'Sorry. It's alright,' said May. 'He doesn't bite.'

Reassured, he produced an ivory-colored calling card from his breast pocket and flourished it before her eyes. 'Edward Theodore Young, the Third, at your service.' He smiled again, filling May with a tingle of excitement that completely banished the cold. 'My friends call me 'Society Eddie'.

With trembling hands May took the card, tongue-tied. She smiled shyly.

'Pretty smile.' Eddie held out his hand. 'Welcome to the Land of Opportunity, Miss -?'

'May,' she blurted out. 'May Sharpe, sir.'

'May. That's a beautiful name. Like blossom on the trees. Young and fresh.' Eddie came closer and tentatively patted Mick's head. 'And what's the little guy's name?'

He was so close May could smell the heady, musky aroma of his scent. She breathed in, a little taken aback. She had never met a man who wore perfume before. The few men she had known growing up all smelt of sweat or manure. 'Mick,' she replied, a little breathlessly.

'Need any help, Miss?'

May turned to see a tall young man in a blue police uniform smiling at her in a friendly, slightly bashful manner. So different to the smile she had just received from Eddie.

'The young lady and I was just having a conversation, buddy,' Eddie said aggressively.

The police officer dismissed Eddie with a look of unconcealed contempt and addressed May. 'You just arrived, miss?'

May tried to stem the panic rising in her throat. What if he sensed she had landed illegally? Maybe he was the second line of defense to catch aliens who had somehow managed to evade the interrogation at Ellis Island? 'I...er...I...,' she stumbled, groping for words.

'Where are you headed?'

Eddie bristled and made to step between them. "Hey, buster, don't you know it's rude to butt into a private conversation?"

The policeman took a step towards Eddie, fixing him with a cold, hard stare. 'The name's Perski. Officer Joe Perski. Now beat it before you read that written down on a charge sheet. That's if you can read.'

Eddie glared back at him, unfazed. 'Buster, I know your chief. I buy and sell guys like you.'

'That I don't doubt. But you can't buy me,' said Joe grimly. Then gently taking May's arm, he shepherded her away from Eddie. 'Sorry about that, miss. But there are some real bad hats hang round here.'

'Bad hats?' May repeated, struggling to understand the strange new accent and language.

'Oh, sorry, miss. You English?'

'No. Irish,' May replied, trying not to display the nervousness in her voice.

'You got folks here?'

Er...yes. Me Uncle Patrick,' said May, repeating the fiction she had told sweet, gullible Henry Rawl.

'You visiting?'

May nodded, distracted, and glanced back. With a sinking heart she saw Eddie getting into his roadster. She had come within an inch of meeting the man of her dreams and now she was being taken god knew where? Most likely the police station where they would find out the truth and sign her death warrant. For she had no illusions what fate awaited her back home.

'Where's your uncle live?' Joe's voice echoed through her racing thoughts. It sounded soft and kind. Maybe her fears were unfounded after all?

'Pardon me?'

'Your Uncle Patrick. He live in New York?'

'No. No...'

May hesitated. Joe waited for her to go on. What had she told Henry Rawl? It didn't matter. He was gone out of her life forever. She clutched at a name she had heard somewhere to do with America. 'Virginia.'

'That's a long way. Is no one meeting you?

'No. No, I'm taking the train.'

'You know where the station is?'

'No, but –,' she began.

'I'll show you.'

The panic rose again in her chest, filling her throat so she could hardly speak. Every minute spent with a policeman risked her flimsy story unraveling and her new life collapsing around her. 'No, really. I'm sure I can manage.'

'I'll show you,' he repeated. 'There are a lot of bad guys round here who'd take advantage of a nice young lady like you.'

May knew that to protest again, with the tension she could feel entering her voice, would only arouse the suspicion of this keen young officer. She forced a smile. 'Thank you. That's very kind.'

Joe smiled shyly, patted Mick's head and said, 'Let's go, buddy.'

CHAPTER TWO

Eddie Young weaved his roadster through the traffic of downtown New York, his handsome features marred by an ugly scowl. That fink cop had just cheated him out of a ripe hit and he was feeling sore. There were plenty of young girls he could entice into his web. That wasn't a problem. But over the years he had developed a keen eye and instinct for the special ones. The ones with a mixture of innocence and beauty that made them irresistible to his 'clients', as he liked to think of the men he made his very good living from. And his instinct told him the young Irish girl at the dock had it in spades. He scowled again and ripped his horn at the stalled traffic ahead.

May's emotions were in turmoil as she travelled with her unwelcome savior by tramcar across the city. She had never seen so many huge buildings, or so many people rushing in and out of them. At another time, she would have gloried, open-mouthed, at the amazing sights and sounds of one of the most dazzling cities in the world. But, sitting close beside Joe in the crowded tramcar, she knew that at any second she could trip herself up with an unguarded answer to his polite questioning. Thankfully, she was able to distract him with a constant stream of questions of her own about the streets they were jolting through, and about his own ambitions for the future, which culminated in becoming a detective, a dream his dead father had always had for his son. As they arrived at their destination, May was very relieved, and secretly amused, that during the entire time of their journey, this young man with high hopes of a career in detection had only learnt her name, and that of her little travelling companion snuggled cozily on her lap.

Grand Central Station took her breath away. It was like a palace or a vast cathedral dedicated to trains and the railway. As she hurried alongside Joe, her head turning to take in the vaulted roof, the towering windows and marble pillars, his voice broke into her tumbling thoughts.

'Which station?'

May stopped dead in her tracks. 'What?'

'Which station in Virginia? Richmond, Lexington, Springfield..?'

She looked around her as if seeking inspiration from the marble walls.

Joe looked puzzled. 'You do know the address?'

'Yes, of course. You don't think I'd travel halfway around the world without knowing where I'm going, do you? I'm not stupid.'

The feigned indignation in her voice convinced him. 'So which station?' he asked again.

'Springfield,' she said confidently. It was a bright, sunny name. 'Springfield,' she repeated.

'Stay here. I'll get your ticket.'

'Wait. I have money.' May dove into the tapestry bag for her purse and rummaged around, puzzled. The contents of the bag were minimal. A handkerchief, a powder compact, a small perfume bottle, a comb and her purse. Which was missing.

'I had it in here,' she said anxiously. She remembered opening her purse on the dockside to offer Henry money for helping her to illegally enter the country. 'It was here. But it's gone. I must have lost it.'

Joe looked concerned. 'Or had it filched.'

'Filched?'

'Stolen.'

May was skeptical. 'Who could have done that? Sure haven't I had the bag with me all the time?'

'Your 'friend' at the docks,' Joe said grimly. 'The grease-ball with the smile and the hat.'

'That nice fella? No. It couldn't be him.'

'It's okay,' Joe said reassuringly. 'I've got money. Let's get your ticket and get you on the train before anything else happens to you.'

Joe bustled along the central corridor of the train holding May's little suitcase in one hand and Mick under his other arm, with a flustered, irritated May following behind. Why couldn't this interfering man just leave her alone? She was about to leave on a train to a place she didn't want to go, but how could she tell him that now? May cursed her luck and herself. Why hadn't she lied that her fictitious Uncle Patrick lived in New York? But it was too late now.

'Here we are.' Joe had found her a vacant window seat looking out over the platform. He stuffed the suitcase on the overhead rack and ushered May into the seat, opposite a severe-looking, middle-aged businessman.

'I guess the dog will have to go in the guard's van.'

'I can do that,' May said hurriedly, reaching up to take the dog from him. 'You'd better get off unless you want to come to Springfield with me.'

Joe smiled. 'Can't say I'd object to that, miss, but my sergeant would throw a fit. Don't worry about the fare. You just mail it to me when you can.' He handed her a slip of paper. 'Here. Officer Joe Perski. Care of New York Police Department, Fifth Precinct.'

May took the slip of paper and tried to sound sincere, through her growing frustration. 'Thanks. Thank you so very much. You've been very kind.'

'You're welcome, Miss Sharpe. Glad to be of service. Enjoy your stay. And if you're ever in New York again...'

The guard's whistle sounded shrilly down the platform.

'I gotta scoot.' He smiled winningly. May noticed for the first time he had an open, handsome face. A shame he was such an interfering busybody. She pasted a smile on her face in response.

Joe hurried down the corridor and disappeared. The train's whistle blew, echoing around the high glass and iron roof of the station. May sprang up with Mick in her arms and grabbed her suitcase from the rack. She still had time to get off the train before it left the station. But before she could take a step, she was halted by a rap on the window. It was Joe outside, grinning widely.

'Don't worry,' he called through the glass. 'The conductor will take him to the van.'

May sat down again heavily as the steam engine blew a first huge sigh and the train began to slowly heave its way out of the station. She waved perfunctorily in response to Joe as he walked alongside waving, then she sat back, staring grimly over the head of the man sitting opposite. When the train had gathered enough speed to leave Joe and the station behind, May tore the slip of paper in two and dropped it on the seat beside her. She noticed the man opposite staring at her curiously, but she was past caring. She closed her eyes in exasperation.

Darkness had fallen before the train slowed sufficiently on a long winding bend on the outskirts of the city. Holding Mick under one arm and her case in the other, May struggled along the train and out of the end carriage door onto the rear platform, just as the train's whistle blew and it began to gather speed once more. Mick struggled in her arms. 'Well jump, you dumb animal!' she shouted angrily.

Mick leapt from her arms into the night. Throwing her case after him May jumped sideways from the moving train. She landed heavily and cried out at a searing pain in her left ankle. Lying winded and hurt in the icy darkness, she watched the lights of the train disappear into the night. Sensing his mistress's distress, Mick appeared and licked her face solicitously.

She lay for a moment recovering from her heavy fall. She knew if she didn't move she would freeze to death by the side of the track. Well, she thought grimly, you haven't traveled all this way to die alone beside a dusty railway line. Pushing herself up, she tested the ankle. The pain shot up to her belly. She cried out, took a deep breath, then bent down to retrieve her case. Mick jumped up at her, barking insistently.

'No, Mick, I can't carry you,' she said, feeling the tears well in her eyes. 'You'll have to walk for a change.'

She set off hobbling along the uneven track, back towards the bright lights of the city, with Mick trotting alongside.

CHAPTER THREE

Joe Perski mounted the stairs to his second floor apartment in almost total darkness. The single light bulb hanging above the staircase had blown and the janitor said he wouldn't have a replacement until the morning. This wasn't the first time. He made a mental note to complain to the landlord about the man's organization skills. He was paying for a service after all.

As he let himself into his room, the cold enveloped him. He cursed silently. The airlock in the heating system was another thing the janitor was supposed to fix. He kicked the pipe hard and heard the water begin to bubble through the heavy iron radiator. In an hour the temperature in the room would be bearable. Until then he'd just have to make himself a sweet black coffee and eat the bagel and cream cheese he had bought at the corner deli for his evening meal.

Ordinarily, when this happened, he would walk a block to the bar on 23rd which was always warm and welcoming, except that, this evening, he had spent his last dime on the food and couldn't afford a beer. Paying the Irish girl's train fare had cleaned him out and he'd have to borrow from his colleagues in the precinct until pay day. But he didn't begrudge her the money. What would she have done without it, after that fink conman had stolen her purse? There were some real scummy people in this city and he was glad to have been able to help her out, even if it meant freezing in his gloomy room instead of nursing a beer in a cozy little bar.

Though he was happy she was out of harm's way, he had felt sad the moment her train left the station. She had gone out of his life as quickly as she had come into it, and it suddenly

15

seemed empty. She had a natural innocence about her, a childlike, yet sensual, quality that made him feel both big and awkward in her presence. It shone out of her face from her beautiful, bright green eyes and, try as he might, he couldn't get those eyes out of his head. Or the pure white skin and the strawberry blonde curls. He shook his head to clear her image from his brain. A girl like her was not for him, or this city. Such an innocent had no place in New York, where the girls quickly learned to be as hard as the sidewalk they strutted on. He bit into his bagel. It tasted stale.

With the arctic wind whipping down the long wide avenues, after midnight, when May at last limped into the heart of the city, its sidewalks were deserted. She was cold, tired, hungry, and in pain from her swollen ankle. She looked again at Eddie's card with the Blackbird motif. The words meant nothing to her.

She looked up at the sound of clicking heels. A young couple were hurrying towards her, huddled together against the biting wind. She held out the card and moved towards them.

'Excuse me - !' she began.

But the couple scurried by without a glance. May looked along the empty avenue, pulled her thin coat around her and carried on.

Down a side street, a block further on, she saw a taxi pull up at a brownstone, and an elderly couple get out. She hurried towards them waving the card above her head.

'Excuse me! Do you – ?'

The couple took one look at the figure stumbling towards them out of the night, with flailing arms, and fled behind the door of their apartment block. May stopped and looked about her, forlornly. In the distance a police siren wailed. In the dead of night it was a scary sound.

Five blocks on, three taxi-cab drivers were hunched around a blazing brazier on a corner. May approached them hesitantly, holding out the card.

'The Blackbird Club? Hang a right two blocks on.'

'Thank you. Thank you!' May said gratefully, almost in tears at the unexpected human kindness.

She increased her pace aware of the lateness of the night. She had no idea whether the club would still be open, or if Eddie would be there. If he wasn't she didn't know what she would do. Staying out all night in the sub-zero temperature could easily kill her. But she was determined not to have travelled all this way, and been through so much, to let that be her fate. The harsh life she had endured growing up in the croft had hardened her. And May Sharpe was not a quitter.

Two blocks on she turned the corner to walk down the street whose number was printed on the card, and her heart sank. Lined with darkened, brownstone tenements, the street was dimly lit and looked deserted. As the light and noise of the city faded behind her, she could hear her heels echoing into the dark, surrounding shadows. Mick suddenly barked. May gave a start as a huddled figure rose out of a doorway and lurched towards her. She was ready to take flight, but stopped at the sound of a familiar accent.

'Spare a dime, miss. For a poor man down on his luck.'

May peered in surprise at the stooped figure, who appeared to be wrapped in nothing but rags. 'You're Irish?'

'That I am. All the way from County Kerry.' His voice was thin and raw. 'Are you from the Old Country yourself?' he continued, hope rising in his voice.

'I am so. And what are you doing begging in a nice town like this?' Despite her own situation May was shocked to see one of her own countrymen reduced to such a degraded level.

The man's laugh was short and bitter. 'A nice town, is it?'

'It is,' May replied. 'And oughtn't you to be getting yourself a job, 'stead of bringing shame on decent Irish folk.' She turned to the dog, anxious to move on. 'Come on, Mick.'

The man grabbed her arm. 'A job? Now wouldn't that be a fine thing! Do you happen to have one on you?'

Mick barked furiously and jumped up at the man, snapping. May tore herself from his feeble grasp and hurried away down the dark street, with the man's harsh laughter ringing after her.

'A job! A job you say! Hah!'

In the warm cozy interior of the bar and late-night drinking club known as The Blackbird, 'Society' Eddie Young was holding court in his favorite booth with his usual group of acolytes hanging on his every word.

'So this rookie cop says "I ain't never heard of you".' He waited for the expected gasps of surprise, then continued. 'So I sez, "I ain't never heard of you either, punk. But your chief shines my shoes!".'

The men around him laughed heartily. Eddie had a reputation for brains and ruthlessness, and he was moving up. It paid to stay friends with the coming men in New York's underworld.

Eddie took a drink of his Manhattan and looked round happily at the familiar interior, with its polished mahogany booths lined with deep red velvet, its ornately etched mirror which ran the whole length of the bar, and the bright, pink-glass chandeliers shaped like tulips. And then he saw her. Her pale face lit from the interior lights, as she stood on tip-toe peering in from the darkness. He stood up and waved at the waif-like figure standing outside the window. 'Hey! Come in here! Charlie, open the door for the lady!'

A broad squat man rose from the booth and crossed to open the opaque glass door, with its etched blackbird motif. Eddie called out from his seat, grinning broadly, and waved again, beckoning the young girl inside. 'Hey, come in! Come in here, out of the cold! What a neat surprise!'

May entered, holding Mick in her arms protectively. She was cold, tired, emotional and frightened, but her anger overrode everything. She hobbled straight up to Eddie's booth and stared down at him, the heat of her anger warming her frozen cheeks.

'Didn't think you'd ever see me again, did you?' she said accusingly.

Eddie spread his arms in an open, friendly gesture. 'Hey, I give you my card, didn't I?'

'Now let me think,' May replied. 'Was that before or after you stole me purse?'

Eddie looked round at his cronies and grinned broadly. 'If I'd knowed it was full of Mick dough, I wouldn't have bothered.'

The group around her laughed loudly. May stood shivering, feeling out of her depth and very alone. She waited for the merriment to subside. 'I want me purse,' she said determinedly. 'Give me me purse.'

Eddie's voice was calm and friendly. 'Hey, relax, doll. Sit down. Take a load off.' He turned to the two men sitting opposite him. 'Make room for the lady. You got no manners?'

As May stood uncertainly she heard a female voice behind her.

'Who's this?' the tone had a trace of suspicion.

The woman who had emerged from the ladies powder room, was in her mid-twenties, blonde and attractive in a hard-bitten way. She was wearing a full-length fur coat with diamonds clustered at her throat and adorning every one of her fingers.

'Met her at the docks today. She'd just arrived. She's got a pretty name. Rose or something.'

'It's May,' May corrected.

'That's right. May.' He waved to a seat opposite him. 'Sit down, May. You look beat.'

May hesitated, shivering with cold and anxiety. She knew she had stumbled into the company of criminals, if Eddie was typical of the crowd, but then she knew what he was already. That's why she was here, to get her only money back. If not she would end up like the beggar she had just met in the street. She was exhausted and frozen to the bone. It was cold and dark outside and she had no money. Nervously, she sat down onto the plush velvet seat of the booth. Immediately her weary body relaxed and said 'Thank you'. Mick, still clutched in her arms, licked her face gratefully.

The woman took her seat alongside Eddie, still looking steadily at May.

'This is Alice,' said Eddie. 'Say hello to May, Alice.'

Alice's cool expression didn't alter. 'You look rough,' she said.

May nodded and gave a faint smile. 'I've been walking a while.'

'You hungry? Eddie asked.

Suddenly, May realized how long it had been since she had last eaten. 'I could eat a donkey and its cart.'

Eddie called over the barman. 'Harry, a special for the lady.' He turned to May. 'And what's your poison?'

May looked across at him puzzled. 'Poison?'

'He means a drink,' explained Alice. 'What do you drink?'

'You mean alcohol?' May asked innocently.

'Well, he don't mean milk, honey,' said Alice.

'I...don't...I mean...I've never...'

'Harry, bourbon on the rocks for the little lady,' Eddie said. 'Make it a double.'

When the heavy cut-glass tumbler filled with thick brown liquid and ice cubes was set before her, May was acutely aware that all eyes were on her. Tentatively she raised the glass to her lips and heard the unfamiliar sound of the ice tinkling against the sides. She looked down at white objects floating in the glass.

'What's up?' Eddie asked. 'You never seen ice before?'

'Of course,' said May quickly, not wanting to appear childish. She had in fact seen some of her fellow passengers onboard ship sipping drinks with ice, but had never had the courage to ask for one herself. Besides she had seen enough of what alcohol could do to people and vowed never to touch it. But this was different. Everybody was watching her. It felt like a test. One she was determined not to fail.

Eddie encouraged her. 'Drink up. That'll soon put the glow back in your cheeks.'

Acutely aware that twelve pair of eyes were watching her, May took a sip and spluttered as the sharp, viscous liquid hit the back of her throat. She coughed at the stinging taste of the drink rising into her nostrils, bringing tears to her eyes. She saw that everyone around her was grinning.

'That hit the spot?' asked Eddie with a broad smile.

Determined not to look foolish, May nodded and tried a smile in return. Raising the glass once more she took a larger gulp and felt the fire erupt in her chest. She gasped, involuntarily, taking in a huge lungful of air to try to quench the flames.

Eddie settled back and smiled to himself. It was fate. Fate had brought this special one back to him, and he wouldn't let her slip away again. He looked at Alice and raised his eyebrows, amused. For the first time Alice relaxed and smiled. This naïve little waif was no threat.

CHAPTER FOUR

It was Joe who found her. In his job he had seen them many times before, but it never got any easier. There was always that same gut-churning feeling deep inside, mingled with sadness and a hopeless sense of waste. They came in all ages, all shapes and sizes. White, black, mulatto, Hispanic, very rarely Chinese. Mostly they were fished out of the Hudson or the East River, but occasionally, like this one, they fetched up in an alley indistinguishable from the garbage. Easy pickings for the rats. She was lying face down, half-naked, and momentarily Joe was jolted by the tangled mass of strawberry-blonde curls. With a shiver of dread he turned the young girl over. It was not her. He felt a rush of relief, and then suddenly very stupid. He had seen her off on the train, hadn't he? By now she would be safe with her folks in Virginia. As he stood guard over the lifeless girl, waiting for the body wagon to arrive, he thought of her. The eyes. The smile. Which he would never see again.

May lay with her eyes tightly closed trying to stop the world spinning. She had no idea where she was and was too frightened to open her eyes to find out. Her first thought was that she had been dumped somewhere and left to die. It felt like she was dying. But then her body became aware that it was warm and comfortable. More comfortable than it had ever been. Part of her felt like she was in heaven. The other part felt like she was in hell.

Slowly she opened her eyes. The room she was in was still spinning, but she could take enough of it in to see that she was in paradise. The whole room was bathed in a hazy sunlight that filtered through delicate net curtains covering the large double windows. The bed she had slept in was huge. Big enough for a whole family. The sheets were so soft she felt she was lying on a cloud. A large canopy over her head was hung with pale pink and ivory drapes whose pattern matched the wallpaper in the large bedroom, the whole effect complementing the white painted door and window frames. An elaborate white dressing table, backed by an ornate gilt-framed mirror, was adorned with a myriad toiletries, perfumes and feminine nick-knacks, little figurines and animals in pretty colored glass. A wall of mirrored doors, rising floor to ceiling, looked like a vast cupboard to hang clothes, if anyone could ever have so many. The whole room was like something out of a fairytale.

Gingerly she raised herself up on the thick soft pillows. The sheets and pillowcases were the same pale pink as the drapes and, when she felt them, she realized they were silk. She gently lowered her naked feet to the floor where they sank into the soft pile of the ivory, wall-to-wall carpet. She put a hand to her chest. She was wearing a pure white silk shift. Was she dreaming? That was it. In a moment she would wake and find herself lying in a gutter with a head feeling three sizes too big and hurting like nothing she had ever experienced.

May struggled to recall the evening before. Slowly images began to filter back into her mind. She remembered hurting her ankle jumping from the train, the long perishing, painful trudge back to the city, the warm club and Eddie's grin. And the drink, the harsh, bitter drink. It must be the drink that was giving her this dream, which seemed so intensely real. How long would it last? Where was she really? And where was Mick? What had they done to Mick? Tears rose in her eyes.

The bedroom door was slightly ajar and she became aware of a sound from the adjoining room. She looked down at her swollen ankle, which had been expertly bandaged. She tested it on the floor. The bandage supported it well. Tiptoeing across the soft, warm carpet she peered warily through the open door and gasped in surprise.

A huge black woman wearing a black dress, white cap and pinafore was dusting the ornaments on a glass table in the centre of the spacious living-room. She looked up on hearing May's involuntary gasp. May ducked back behind the door, her heart pounding.

'Morning!' the woman called. 'Beautiful morning.'

Nervously, May emerged from her hiding place and stood in the doorway looking around her in amazement. The large living room of the apartment was decorated in the same color scheme as the bedroom, giving the sumptuous apartment an overwhelmingly feminine touch. The room, which was carpeted throughout with the same carpet as the bedroom, was dominated by two voluminous ivory-colored couches, filled with pink cushions, arranged around the glass-topped table. Ornate gilt-legged occasional tables topped with expansive displays of pink and white flowers were arranged about the walls. Pink drapes framed the ceiling to floor windows, which led out onto a balcony overlooking trees laid bare by winter. Through the branches May could see glimpses of the city and a shining river beyond. The black woman had stopped her dusting and was looking at May, wearing a broad grin. Her teeth seemed unnaturally white against her black cheeks. 'You sure had a good sleep,' she said kindly. 'Snoring fit to raise the dead.'

May found her voice at last. 'Pardon me?'

'Yessum?'

'Where am I? Am I dreaming?'

The black woman's huge body shook with a gale of laughter. May stared at her, a little afraid, until the convulsion subsided.

'Folks where I live might think so. But no, you ain't dreaming, missy,' she explained. 'You in Miss Alice's apartment.'

May suddenly remembered the hard-looking, attractive blonde in the club. 'Where is she?'

'She coming over soon. Told me to tell you there's fresh coffee in the kitchen,' the maid added, nodding towards a door on the opposite side of the room.

Still half convinced she was dreaming, May made her way across the room and entered the open door leading to the kitchen. At least she assumed it was a kitchen, for the woman had called it that, but she had never seen anything like it before. The whole room was bigger than the entire croft where she had spent the first sixteen years of her life, and so bright in its whiteness that she had to shade her eyes for a moment to let them adjust to the brilliance. Her eyes hurt and her head swam with a dull ache.

A round, gleaming, ivory-colored table with six matching chairs dominated one half of the room. In its centre stood a tall white vase filled with the ubiquitous pink and white flowers. The other half of the room was devoted to a state of the art kitchen. Long stylish cupboards topped by white marble work surfaces, with matching wall cupboards above them, were ranged on either side of the room. A shiny cooker with six electric burners was in the centre of the third wall, with cupboards and work-surfaces on both sides.

May ran her hand over the smooth cold marble and pressed her cool fingers to her temples. Then, curiosity getting the better of her, she began to open each cupboard in turn to reveal masses of shining pans and pots of all shapes and sizes. The wall cupboards contained sparkling crystal glasses and white china crockery prettily decorated with a pink flower motif. She approached the bulky white, cupboard-like structure standing alone. Tugging on the metal handle, she opened the heavy door and blinked at the cavernous, glowing interior stuffed with weird and wonderful foodstuffs of every conceivable kind. May reached inside to touch some of the unfamiliar objects, flinching a little at the coldness. A voice behind her made her start.

'You surfaced.'

May spun around guiltily. Alice was standing in the doorway, resplendent in a full-length fur with matching hat. In her arms she carried a miniature, manicured white poodle with a pink bow on top of its tiny head. May flushed guiltily.

'Oh, I was...er...How did I..?' she stammered.

Alice smiled. 'You were whacked. We put you in here. I slept over at Eddie's...You eaten?'

May was still in a daze. 'Eaten?' she repeated lamely.

'Yeah, you know, like food?'

'No, no,' May replied. The thought of food suddenly made her stomach turn. 'I, er...I'm not...'

'I'll fix you breakfast,' said Alice, gliding into the kitchen and thrusting the dog and her fur into May's arms. Businesslike, she turned a knob on the cooker, then took a tray of eggs and a jar of cooking oil from the open refrigerator.

The little dog in May's arms made her suddenly remember with a stab of dread. 'Mick!' she exclaimed.

Alice turned from lightly basting the grill on the cooker top with oil. 'Say again?'

'Me dog, Mick. What happened to him?'

'He's okay,' Alice replied reassuringly. 'We left him with Harry. Don't worry, he won't wind up in the club sandwich. One egg or two?' she asked, cracking an egg onto the grill. She looked at May. 'Two. You need fattening up.'

May watched as Alice cracked another egg onto the grill. The transparent, glutinous placenta slowly turned white and opaque, around the deep yellow yolk. The smell of egg and oil hit May's nostrils. She retched and dropped the dog and fur onto the floor, clutching her mouth and stomach in panic. The little dog yelped, affronted.

'In the bathroom,' said Alice calmly, indicating the doorway with the metal spatula in her hand.

May hobbled into the living room, looking about her wildly.

'There!' cried the maid, pointing to a door May hadn't noticed before. She headed for the bathroom, but it was too late. The entire contents of the Blackbird's Club Special landed in a messy, multi-colored heap onto the pristine carpet.

For the second time that day May woke in the sumptuous bedroom. The sunlight, which had been streaming in earlier, was fading to dusk. The pills Alice had given her, after the accident on the carpet, seemed to have worked and she was feeling much better physically. But when the memory of what had occurred flooded back she shrank down into the comfort of the bed wishing she had died.

She listened intently for any sound from the next room. The apartment was silent. May guessed her clothes had been put into the large, mirrored cupboard which covered the entire length of one wall. If she could get dressed and slip out of the apartment without being heard she could fade away without having to face Alice. She had been so kind to her, a total stranger, and May had repaid her by doing an awful thing in the middle of her beautiful carpet. Trying to tell herself that it was really Eddie's fault for plying her with so much 'booze' as he called it, didn't help. She knew she could never face Alice again.

Hardly daring to breathe, she slipped silently out of bed, crossed to the cupboard and tugged on one of the gold knobs. She stumbled backwards, surprised, as the whole length of the mirrored doors concertinaed, each one folding back onto the next, revealing more clothes hanging in neat rows than she had ever seen before. Glancing nervously at the door behind her, she searched feverishly for her own clothes amongst the elegant, designer gowns, dresses and furs. Her heart sank as she realized that her cheap suit and under garments were not there. Would she have to add insult to injury by stealing one of her benefactor's dresses to escape in? She let her fingers trail over the soft silks and furs in wonder. And, for the second time that day, jumped guiltily at a voice behind her.

'Looking for something?'

May turned to face Alice, feeling her face flush bright crimson. 'I er...no...yes, me clothes.'

'Molly threw them in the garbage,' said Alice matter-of-factly.

'Molly?'

'My maid. You saw her cleaning the apartment this morning.'

May was at a loss. 'She threw them..?'

'In the garbage. Like I told her to.'

'But...' May couldn't form the words. She guessed that 'garbage' meant rubbish, and that her clothes had been thrown away, but she didn't know what that meant. Was it a punishment for what she had done to Alice's carpet? And where was her case with the rest of her things inside?

'You can't wear trash like that when you work for Eddie,' Alice said enigmatically.

'Work?'

Alice smiled teasingly, 'Oh sorry, your Majesty. You don't work where you come from?'

'No, I meant...' May didn't know what she meant. Things were happening so fast. Everything was strange and new.

'I'll run you a bath,' Alice was already moving towards the adjoining bathroom. 'You smell like a stable.'

CHAPTER FIVE

Alice stood in the spacious, pink and white tiled bathroom watching May with an amused grin. Her new protégé, the pretty young Irish girl, was standing staring down in child-like wonder at the steaming bathtub, with its mass of winking bubbles. 'Are you going to look at it all day, or get in?'

May looked at her and then back at the alien bubbles. 'In there?'

'What's the matter? Ain't you never had a bath before?'

'No. I never did.' May looked down at her bare feet nestling in the thick white rug, feeling very foolish.

'Jeez,' Alice exclaimed. 'You are gonna be one heck of a challenge.'

May looked at her, puzzled. She didn't understand what was happening to her. But whatever it was, it felt exciting.

'You just step in. It'll do your ankle good.' said Alice reassuringly.

Alice had taken off the bandage and the swelling had already begun to subside. After a moment, May lifted the hem of her slip and lifted one leg over the side of the bath. Her dainty foot and milky calf disappeared through the bubbles into water that was like a warm caress. She let out a little sigh of pure pleasure. Stepping in with her other leg, May stood holding up her slip, looking down at the bubbles coming up to her knees. Alice watched, at first with amazement, then amused, as May slowly sank down into the bubbles still wearing her slip. She looked up, startled, as Alice's laughter echoed round the brightly-lit room.

'You kill me!' roared Alice.

May was in heaven. She had luxuriated in the deep, warm water while Alice shampooed her hair, cut and polished her toenails, and then dried off her glowing young body with a huge fluffy white towel that had been warming on the bathroom radiator. Now she was seated beside her new friend and mentor on one of the enormous sofas in the lounge swathed in a pink satin robe with a white towel wrapped around her head. They were leafing through a glossy fashion magazine on Alice's lap. May pointed to a drawing of an elegant young woman standing at the rail of a luxury liner. 'I had a picture just like that at home. On me wall.'

'*My* wall,' Alice corrected.

May looked about her at the room. 'No, I meant back in Ireland. I pinned it on the wall in me bedroom.'

'*My* bedroom.'

May smiled prettily. 'Oh, I see!'

'No point wearing a pretty dress if what comes out your mouth is ugly.'

'Will I have a pretty dress?' She was beginning to understand that, in order to work for Eddie, she was to be transformed. The prospect filled her whole body with a tingling sensation. She couldn't wait to find out what exactly the work entailed.

'First things first,' Alice said, closing the magazine and standing up. With a nod of her head she beckoned May back into the bedroom.

May was only five when her mother died. She didn't have many memories of her to draw on, but one in particular stood out, which happened not long before her mother passed away. There was going to be a big event in the village seven miles away over the bog. At this distance in time May couldn't remember what it actually was, but it must have been to do with horses she guessed. The rural Irish were obsessed with horses. It was a long trek over the peaty fields and down a stony cart-track, but, for once, it promised to be a bright, sunny day and her mother was determined to go and take her little daughter with her.

Before the sun was up her mother had woken May in her little bed. She had boiled a pan of water over the open fire in the grate and had stood May naked in front of the flames, while she wiped her body all over with a warm, wet cloth. Then, after dressing her daughter in her best dress, which she herself had worn as a child, she sat May on a stool before the dying embers, with the door wide open to catch the early morning sunlight, and started to comb her hair. May could still remember the warmth of the sun on her face, and the tug of the comb pulling through her thick curls. It had made her eyes water, but she was so thrilled at the prospect of the day ahead, that she didn't cry out. When her mother was finished she took a little pink ribbon from her apron pocket and tied it on top of May's bright yellow curls. Then she stood back to admire her pretty little daughter sitting in the ray of sunlight, and beamed. It was the last time May ever saw her mother smile.

She had tried to erase the memory of her father's rage, but the brutal images crept in when she wasn't on her guard. The frightening loudness of his voice bouncing off the bare stone walls of the tiny croft, her mother's plaintive protests turning to shrill, agonizing cries of pain as her father's angry fists pummeled every inch of her body. The hours of heart-broken sobbing behind the closed wooden door of her parents' room, as May was made to bring in the logs, sweep the bare earth of the living room, and finally, feed the pig in her new best dress.

'Hold still, said Alice, as she stroked the ivory-handled brush through May's hair. May was seated happily on the padded stool before the large mirror of the dressing table watching excitedly as Alice fussed over her curls. 'You have great hair.'

'Me mammy said so. *My* mammy,' she corrected, proud that she didn't have to be prompted this time.

'She back in Ireland?'

May shook her head. 'She died.'

'Poor kid. You got any brothers and sisters?'

'No,' said May shaking her curls.

'Me neither. I always wanted a kid sister.' She stood back to admire her work. 'How's that?'

May looked at herself in the mirror and smiled. 'It looks wonderful. You're so clever.'

Alice pursed her crimson lips, 'Mmm. Maybe...' She started to refine the style, grooming the curls into smoother waves. May sat meekly, soaking in the unaccustomed feeling of being pampered.

'Is this place all yours?' she asked.

'Bought and paid for by yours truly.' There was no mistaking the pride in Alice's voice.

'It's wonderful,' May said, still a little breathless that all this hadn't turned out to be a dream.

'It'll do till Eddie and I get a place together.'

'You're moving out?'

Nodding at May's reflection in the mirror, she said, 'When we get married.'

'Oh, are you two..?'

Alice thrust her hand in front of May's eyes. The huge diamond, caught in the glare of the chandelier, threw out a shower of tiny colored lights.

'That's wonderful. But I can't imagine anyone ever wanting to move from here,' she said innocently. 'I'd die for a place like this.'

A wry smile tugged at Alice's lips as she gave May's hair one last touch. 'Some people have,' she said cryptically.

Alice grazed through the lines of clothes hanging in the 'closet', as she called it, while May stood obediently in the centre of the room wearing a short satin shift, garter-belt and silk stockings. She had watched in wonder as Alice dressed her, showing her how to smooth the gossamer fabric of the stockings up the long length of her legs so as not to tear them.

'Class is the thing,' said Alice over her shoulder. 'No good looking like a two-bit hooker.'

'Hooker?' May repeated uncomprehendingly.

'You don't wanna know, kid.'

Alice took a simple pale green dress from a hanger and held it against May's body. She cocked her head on one side and pursed her lips. 'Yeah. Matches your eyes.'

'Alice,' May said in a little voice.

'Yeah?'

'This work...for Eddie..?'

'You're a natural. You're gonna love it.'

As Alice manicured May's nails and painted them a delicate shade of pink, she explained the details of the work that they would be doing together. May listened with a ball of panic expanding in her stomach, squashing the breath in her chest.

'And that's all there is to it,' Alice said brightly.

May sat for a moment in silence, watching the deft moments of Alice's fingers applying the nail varnish with a tiny brush. She could hardly breathe, but she had to speak. 'But isn't that against the law?' she said timidly.

Alice raised her head, looked into May's eyes and smiled kindly. 'It's a tough world out there, kid. They're all on the take anyhow. They'd sell their grandmothers if they could make a buck,' she said, resuming her work transforming May's peasant hands to those of a young lady of leisure. 'Don't worry, I'll look out for you.'

'It sounds so simple,' May said. 'Does it really work?'

'You betcha, kid. Men *are* simple. Show 'em a nice ass and they're putty.'

May frowned, puzzled. 'Ass? Do we have a donkey as well?' she asked innocently.

Alice's body shook with laughter. 'You kill me!'

Placing a simple string of pearls around May's slender white neck, Alice spun her round to face the full-length mirrors on the closet doors. May gasped in surprise and delight. It was a miracle. Never in her most vivid fantasies, lying huddled in the cold, dark bedroom of the croft, did she imagine she could look like this. She was like a lady. More than a lady, a princess. Alice stood back, admiring the transformation she had brought about.

When May could get her breath, still unable to tear her eyes from her reflection, she asked in wonder, 'Is that me? That can never be me!'

Tears shone in May's eyes, as Alice folded her arms around her. 'It will be, kid. It will be.'

CHAPTER SIX

In the early evening the Blackbird Club was buzzing with pre-theatre diners who liked to eat well, but on the cheap. Harry served some of the best hot pastrami mash, topped with golden-yoked fried eggs, in town, and his Martinis were legend. New Yorkers and out-of-towners sat shoulder to shoulder in the cozy booths in animated conversation, looking forward eagerly to the evening's fun. After the prolonged gloom of the war New York was coming alive again.

Seated in his favorite booth, at the rear of the club, a stone-faced Eddie faced a frightened young woman no more than eighteen years old. In front of him his pastrami was growing cold as he listened to the girl's stumbling explanation.

'You trying to piss me?' he hissed, interrupting her in mid-sentence.

The girl's face turned paler. 'No, Eddie. I swear to God.'

'He ain't gonna help you,' Eddie snapped. 'Just remember, if I catch you creaming off the top you're gonna be swimming with the fishes in the river, with your hands tied to your ankles.'

'Eddie, please –,' she began, terrified.

'Get out of my sight! You're giving me gas!'

He dug his fork into the mash and shoved it into his mouth. The girl stood up, trembling, and hovered at the edge of the booth, trying to think of the words to smooth over the situation. But nothing came. Eddie looked up from his plate, his mouth full, his eyes cold and hard.

'You still here?'

The girl turned and hurried away shaking, almost stumbling into another booth in her desperation to get away. At the door she pushed blindly past two young women entering the club from a taxi, which was pulling away into the thronging traffic.

'Francis?' said Alice, surprised. 'What's up?'

Wrapped in her cocoon of panic, the girl hurried away into the night, deaf to Alice's voice. Alice glanced at May beside her and shrugged. Then, taking May's arm, she led her young charge down the central aisle of the club to where Eddie was seated eating. May was aware of all eyes turning as the two women passed by each booth. Alice shot her a sly smile, reveling in the stir the two glamorous women were making. Eddie glanced up, did a double-take and watched May intently as they approached his booth. Alice stopped beside the table. With both hands she opened May's fur to reveal the stylish, pale emerald dress that perfectly matched the young girl's eyes and fitted her slim figure like a glove. Alice raised a white-gloved hand as if presenting her to Eddie, and watched his reaction closely. 'Well? What did I say?' she said proudly.

Eddie slowly looked May up and down, drinking in the stunning young girl before him. May looked down at her feet, self-consciously. 'She scrubs up real neat.' He shoved another forkful of mash into his mouth and gestured for them both to sit. As May and Alice slipped into the booth opposite Eddie, a young man in a waiter's apron glided to their table.

'What'll it be, Miss Alice? Your usual?'

'Right, Tom and...' She turned to May questioningly.

May hesitated. 'Do you just have...water?'

'Water?' Eddie nearly spat his mouthful out onto the table in amused surprise.

'The kid had a rough time, Eddie.' said Alice coming to May's rescue. 'With all the booze you fed her last night,'

May smiled at her gratefully. Eddie shrugged and nodded at the waiter. 'Water it is. But tell anybody and you're dead,' he added with a grin to the young man.

When the waiter had gone, Eddie looked hard at May. 'Alice, brung you up to speed?'

May looked at him, perplexed. 'Speed?' She turned to Alice for help. There was a whole new language she would have to learn and fast.

'I told her the routine. She's game.'

Eddie fixed May with a warm smile that made her flutter inside. 'You ready to earn some real American dough?'

She smiled prettily in return. 'You betcha!'

The bar of the Ritz-Carlton Hotel was the grandest place May had ever seen. Alice and May had left Eddie at the Blackbird Club and traveled by taxi down the wide, busy avenues to arrive at the elegant frontage of one of the city's premier hotels. They were helped from the taxi-cab by a livered doorman and ushered obsequiously through the gilded, swing doors, where a porter, dressed in a red jacket with gold trimmings, escorted them into the large brightly-lit room. At Alice's request, the porter seated them at a pink marble-topped table, in a corner shaded by palms. As if by magic, a white-jacketed waiter appeared at their side and Alice ordered a martini for herself and spring water for May. Then the two women surveyed the room, but with very different eyes.

May drank in the space, flushed and thrilled. If Alice hadn't told her it was a hotel, she would have thought they had entered a royal palace. Rows of marble columns, topped with garlands of golden leaves, reached upwards towards a stucco ceiling painted with murals, large and small, depicting classical scenes of heavenly hosts and rural idylls. The whole room shone from the crystal chandeliers hanging from gilded chains. Not for the first time since she had landed in New York did May feel her breath taken away.

Having seen the room a hundred times, Alice was surveying the customers with a practiced eye. With the theatre shows having started all over town, there were few drinkers in the bar. It would fill up much later with chic women and their wealthy escorts. Alice homed in on a man in his mid-forties, seated alone at the bar, nursing a whisky sour. From his suit and briefcase she picked him as a travelling salesman, most likely from out of town. She had seen him notice May with interest when they entered the room, but he had returned to his drink, looking a little hang-dog. She leaned over to May and confided in a low voice, 'Don't look now, but that's our john.'

Alice had become one of Eddie's girls shortly after leaving the orphanage. A bright, ambitious young girl from Brooklyn, she quickly rose in the pecking order, and for the past three years had been Eddie's best girl and lover. She enjoyed the feeling of power she got through her work. And the money gave her a feeling of security she'd never known since her mother died, leaving her only child an orphan at nine years old. Now, in the swank hotels and bars of New York, Alice was queen.

May watched with growing admiration and nervousness as Alice slipped a long filter cigarette from her diamond-encrusted case, then shimmied over to the man and asked him for a light. A couple of minutes' conversation later he had joined them, beaming broadly, at their table. They were now into the round of drinks that Bob had ordered for them and he was becoming expansive, focusing all his attention on May.

'An actress an' all,' he said in his high mid-Western whine. 'I ain't never met a real actress before.'

'So you said, Bob,' said Alice wearing her false smile.

Warming to the game, May was happily trying out her new Irish-American accent. 'But surely, Bob, with all the travelling you do...'

'Oh sure,' he said with a peacock grin, 'I've met plenty of girls. Some might have said they was actresses, but hell - pardon me,' he apologized, touching May's hand. 'They was none of them on Broadway!'

May feigned a modest blush. 'It's only a very small part.'

'But I bet you'll be great!' Bob gushed. 'Finish up. Let's drink to success!' He turned to the tuxedoed waiter hovering nearby. 'Hey, buddy, hit us again!' Turning back to the table he looked at May's empty glass with raised eyebrows. 'Boy, that was quick.'

'I don't like the taste,' she replied, a little flustered.

'Just the effect, eh?' He grinned, a touch too lasciviously.

Alice watched as May smiled shyly and fluttered her eyelashes. She looked at the tiny gold watch on her wrist. 'Goodness, is that the time? We have to go, May.'

'Oh gee, really?' Bob's dismay was genuine. 'You can't. I've just ordered drinks.'

'You have mine, Bob. I really have to go.'

'Do you have to go as well, May? I kinda like talking to you,' said Bob, looking at May like a lost dog looking for a home.

May glanced at Alice. 'Well..'

'I guess you don't have to go,' Alice said. 'They're not expecting you.'

Bob's smile was from ear to ear. 'That's settled then.'

Alice rose, gathering up her jeweled handbag. She kissed May lightly on the cheek. 'See you later.' Then, with her lips so close to her ear May could feel Alice's warm breath, she whispered, 'Kill.'

May watched as Alice walked away, turning at the doorway to give her a wink, unseen by Bob who was still beaming, hardly able to believe that this beautiful young girl had dropped into his lap. May returned his smile, suddenly nervous again, now her mentor had gone. Would she be able to go through with this? She was excited and terrified at the same time. It was a heady mix of emotions that made her feel very alive.

The waiter arrived from around the palms, and put down their drinks. Bob picked up his glass and held it out to May. 'Here's to us.'

Picking up her drink, May touched his with hers.

'Down the hatch,' he said and downed his whisky sour in one. He put down his empty glass just as May was putting down hers. Bob grinned, surprised. 'Boy, you sure don't like the taste!'

May smiled, secretly thrilled how easily the trick Alice taught her had worked. But she knew that the real test was yet to come. And that would be a whole lot harder than tipping martinis into potted palms.

CHAPTER SEVEN

The taxi pulled up at the brownstone building that had been converted into a low-cost hotel sometime after the turn of the century. Bob peered from the cab window at the dimly-lit doorway, skeptically. 'This is the place?' he asked, frowning.

'I did say it's only a very small part,' May answered in explanation. 'It was so good of you to see me back,' she added touching the sleeve of his overcoat lightly.

'No, no. I had to see Sarah Bernhardt back to her hotel, didn't I?'

There was a slight pause. May could hear his heavy breathing in the darkness beside her. 'Well, Bob, it's been very nice meeting you.'

His reply sounded slightly strangled in his throat. 'Well, I think I better see you inside the hotel. This doesn't look like the kind of neighborhood for a pretty, young girl to be alone in.'

May led Bob down the dimly-lit corridor, her trembling legs hardly able to support her. With her heart pounding in her chest, she turned the key in the lock. She opened the door, turned on the light and stepped into the cheaply-furnished room. Apart from the double-bed, which dominated the room, the only other furniture was a bedside table, a wooden chair and a large, double-doored wardrobe. She turned to Bob, who was standing in the doorway, grinning nervously.

'Thank you, Bob.'

Bob glanced at his watch. 'Would you look at that? I missed my train.'

'Oh, I'm sorry. That's all my fault.'

'There's one later...' He paused, looking this way and that along the corridor. 'I guess...I guess I couldn't wait in here?'

Despite her own nervousness, May's heart went out to him. He suddenly looked like a small boy, asking a favor he desperately wanted, but didn't expect to get. May looked around at the bare, gloomy room lit by a single light bulb. 'Well, it's not much,' she said apologetically.

'I really like talking to you May,' he blurted out, anxious to scotch any suggestion that something else might be on his mind.

She pretended to deliberate his request. 'Well, I suppose...of course, come in,' she smiled.

Bob stepped inside eagerly, in case she was about to change her mind. May closed the door and turned back to him, feeling her face heat up, despite the chill of the room. He stood awkwardly in the centre of the room holding his hat.

'Can I take your coat?'

'That's okay,' he said, and produced a brown paper package from his pocket. 'Scotch?' he asked, offering the package to her.

May shook her head. 'I *really* don't like the taste of that.'

'Gee, I'm sorry. I don't have anything else. I didn't expect...' he hesitated.

'That's okay. You go ahead,' she encouraged.

Bob smiled his thanks, guiltily, and took the top off the bottle, still wrapped in the paper bag. 'Good health.' He took a pull on the bottle and swallowed hard. Replacing the top he put the bottle back inside his pocket and looked at May sheepishly.

May was convinced he could hear her heart thumping against her ribs. 'I'll light the fire,' she said, crossing to the gas fire on the wall.

Here. Let me.' He produced a lighter, bent down to turn on the gas tap, then applied a flame to the single burner. The fire popped into life. He straightened up and they both stood watching the mantel begin to glow red.

'That's better,' May said lamely. 'Soon be warm now.'

Bob nodded. He took the bottle from his pocket once more. 'You sure..?' he said, holding it out to her.

May shook her head. 'No. Really. But, please, you go ahead.'

He drank more deeply this time, and wiped the back of his hand across his lips. 'I...er...' he began and faltered.

'Yes?' May encouraged, nervously.

'Well, I know I said back there, in the bar...' he continued haltingly, looking down at the glowing fire. 'Well, I sorta implied that I...well...I...Darn it, the truth is, May, I ain't never cheated on my wife Marybelle. Not never in fifteen years.'

May felt a warm swell of relief wash over her. For the first time that evening, her smile to him was genuine. 'I'm sure glad to hear that, Bob.'

The woman and two young children in the photograph smiled out at her. 'They're lovely. You have such a beautiful family. You're very lucky, Bob,' May said, handing the photograph back to Bob who was seated on the bed beside her.

'Yeah, yeah,' he agreed, taking another slug from the bottle, which was now half empty.

They were both propped up with their backs against the wooden bed-head, fully clothed. May was relaxed now, feeling very much in control. 'You must miss them though. Traveling about like you do.'

Bob nodded morosely, turning the family picture round and round in his fingers. He turned to her, his face sad and plaintive.

May straightened up, concerned. 'What is it, Bob?'

'I'm sorry, May...' he paused, sniffing back a tear.

May turned to face him fully, putting a hand on his arm. 'What for?'

'I lied to you..'

'What about?'

'I'm out of a job. Two months now...' He continued, his voice breaking, 'Haven't had the guts to tell Marybelle.'

'Oh Bob...' She took his hand in hers as the tears rolled down his cheeks.

He raised the bottle to his lips once more, and drank deeply. Cradling the bottle in his lap he let the tears flow silently, his lower lip trembling. May continued holding his hand and stroked the back of it with her fingers. She wanted to take this sad man in her arms and hug him, but she had never held a man before and was uncertain, wary. The man closest to her in her young life had never been a man to show affection to.

'Ten years,' he said suddenly, bitterness stifling the tears. 'Ten years I worked for them. Ten years they sucked the blood out of me...And know what..? I got ten lousy bucks to my name...I was going to the track when I met you...'

'The track?'

'The dog track...Thought if I could pick a winner Marybelle wouldn't have to know. Leastways not for a while.'

'No, Bob. You can't do that. What if you lose?'

He turned to her, eyes glistening with tears. 'Throw myself in the river.'

May pulled back, shocked. 'Bob! You have a lovely wife. Two lovely children. You can't do that! You can't leave them to fend all on their own..! You can beat this, Bob.' she said urgently. 'You can beat this for them. I know you can.'

His eyes never left hers, as if in some way he could draw the strength he saw in her face into his own body. 'Yeah..? You really believe that, May?'

'I do!' she said passionately. 'I do..! But the first thing you have to do is go home and tell her. Tell her everything. It's nothing to be ashamed of...She'll understand. She loves you, doesn't she?

Bob nodded tearfully and put his fist to his mouth to stifle a sob.

'Then she'll help you. You can beat this together.'

He continued to gaze at her, wiping his cheeks with the sleeve of his overcoat.

'Now go,' she said gently. 'Go straight home and tell her.'

He looked at her for a long moment. 'You're a wonderful young woman, May,' he said at last.

'Ah, away with you,' she said lapsing into her Irish brogue, forgetfully, caught in the genuineness of the moment. 'Come on now.' She slipped off the bed and helped him to his feet. He swayed unsteadily to the door, holding her hand.

'You're an angel, May,' he said, his voice thick with gratitude. 'You know that?'

May smiled. 'I don't know that the Good Lord would agree... Wait.' Taking her purse from her pocket, she took out a five dollar bill and slipped it into his hand. 'Here.'

'What's this?'

'Take a cab. So you don't miss your train.' She straightened his tie and smoothed down the collar of his coat. 'Your family's waiting for you, Bob McLeish.'

He smiled sadly at her, regretful. 'You're a wonderful girl, May. You deserve your name in lights. I'm sure I'll see you up there someday.'

May smiled guiltily. Bob leaned and kissed her on the cheek. She opened the door. He swayed out into the corridor and turned to her one last time.

'God bless you, May. God bless you.'

She watched him make his way unsteadily down the darkened corridor and then closed the door. As soon as the door clicked shut, the doors of the wardrobe were flung open and a furious Alice burst out, stumbling into the room aching from being cooped up inside the cramped space for so long. She glared at May, face red with anger. 'What the hell do you think you're playing at!' she yelled.

In his showy penthouse apartment overlooking Central Park, Eddie lay back on the black leather sofa holding his sides with laughter. Alice sat beside him, a smile playing about her crimson lips, seeing the funny side now. May stood before them sheepishly, eyes cast down, feeling deeply humiliated. After a moment Eddie regained his power of speech. 'You're supposed to fleece the guy, not pay his cab fare!'

May looked up, her eyes beginning to regain their natural fire. 'I couldn't take his money. He was so sad. He was going to jump in the river.'

'He was probably shooting you a line', Eddie grinned. 'You've been had, doll.'

Alice joined in the humiliation. 'All you had to do was get his clothes in the closet. I'd have done the rest.'

'You do *know* how to get a guy's clothes off, I suppose?' Eddie said, searching her face with his penetrating ice blue eyes.

May looked at the floor then around the room, avoiding his gaze, feeling the hot flush of embarrassment flood her throat and cheeks. Eddie looked at Alice and raised his eyebrows.

'It's not right anyway,' May said defensively. 'It's stealing.'

With another glance at Alice, Eddie rose and took May's chin in his hand. May flinched away instinctively, with a tiny stifled cry. Eddie held her chin firmly. 'Hey. It's all right. I ain't gonna hurt you. I don't hit broads.' He looked deep into her eyes and continued in a stern tone, as if lecturing a child, which indeed he was. 'Where do you think you come from, May? A frigging palace? You wanna wind up like them bums sleeping in shop doorways?'

May wrenched her face from his grip, angrily, her eyes flaring. 'I could have! You stole me money! I'd done nothing to you! I could have froze to death that night! And I'd done nothing to hurt you!'

'You're a sucker,' Eddie said sharply. 'Suckers hurt everybody.'

He crossed to an elegant mahogany bureau, opened the top drawer and took something out. Turning back to May he held out the object in his hand. It was the purse he had stolen from her. 'Here. You want this? It's still got all your Mick money in it. Go out there. See how far it gets you.' May stood silently, eyes cast down at the expensive carpet at her feet. Eddie offered it again. 'Take it...'

Cornered, May looked at the purse, tears stinging her eyes. She had seen the way Alice lived, the way Eddie controlled his world, glimpsed the life she was being offered. It was the kind of luxury she had dreamed of for so long. She could have it, and for what? A little deception. A little dishonesty. Hadn't she done worse back in Ireland to make her escape?

'Or do you want in?' Eddie said gently.

CHAPTER EIGHT

Snow lay thickly on the sidewalk, being steadily trampled into slippery, grey slush by the passersby outside the Blackbird Club. In the warm, welcoming interior, Harry wiped the bar and looked idly around at the customers eating and drinking. It was the lull before the theatergoers flocked in after the shows to drink the night away. The few customers were mostly regulars, locals happy to eat at Harry's prices rather than fix a meal for themselves in their lonely apartments. New York was a great city, but it could be a cruel, uncaring place if you weren't in control of your life. Harry glanced at Eddie, seated alone in the shadows at the back of the club, engrossed in the sports pages of a newspaper. Eddie Young was in control. He was going places.

'Society' Eddie had first made the club his 'office' about five years ago, as a fresh-faced twenty-three year old. A shrewd, wise-cracking kid who had risen from the tough streets of the Bronx, Eddie was a mixture of warm geniality and cold menace. The coterie of associates who gathered around him nightly laughed uproariously at his jokes, happily drank his whisky, and feared his wrath. It was only a rumor, never confirmed, that at least one unfortunate conman was rotting at the bottom of the East River after trying to double-cross the handsome, self-styled 'King of the Grifters'.

The front door opened letting in an icy blast from the street. Two young women entered, dressed head to toe in furs with matching hats. They closed the door quickly and walked arm in arm towards the rear of the club, their heels clicking on the tiled floor that ran alongside the cozy, carpeted booths.

'Hi, Harry,' said the older of the two.

'Alice,' he replied.

'Hi, Harry,' parroted the younger, prettier girl. Unlike her companion, she was a girl. Beneath the sophisticated makeup and clothes, Harry guessed May was no more than sixteen or seventeen. But what a difference from the starved, innocent, frightened young child who had stumbled into the club that cold, late night only a few days ago. No longer innocent. No longer scared. May was beautiful, she was ambitious and she was class. Harry sensed trouble down the line.

Alice and May slid into the booth opposite Eddie. Laying his paper aside, he grinned at them expectantly. 'So whad'ya know?'

From her handbag Alice produced a wad of dollar bills of various denominations and handed them to Eddie. May looked on smiling, feeling pleased with herself, as Eddie counted the bills. She had done it. Just as Alice had taught her. It had been scary and exciting, but she had done it!

'Not bad,' he said when he had finished counting. 'For your first real day, not bad.'

'May's a natural,' said Alice. She took off her hat and shook her hair. May did the same, shaking her curls free.

Eddie peeled off a few bills from the wad, dropped them in front of May and slipped the rest of the money into his inside pocket. May looked down at the money, a frown furrowing her creamy-white brow. It was only a small fraction of the total amount she had earned that day.

'But that's...' she began, then stopped, sensing both their eyes were on her.

'Problem?' Eddie was looking at her steadily.

May glanced at Alice. She returned May's look, impassive. May fingered the bills for a moment, then biting her tongue, she picked them up and put them into her handbag.

'Good girl,' said Eddie, with a significant glance at Alice. 'Let's eat.'

The next day, May followed Alice up the stairs of the apartment block with a sinking feeling. This neighborhood wasn't nearly as smart as where Alice lived, and the apartment block itself was dark and gloomy even on such a bright, crisp winter's morning like today. On the third floor landing, Alice paused beside a door and produced a key from her pocket. Turning the key in the lock she opened the door and went inside. May followed her and her heart sank.

The apartment was little better than the creep-joint room where Alice and she did their business. There was a single bed, a closet, a table with two chairs, a sink and small gas cooker, all occupying a space smaller than Alice's kitchen. Alice opened another door and looked inside. 'Hey, you've got your own john,' she said brightly. 'Stead of sharing with a dozen bums down the corridor.'

Glancing inside the tiny room, May glimpsed the toilet bowl beside a scruffy shower cubicle with a faded shower curtain. When she turned back to the main room her expression said it all.

Alice read her face. 'Kid, you could be sleeping on the sidewalk.'

May felt the mattress on the bed. It was old and thin. The cooker top had a coating of burnt-on grease and the thick porcelain sink was stained brown by a dripping tap. She thought of Alice's apartment and felt like crying.

'It's what you get for the dough,' Alice explained sympathetically.

Picturing the wad of money they had given Eddie the previous evening, May asked. 'Why does Eddie have to take so much? We do all the work.'

'He's your protection.'

'Against what?'

Alice looked at her with a worldly smile. 'Everything. It's a tough world out there, kid.'

May sat down heavily on the lumpy bed, pouting. 'I don't need protecting. I can look after myself.'

'Sure you can. You and your cute little donkey.' Alice teased.

May looked up at her. Alice chuckled. May gave a rueful smile, remembering her naivety of only a few days ago. Alice sat down beside May and put an arm around her shoulders, reassuringly. 'Give it time, kid. Rome wasn't built in a day. You're doing great.'

'I want a place like yours, Alice. I'll never have that if Eddie takes all the money.'

Alice lifted a lock of May's curls from her eyes. 'This place isn't so bad. Just needs a little loving that's all. A few curtains, a lick of paint.'

'I can't even afford that,' May replied sulkily.

'Want me to show you a short cut?'

May looked at her curiously. 'What's a short cut?'

Macy's on Herald Square was the first department store May had ever been inside. Having everything you could ever want in one shop was a revelation, almost like a miracle. She wandered wide-eyed along the aisles, past counters laden with goods of all descriptions, with Alice at her side, amused at May's childlike wonder at something she had always taken for granted. At least since she had met Eddie. Her own life till then had not been so great, which was why she had taken a special liking to May, she guessed. She sensed a deep sadness in the young girl that could only have come from a childhood deprived of the pleasures all children ought to have. Well, she would do her best to remedy that for May.

Casually, Alice looked about her and noticed the young man in a cheap grey suit lingering at a counter a couple of aisles away. There was something too studied about the way he was examining the goods to mark him out as a genuine shopper. She smiled to herself. At another counter May had picked up a pearl-backed hairbrush and was turning it this way and that, marveling at the myriad colors the surface created as it caught the light. She turned to Alice.

'Isn't this just beautiful? Wish I could afford it.'

'Let me see,' said Alice.

May handed her the brush. Alice turned it admiringly in her hand and then, with one swift movement, slipped it inside her fur coat.

'Ahh!' May gasped, involuntarily.

Alice saw the young man glance their way. She smiled prettily in his direction. He looked away shyly. Taking May's arm, she led her away.

'Alice, you stole that,' whispered May incredulously.

'Stop looking like you expect the sky to fall in,' Alice said calmly. 'Let's see what else you need.'

On each level of the store, at several counters, Alice slipped items into the large purpose-made pockets inside her coat, as May looked on amazed and terrified, with flushed cheeks and the pulse pounding in her throat. They returned to the ground floor and were browsing the handbag section when Alice turned to her. 'Okay, your turn.'

'What?' May asked, hoping she had misheard.

'My coat's full. Don't you just love that snakeskin bag?' She picked up the small leather handbag and handed it to May. May's mouth had gone dry. She felt her face growing so red and hot she felt it would catch fire at any moment. 'Don't wait too long. Looks suspicious.'

'I can't,' May implored, her voice barely a murmur.

Alice looked about her. 'It's okay,' she said coolly. 'Do it now.'

Scarcely able to breathe, May opened her coat, slipped the bag inside and panicked. 'There's no pocket!' she gasped, her heart hammering in her chest.

'Hold it under your arm. We're going now anyway.'

With her legs trembling so violently she felt hardly able to stand, May allowed Alice to shepherd her towards the front entrance where a uniformed doorman opened the door for them to exit. Alice calmly nodded her gratitude and stepped to the edge of the sidewalk awaiting a taxi. Glancing behind nervously through the double glass doors of the store, May could see a young man looking out at them strangely. She turned to Alice who was preoccupied looking up and down the avenue searching for a cab in the bustling traffic. 'Alice!' she hissed.

May turned again and saw the young man approaching the entrance. The doorman put his hand on the handle to open the door for him. Panicked, May stumbled away down the crowded sidewalk, dropping the handbag from her coat as she went.

The yell came loudly behind her. 'Stop thief!'

Turning to look back as she ran, she felt her body collide with a solid object and a pair of strong, masculine arms wrap around her. Alarmed, she looked up, straight into the deep brown eyes of Officer Joe Perski.

CHAPTER NINE

All the way to the 5th precinct station May cried silently, alone in the back of the police van. Joe sat up front with the driver, seemingly not having recognized her, which was testament to Alice's genius.

She couldn't stop crying or her whole body from trembling. Now it would all come out. The police would discover who she really was, and she would be shipped back on the first boat to Ireland. With modern wireless telegraph they would be able to contact the police in the nearest town. They in turn would relay the news to the constable in the village. He would make the long trek across the bog to tell her father, and he would be waiting for her, murderous with rage, when she stepped ashore. Except that she wouldn't be on the boat. She resolved that she would throw herself into the cold, grey waves rather than face the fate that awaited her at home. That thought alone gave her a crumb of comfort. She was still in control of her destiny. But what if they kept her locked up on the boat? She was a criminal after all. She wouldn't be given a chance to take her own life. They would leave that to her father, who would use and abuse her to an early grave, as he had her mother.

May stood, handcuffed, before the sergeant's desk with Joe Perski and the young store detective standing at either side. The small snakeskin handbag lay on the desk in front of the sergeant's nose. The handcuffs felt heavy and cold around her slender wrists. 'We want her charged, sergeant,' said the young man self-importantly. 'This is happening all the time. We got to set an example.'

The sergeant picked up the bag and turned it over in his hands. 'You know she'll go down for this?'

'She should have thought of that before she stole it,' the man replied coldly.

The sergeant looked at the fresh-faced young man. He guessed he was new to the job. Maybe he had just returned from the trenches, hardened by the horrors his young eyes had seen. Or maybe not. Surely that experience would have taught him compassion. He looked at Joe and shrugged. What could he do? Help ruin another young life that was already on the way to ruin anyway. He had three years to go before his retirement. It couldn't come too soon. He turned to May resignedly. 'Name?'

The young girl's eyes remained fixed on the floorboards, where the tears and the snot dribbling from her nose were making a tiny dark stain on the wood. She sniffed and mumbled something unintelligible.

'Say again?' the sergeant asked kindly.

The voice was tiny. 'May...May Sharpe.'

Joe stirred beside her. He peered down at her lowered face, shrouded by the brim of her hat. At that moment the double doors to the station were flung open with a crash and Eddie Young burst in, immaculate in double-breasted suit, silk bow-tie, homburg and white spats. He strode up to the sergeant's desk like a prize-fighter entering the ring. 'Frank! Frank! What gives?' Eddie put his arm around May's shoulders in an affectionate hug. 'You okay, sweetheart?'

'You know her, Eddie?' Things were suddenly clicking into place in the sergeant's brain.

'She's my niece.' He turned to face the store detective. 'Who's this bum?'

'He's the detective who caught her thieving at his store,' the sergeant explained.

Eddie bristled. 'Sez who?!'

'She stole this,' said the young man picking up the handbag from the desk.

Cutting him short, Eddie snatched up the bag from his hand and brandished it like a weapon. 'This? My niece steals cheap junk like this! Gimme a break, Frank!'

'She's not his niece, serg,' Joe cut in.

'Who asked you?' snapped Eddie, looking at Joe as if he'd just found him on the bottom of his shoe.

The store detective pressed on. 'It was under her coat. She dropped it when she ran.'

'These two guys saw it, Eddie,' the sergeant said patiently, already knowing where this situation was headed.

'It was a mistake. You pick it up. You forget to pay.' He spread his hands to the sergeant, appealing. 'You got daughters, Frank. You know what young girls are like.'

The sergeant shifted uneasily. Eddie pressed home his advantage. 'What can I say? I promised my only sister on her death bed I'd take care of her daughter. I do my best, but I'm a businessman. I can't be with her every minute of the day. She's new to the city. She doesn't understand.'

Head bowed, May stood listening to Eddie weave his spell, her hopes rising. 'I'm sorry, Uncle Eddie,' she said contritely, almost beginning to enjoy the novel experience. 'I just forgot it.'

The detective could feel things slipping from his grasp. 'My store has a policy of prosecuting thieves,' he said stiffly.

'Thieves?' Eddie rounded on him. 'You calling my niece a thief?'

The young man stood his ground gamely, 'She stole...' But then took an involuntary pace back as Eddie shoved his face close to his.

'Listen, pal,' he hissed venomously. 'You heard what she said. It was a mistake. You lay a finger on my niece again and I'll break both your legs!'

'Eddie,' cautioned the sergeant. In his domain he could only allow things to go so far, no matter what Eddie's connections.

Eddie backed off and relaxed. 'Get them bracelets off,' he ordered Joe.

Joe looked at the sergeant, who shrugged. The store detective stood cowed. He watched meekly as Joe produced a key and began to unlock the manacles from May's pale white wrists, trying to catch her eye as he did so. But May's eyes remained resolutely downcast, avoiding his gaze.

'Catch you later, Frank,' Eddie said familiarly, putting his arm around May's shoulder's to escort her from the station. As a parting shot, he turned back menacingly to the detective, who was standing open-mouthed, but speechless. 'You watch it, pal. I got my eye on you.'

The three men watched in silence as the double doors closed behind Eddie and his young companion. After a moment Joe followed them out and stood on the steps looking on as Eddie opened the door of his waiting roadster for May to get in. Then with a parting wave to the young officer, Eddie slid behind the wheel and started the car.

Relief was flooding over May like a warm ocean breeze. She had failed, but Eddie had saved her. 'Thank you, Eddie,' she said, her voice catching.

Eddie fixed her with an arctic stare, 'Forget it. Just remember next time when you beef about my cut.'

Joe's head was swimming as he watched the car speed away with a squeal of rubber. If he didn't know better he'd have believed May really was Eddie's niece. She had picked up the lie as deftly as a bum picked up a cigarette butt from the gutter. What was May Sharpe doing back in the clutches of a criminal like Eddie Young, when he had put her on the train to Springfield? As he watched the roadster disappear around the corner, the concern on his young face turned to determination.

CHAPTER TEN

Eddie was silent on the journey back to her new apartment. When May tried, stumblingly, to explain what had happened at the store, he didn't seem interested, responding with unintelligible grunts. He dropped her off without a word. She mumbled her gratitude once more, but he was speeding away before she could finish.

Feeling miserable and rejected, she climbed the gloomy staircase to the third floor and let herself in. Mick ran to greet her, yapping excitedly. She picked him up and sat on the bed, stroking his head for comfort.

'And I thought I was doing so well, Mick,' she sighed. The dog, sensing her mood, nuzzled his head in her lap and looked up at her with sad, soulful eyes. May sighed again, heavily. Her relief at having escaped being sent back home was mingled with concern that she was now skating on thin ice with Eddie. She recalled the tearful girl who had pushed past them as they entered the Blackbird Club. She didn't want to be out in the cold, alone.

There was a knock on the door. Putting Mick under her arm, May went to open it. Alice was standing outside with a wide smile on her face. May looked down at her coat, puzzled. Alice looked heavily pregnant. She bustled inside and May closed the door behind her. 'Sorry about the bust, kid. I brought you a little present to make up for it.' Opening her coat she pulled cushions, silk sheets and finally a bolt of pink silk curtain fabric from the voluminous pockets. May stood with her mouth wide open in astonishment. 'You know how to make curtains?' Alice asked.

The lights were being lit all over the city. In the final flourish of a vivid sunset the brownstone tenements opposite May's apartment glowed like fire. In the tiny room the woman and the girl worked happily, bathed in the pool of light from a single lamp, surrounded by the flowing material. Mick had long since tired of playing hide-and-seek in the folds, and was sleeping peacefully beneath the cloth on May's feet. Alice suddenly sniffed and wiped her eyes with her free hand.

'You okay?' asked May.

Alice nodded and sniffed again, this time producing a white cotton handkerchief to blow her nose. She looked at May and smiled, a sad smile. 'I haven't enjoyed sewing since my mom died.'

'When was that?'

'I was nine...We used to sew together. Little dresses, cushions for the apartment.' Her expression suddenly changed and became hard. 'They used to beat us in the orphanage if you didn't sew fast enough.'

May felt privileged. It was the first time Alice had revealed anything about her past life. 'What did they make you sew?'

Alice gave a bitter laugh. 'What didn't they? Mailbags, corn sacks, kitbags. They made a fortune out of us. Not that we saw any of it...Your mom teach you?'

May nodded her head. 'I'd only just started when she died. I was five.'

'I'm sorry...What did she die of?'

'Hard work...That and the beatings.'

Alice nodded understandingly. It was an all too familiar story at the orphanage.

Lost in her memories, May went on, 'Me Da wouldn't pay for a decent burial. Though I knew he had the money...She was buried in a pauper's grave. No stone. Not even a little cross.'

Alice was shocked. 'Gee, that's awful! Imagine not having anything to be remembered by. When I go I'm gonna have me a big white marble headstone. A pretty, smiling angel.'

May smiled at the image, tears close by. Looking at her, Alice smiled. 'Yeah. Kinda like that.'

She opened her arms. May moved to her and nestled to her breast, the tears flowing now. Alice stroked the soft curls of her head. As the light finally faded from the sky, they stayed in silence, cocooned together in the nest of soft, pink silk.

The next afternoon, when May returned from the errand downtown she had been sent on, Alice made her stand on the landing outside the door. It had been exciting negotiating the big city by herself for the first time. The subway was strange, noisy and scary, but she had braved it. It was almost dark by the time she had made it back and she was feeling very proud of herself. Now she was cold and ready for a hot drink.

'Are you ready?' Alice asked from inside.

'Just open the door, Alice. I'm cold.'

'Okay, but close your eyes and no peeking until I say.'

May was intrigued. 'Open the door!'

She closed her eyes and heard Alice open the door. Feeling Alice take her hand, she allowed herself to be led into the room. The door closed behind her.

'Okay, you can open your eyes.'

May did as she was told. The room was in total darkness. Then suddenly it was flooded with light. May gasped in surprise and delight. 'Aaaaeeehhh..! Alice!'

The shabby room had been transformed. The sofa, cushions and lampshade had been covered in the material Alice had brought and the curtains they had made together now hung prettily at the window. 'Alice! She repeated and hugged her hard, spinning them both round and round laughing. May broke away and went around the room touching the new coverings.

'You like it?'

'It's marvelous! A beautiful room all of me own.'

'*My* own,' Alice corrected.

'Sorry, yes, *my* own!' She took hold of Alice's hands. "I am truly, truly grateful, Alice. You doing this for me.'

Alice smiled happily, 'It's my pleasure, kid.' Then her expression clouded as she decided to say it. 'Anyway, it's the least I could do...for setting you up.'

May frowned, mystified. 'Setting me up. I don't understand.'

Alice was unable to look her in the eyes. 'The store. Eddie wanted to teach you a lesson,' she confessed guiltily. 'He doesn't like to be challenged about his cut.'

'The store..?' Suddenly it all made sense to May. She let go of Alice's hands.

'I'm sorry, kid,' Alice shrugged. 'I hated to do it, but that's the way it is.'

A shiver ran down May's spine. She would have to be very careful around Eddie from now on.

CHAPTER ELEVEN

Spring had come early to the city. Under the warmth of the brightening sun, buds were bursting on the trees that lined the avenues. After the long months of hibernation, flowers had started to emerge, blinking, in the tiny front gardens of the brownstones and children were once again playing in the street, their happy cries echoing up into the bright blue sky. It was Sunday morning. In her apartment, whose transformation she had added to week by week as she became more and more adept at her new profession, May was preparing herself a leisurely fried breakfast. In a patch of sunlight streaming through the window, Mick lay expectantly at her feet as the sausages sizzled in the pan.

May was wearing a fetching cream peignoir, a present from her best friend Alice. No matter that it had undoubtedly been stolen rather than paid for, it was the thought that mattered. She smiled to herself remembering how, only a few short weeks ago, stealing had seemed to her like a mortal sin. But, back home in Ireland, fear and desperation had driven her to committing that sin herself and it had led to the life she was now living. Happy, secure, safe and, what was more, exciting. Stealing was now her way of life and it felt good. Since the first embarrassing evening when she had given Bob McLeish five dollars for his cab fare, May had hardened her heart to the many sob stories she was told nightly. Of frigid wives who didn't understand their husbands needs, of ungrateful children who demanded more and more of their hard-pressed fathers, of careers blighted by ambitious rivals, or successes that had led to deserved windfalls. Windfalls that May had become expert at seeking out and picking from unsuspecting pockets. She enjoyed the teamwork that she and Alice had developed and was secretly proud that they had become the talk of their little patch of the underworld. The toast of the nightly revelries at the Blackbird when the gang gathered to celebrate the day's work.

The doorbell chimed. May frowned. She wasn't expecting anyone this early in the day. Most of her crowd were night owls, rarely surfacing before noon. Sliding the pan from the flames, she wrapped her peignoir more tightly around her and, with Mick at her heels, went to open the door. Outside, in uniform, stood Officer Joe Perski.

For a brief moment panic gripped her. Not long ago it would have reduced her to a trembling wreck, but through her work she had developed a hard carapace and, as quickly as it came, the fear subsided. She stood tall and looked him boldly in the eyes. 'Oh, you,' she snapped coldly. 'What do you want?'

The concern on his face was transparent. 'I thought you were going to live with your uncle in Virginia? I put you on the train.'

Unlike their first encounter at the docks, May was now very skilled at thinking on her feet. She decided to play along and looked down at her pretty bare toes, feigning embarrassment. 'I did...I went there...but...my uncle...he tried to...It wasn't my fault. I didn't encourage him or anything like that. But my aunt caught us and threw me out.'

'Oh. I'm sorry to hear that. But what're you doing back here? With Eddie Young?'

'I didn't know anyone. I had nowhere to go,' she said, playing little girl lost to the hilt. 'I had his card...Eddie's been very kind to me. He lent me this apartment.'

Her act had clearly worked. Joe's face became grave. 'Miss Sharpe. I gotta tell you. This guy is bad news. He ain't doing nothing for nothing.'

May looked up at him innocently. 'I don't understand.'

'There's no way to butter this,' he said uncomfortably. 'He's a crook. You gotta get away from him.'

May widened her eyes even further in mock disbelief. 'A crook? No, never, he can't be!'

'I seen you hanging with that gang of his at the Blackbird. He calls them 'business associates' but they're all just cheap crooks and hoodlums, believe me. Pretty soon he'll have you thieving or grifting or worse.' He hesitated for a moment, then added a little shyly. 'I'd hate to see a pretty face like yours behind bars, Miss Sharpe.' He looked down at the shine on his regular issue boots to hide the flush he felt rising in face.

'Grifting?' May asked disingenuously. 'What's that?'

'Conning guys. Telling lies. Stealing their money. I don't know what happened with you at the store, but that's how he starts people out.' He looked up at her again, holding her gaze this time. 'I sure hope you ain't got into that.'

Inwardly May smiled. In the past weeks she had spent so much time with so many different men she had learnt to easily read the signs. She felt totally in control. 'But I don't have any place else to go,' she said disarmingly.

A light of hope ignited in his eyes. 'There's a church hostel I know, in the next block.'

It was all May could do from breaking out in peals of laughter. If he only knew her experience of churches and priests! 'A church hostel?' she repeated mildly.

Joe nodded, hopefully. 'They know me. I could put in a word.'

May smiled, enjoying herself. 'Have you had breakfast?'

'Pardon me?'

'I was just cooking breakfast. Maybe we could talk it over while we eat? About the hostel?'

He hesitated, sniffing the tempting aroma of the sausages. 'Well, sure smells good. I'm due off anyhow. You was on my way home.'

'And there's no one at home waiting to cook you breakfast?'

'No. I live on my own.'

May stood aside to let him enter. 'Be my guest.'

'If it's no trouble,' he said, stepping inside and taking off his cap.

May closed the door and took Joe's cap from his hand with one easy motion. It felt just like working over a john. 'You never cook breakfast, I suppose?'

'Never had no-one to teach me. My mom left when I was still a kid. Policing can be tough on a family. Hard to leave it on the outside, y'know?'

'So I see,' May said with a grin.

Joe smiled bashfully in response.

A shaft of the spring sunshine lit up the table where May had seated Joe. The damask tablecloth, napkins and silver cutlery shone brightly in his eyes. He stroked the rich material of the cloth with his fingertips. After his mother had walked out of the family home to live with the travelling salesman, his father had never bothered with the finer touches of home life, and Joe had followed his example. He made a mental note to buy a table cloth, just in case.

He watched May serving his breakfast onto a china plate. She was so young, yet so much more assured than the timid young girl he'd met at the docks. That must have come from Eddie. He hoped he had found her again before it was too late. Since the moment May had stumblingly told the sergeant her name at the station Joe had lived in a state of perplexed, high excitement. He didn't know how or why, but she was back in New York. And mixing with a hoodlum.

Joe's sergeant had refused to tell the young cop where Eddie lived or hung out. The old cop knew Eddie had contacts that could make life unpleasant for anyone daring to ruffle his feathers. He'd heard the rumor about the young man fished out of the river a few years back and he didn't want Joe winding up the same way. So it had taken Joe longer than he'd hoped to track down the conman 'Society' Eddie Young to his favorite haunt at the Blackbird Club. But last week he had finally seen her show up there, and the previous night had at last managed to follow her home. He had a second chance to rescue her, and he was determined not to fail this time. 'Did Eddie give you all this stuff?'

May looked up at him and nodded. 'I told you he's been very good to me.'

'You ever wonder how he can afford all this?'

'He said he's in business.'

'Yeah, the crime business. And in his case it pays. Least till I catch up with him,' he added with a steely edge to his voice. He went on ruefully, 'Even if I make detective it'd take me six months pay to buy just what's in front of me,'

'I'm sure you'll make detective.'

'I sure hope so. I promised my dad. He never got the badge. Wouldn't take the bribes.'

'I shouldn't think you will either,' May said truthfully.

'No, sir. I'm gonna make it the hard way or not at all.'

May put the plate in front of him. Sausages, bacon, two eggs and hash browns. He breathed in appreciatively. 'Mmm. Smells good.' He picked up his knife and fork.

'Ah, ketchup!' May exclaimed. Snatching up the bottle from the table she shook it vigorously, all over Joe's uniform. 'Oh goodness!' Grabbing a napkin she tried to wipe the globs of red sauce from his tunic, making it considerably worse in the process. 'Ah, I'm sorry! I'm so sorry!' she gasped, managing to spread the mess onto his trousers.

'It's okay,' he said, flustered. 'It's okay. It was an accident.'

'Oh, but you can't go outside like that,' she insisted. 'Take off your uniform. I'll sponge it down for you.'

'No, really, it's no trouble.'

'Oh, please, I feel terrible.' She looked almost in tears. 'Please. Use the bathroom. I'll keep your breakfast warm for you.'

Joe shrugged and rose from the table. 'Here,' she said, slipping his jacket from his shoulders. She smiled at him guiltily and opened the bathroom door for him. 'Hand your pants out to me. I won't be long. I'm so very sorry.'

With another compliant shrug Joe stepped inside and closed the door. He unbuckled his belt and slipped down his pants, only then remembering with consternation that he'd forgotten to collect his laundry from the old Chinese woman in the apartment below him, who helped him out. Holding his shirt down to cover his nakedness, he opened the door just wide enough to hand his pants to May standing outside. She took them.

'Thanks. I won't be long. I'm so sorry.'

As she closed the door Joe heard her sneeze loudly.

'Bless you!' he called, not having heard the key as it turned in the lock.

Feeling uncomfortable half naked in May's bathroom, Joe wrapped a towel round his waist. 'Don't go to too much trouble now!' he called through the door. 'I gotta neighbor in the dry-cleaning business!'

Joe looked around the tiny room then out of the small window which was half-frosted at the bottom. In the street below two urchins were playing with a makeshift football made of paper and string. Joe smiled at the scene and then turned back to the room. He checked his hair in the small mirror hanging above the water closet and smoothed it down with some water from the tap. May's toiletries were ranged in a neat row on a shelf by the shower. He picked up each one in turn, relishing the knowledge that she touched them too, in her most intimate, private moments. Taking the top from a perfume bottle he inhaled deeply of the exotic aroma. Raising the bottle to read the label he felt it slip in his fingers. He made a couple of frantic grabs at the tiny bottle and managed to catch it before it hit the tiled floor, but not before most of the precious liquid had splashed liberally down his shirt front. Wiping himself down with his hands, he sniffed himself. He smelt real nice. Joe smiled to himself, knowing that when he took his nap that morning, he would doze off smelling her fragrance.

'How you doing?' he called. There was no reply. 'Miss Sharpe?' Still no response. A little impatient now, he glanced out of the window once more and did a double-take. Three floors below, May, now dressed in day clothes, was getting into a cab. It took a moment for it to register. Then he saw the two little urchins. They had abandoned their game for another. One was strutting around wearing Joe's jacket and cap, while the other flourished his police baton in the bright morning sunshine.

The sergeant was seated at his desk engrossed in the sports pages. Sunday morning shifts were dull and endless. Not like Saturday nights which were hectic and sped by in the blink of an eye. He missed the days out on patrol, doing a real policing job, caught up in the life and energy of the city streets, the characters, the excitement, the danger. Reaching out for his mug of coffee, he looked up and frowned. An officer was dragging a young urchin through the front entrance of the station. The little boy was almost engulfed by an officer's jacket and was wearing a patrolman's cap at a jaunty angle.

'What the..?'

The officer took the jacket from the boy and handed it across the desk.

'Joe Perski's,' the officer said grimly. 'Found dumped in the street.'

The sergeant looked at the thick dark red smear across the chest of the jacket. A knot twisted in his stomach. He felt the stain. It was sticky and wet.

The winter had been long and bitter, and at her age it wasn't prudent to chance walking on icy sidewalks. Old bones broke easily. But today spring was really here and she was determined not to spend another morning cooped up in her apartment. She had dressed in her Sunday best, pinned on her favorite hat, fastened the new diamante-studded lead on her darling little Rufus and had stepped out happily to greet the new day.

Turning the corner into the bright sunlight, she saw him. He was young and well built she could tell at first glance as he was wearing only a shirt, with a white towel wrapped around his waist. The young man was perched precariously on the ledge of a small window, stretching out with one hand for the fire escape just tantalizingly out of reach. She watched with alarm as he suddenly made a lunge through the air reaching out with both hands for the iron stairway. As the towel dropped from his waist, she screamed.

CHAPTER TWELVE

Eddie had sent his own car round for her. Since the lesson she had been taught by the department store incident, May had toed the line, accepting the dollars she was given by her boss with good grace and a winning smile. She found she could get by on what she was allowed to keep of her earnings. Whatever else she wanted, but couldn't afford, she stole, often working in tandem with Alice. They had formed a good team in their main profession and were grudgingly acknowledged by the rest of Eddie's girls as the best in the business.

Generally May acted as the bait. It seemed the older men got the younger they preferred their female company. As the two women naturally chose successful men as their 'clients' these tended to be of a more mature age. If Alice resented this division of labor she never showed it. Younger johns occasionally went for Alice, probably working out some dark Oedipal issue of their own, and then May took her turn hiding in the closet. But she preferred being the performer, onstage, in the limelight. She had a natural flare for role playing and enjoyed adapting her character to meet each fresh circumstance. Each john had his own vision of the perfect girl and she endeavored to be that goddess for him for that brief moment. Sometimes she toyed with the notion of becoming an actress. But that was a tough profession and she had seen many young hopefuls reduced to very degraded lives, striving to fulfill their dream. By contrast she never felt debased by what she had chosen to do. She was in control, the abuser not the abused. Perhaps in some way she was gaining revenge for her poor mother, but she didn't hate all men. Only her father.

Well aware by now that she wasn't the only girl in Eddie's 'stable', she had redoubled her efforts to be the best. She took pride in the fact she had learned to work more johns for more dough in a day than any of the others. With a john you never took anything for granted. What you got you worked for. May worked hard. And it was paying off. Eddie had sent his brand new limo and chauffeur to collect her. She felt on the verge of something special.

The young policeman at the intersection held up his hand to stop the traffic on the main avenue. A light drizzle had started to fall like a grey mist and he could feel the rain running inside his sleeve and dribbling down the back of his collar. He sighed inwardly. Being demoted to traffic duty was going to be a big stumbling block against his dream of becoming a detective.

Joe waved on the vehicles waiting on the cross street. Since he had stood before the sergeant's desk wearing just his shirt, towel and boots, smelling, as the sergeant put it 'like a whore's bathroom', he'd become the butt of all the station jokes. He would have laughed too if it didn't hurt so much. It was painful to remember what a fool he'd been. He had been well aware that the beautiful Sharpe girl had already been sucked into Eddie's web when he called on her that fateful Sunday morning. What had he been thinking of? Had he thought he could work a miracle? If he was going to be that naïve, maybe he should have become a priest instead of a cop.

What was it about her that felt so special? On that first day at the docks, why had he had risked a reprimand, or worse, for leaving his patrol to escort her halfway across town to catch a train? A train, he now knew, she never had any intention of leaving town on. He knew why very well. And it hurt even more to admit it to himself, because the feeling wouldn't go away, no matter how much he tried to ignore it. He thought about her lying in bed at night. He dreamt of her, sleeping and waking. It was a feeling he'd never felt for anyone in his life before. He was in love. And it had probably cost him his dream.

He had thought of going round to see her again after that embarrassing event, angry and self-righteous. But the sense of humiliation was stronger than his outrage. She would probably make a fool of him a second time. Third time, if you counted the train.

The honking horn brought him back to the present. A black limo, glistening in the rain, was waiting impatiently at the head of a long line of traffic on the main avenue. The cross street was almost empty. Joe turned and held up his hands to stop the cross street traffic and waved on the main stream. As the limo approached the rear window slowly wound down. Despite his low spirits and his damp uniform, which would be sodden by the end of his shift, Joe's heart skipped a beat. Seated comfortably in the back seat, looking more beautiful than ever, May Sharpe gave him an ironic little wave as the car passed by. As Joe watched the limo glide away up the avenue his handsome face set hard. He was resolved.

May was surprised to find, when she recalled her actions on that Sunday morning, she did so with a tinge of guilt. Surprised because she'd assumed that emotion had been dead and buried long ago. She certainly didn't feel it for any of her 'johns', or the stores she stole from on a regular basis. They were out for what they could get and she exploited that. But the young policeman, Joe, had genuinely seemed like he wanted to help, and she had repaid him with cruelty. Of course he fancied her, that was obvious by the way he blushed whenever his eyes met hers, but fancying someone wasn't a crime. *She* fancied Eddie.

He was handsome, dashing, exciting and daring. May amused herself sometimes thinking up more and more words to describe him. Trustworthy? Only if you didn't cross him. She had made a mental note never to do that again.

But Eddie was with Alice. And Alice was her best friend. Though many people would call her immoral, May was deeply moral where it counted most. Friendship. Alice was the first person she had ever known who gave so freely and without strings attached. May didn't know why she had been singled out among all the others to be the recipient of her friend's largesse, but she would be eternally grateful. And her gratitude meant that, no matter how much she fantasized, she would never make a move for Eddie. Or encourage him if he ever made a move on her.

She was jolted out of her reverie as the car turned a corner and was suddenly engulfed in a seething mass of men fighting furiously outside the closed wrought iron gates of a factory. It was clearly a demonstration of some kind that had turned into a pitched battle. Some men were using their placards as weapons against their opponents, big, brutal-looking men wielding baseballs bats and pickaxe handles. Bloodied bodies milled around the car, screaming and yelling. As May watched in horror a body crashed against the rear side window. May recoiled with a scream and covered her face. Grim-faced, the chauffeur leant on the car horn and bulldozed the limo through the sprawling mob. When the car was clear, May looked back at the mayhem out of the rear window. Her voice was shaking. 'What the hell was that, George?'

The chauffeur spoke over his shoulder, nonchalantly. 'Just some commie bastards getting what's coming.'

'Commie bastards?'

'Strikers. Scum who don't wanna work.'

May turned back to gaze at the scene. It was like a battlefield. As she watched, a slight young man in working clothes and a cap was floored from behind by a brutal blow from a baseball bat. She put her hand to her mouth to stifle her cry. The car sped on down the deserted avenue.

They had arrived to protest peacefully at the factory, having been locked out when the owners brought in scab labor to break their strike. The thugs had been waiting for them, hiding in two trucks parked at the gates. The slight young man's guts had turned to jelly when the battle started. He had been here before, in a land far away, fighting for the future. Now he lay motionless, face down in the road, blood oozing thickly though his blonde hair. As the battle raged around him, darkness enveloped Henry Rawl.

CHAPTER THIRTEEN

With the short, dark wig covering her own abundant curls, May paraded up and down the aisle alongside the booths. Her heels clicked on the tiles. Her hips swung. All eyes were on her. She was in her element.

The Blackbird was closed to casual punters that night. Eddie had booked the entire club for a special Fourth of July party. It was a rare night off. No self-respecting 'john' would be playing the field tonight. The more successful the businessman, the more he would be safe at home, masquerading as the loving husband, caring father, generous, warm-hearted host and friend. Tomorrow was another day.

The champagne had flowed all evening into the early hours. Along with everyone else May was high. The party was fancy dress and she had chosen a short Greek style tunic in ivory coloured silk that showed off her graceful, slim white legs. It gave her a secret thrill that Eddie's eyes had hardly left her all evening, but that was as far as it went. Or would ever go. Diving into her bag, she produced another wig, with flaming red waves. Whipping off the dark wig she deftly fitted the other, having fun dressing up, playing the little girl she had never been allowed to be as a child. She posed for Alice, sitting in the booth beside Eddie. 'What d'you think, Alice?'

'What about?'

'The disguise. Y'know, for the job?'

Alice looked at her critically. 'What's the point?' she slurred.

'So if I bump into any of the johns I've rolled, they won't recognize me,' she grinned.

There was an edge to Alice's voice that May in her happy state didn't catch. 'So they recognize you, what they gonna do? Tell the cops and have their wives find out?' Alice drained her glass. 'I'm pooped, Eddie. Let's split.'

'I think it's neat, kid,' said Eddie to May. 'Why didn't you think of that, Alice?'

Alice pursed her lips in reply.

Eddie rose. 'Don't stay up too late, kid,' he said in a fatherly tone to May and gave her a peck on the cheek. 'You got work tomorrow. I'll send George back to drive you home.'

May spun round theatrically, arms aloft. 'It's a beautiful night. I want to walk home!'

'And wind up fucked and dead in a back alley?' he snapped. His tone brought May up short. 'I'll send George back.'

They left May standing, playing with the long tresses of her wig a little sulkily. Alice looked back at her. It was a look that said maybe fucked and dead in a back alley wasn't such a bad idea.

Judge Bennett Palmer the Third was ushered from the limousine by a fawning doorman to be greeted by a crush of waiting photographers and reporters. He turned back, holding out a hand for his sour-faced wife in the rear seat. She stepped from the car, blinking and waving an irritated hand at the puffs of white smoke as the flash bulbs popped. Mounting the steps of city hall, the couple turned to pose stiffly and impatiently for the photographers. Dubbed the 'hanging judge' for the severity of his sentencing, Bennett Palmer stood statesmanlike, every inch the Supreme Court judge he expected soon to become. Behind the stern mask of gravity the judge was delighted to be back in sin city.

The photograph showed a distinguished, silver-haired man in his late-sixties standing beside a grumpy-looking woman. 'Judge Bennett Palmer the Turd is back in town!' said Eddie with a gleeful expression, holding up the front page of the newspaper for the rest to see.

Eddie and his acolytes were gathered in their favored spot in the rear of the Blackbird. Alice was seated in the booth alongside Eddie with May sitting opposite. 'I know him, the bastard,' Alice scowled. 'Gave me three months one time. If I ever see him again...'

'He'd know ya,' said Eddie.

'You bet he would.'

Eddie folded the newspaper. 'Which is why I'm gonna do the hit with May.'

May was suddenly alert. 'Me?'

Alice turned to him sharply. 'What hit?' Her expression was stony.

'Judge Bennett Palmer ain't in town for his health. Word is he's getting a big payout from the mayor in large bills. So May's gonna get to him before that ugly sow of his wife goes on one of her spending sprees...' He sat back expansively. 'I got some scores to settle with him too.'

'May ain't done the time to hit the judge,' said Alice sharply. She looked at May with a cool smile. 'No offence, kid.'

'She's the best in town,' Eddie said, giving May a smile.

'Eddie, she's too young,' Alice pressed.

'From what I heard he likes 'em young.'

Alice tried another tack. 'It's too dangerous. If May gets caught Bennett Palmer will throw the book at her. She won't get out till she's an old lady!'

Ignoring Alice, Eddie looked at May. 'Well, what d'you say, May? Wanna take the risk with me?'

May leaned over the table to look at the front page photograph. 'Aw, he looks cute,' she said.

Eddie's laughter rocked the chandelier above their heads, making the crystal beads tinkle. 'Cute!' he guffawed. 'That poor bastard ain't gonna know what's hit him!'

As the others roared their approval, Alice pasted on a smile.

May had been thrilled when Eddie had singled her out for the biggest hit of her career to date. Usually the 'johns' were anonymous businessmen from out of town, but from time to time when celebrities breezed into the city, they would be targeted for the special attentions of Eddie's girls, or boys, depending on their sexual preference. It was always more risky hitting on the famous. If things went wrong, they could pull strings with the police and the press to keep their good name out of the case. But the offender would be made an example to others, getting the maximum penalty the law would allow, and then some.

So, after May's initial excitement had subsided, the reality of the task Eddie had chosen her for set in. As Alice had rightly said, the average Joe Businessman would just take the hit in secret, fearful of the publicity a complaint to the police would create. But would Judge Bennett Palmer take it lying down? Even if the hit went to plan, the judge could set the police to track May down. And, with police stooges rife in the underworld, she wouldn't be hard to find unless she left town.

'Don't worry about it, kid,' Eddie had said reassuringly, when they met to go over the details of the hit. 'He's busting his balls to get to the Supreme Court. And you can bet your bottom dollar he's got enemies who'd cream themselves to piss on that.'

May was sure Eddie was right. He knew all the angles. But her excitement was tinged with a trace of fear as she stepped out of the cab and entered the hotel.

CHAPTER FOURTEEN

Judge Bennett Palmer was bored. Sitting in the elegant bar of the hotel with his sour-faced wife seated opposite, he was thinking of a plausible reason to excuse himself for the evening. The day had gone well. He had received the mayor's public support for his political ambitions and, privately, a sizeable wad of high denomination bills as a sweetener for when he attained the Supreme Court. Now he wanted some fun.

He looked across at his wife with a heavy heart. Politically it had been a good match and he had done very well by marrying into the state's most influential dynasty. But it had never been a love match. The family had been only too pleased to divest themselves of their plain and rivetingly dull daughter to the handsome Yale graduate. But forty years had been a long sentence for his crime.

The couple were due to return home the next day. What he desperately needed now was a few hours pleasure to tide him over the tedious weeks ahead. In his home town he was too high-profile a figure to get away with what he did in 'sin city', as he liked to call it in his own mind. As long as he could get away every few months to indulge his personal vices he could endure the tiresome façade his high office forced him to adopt day to day. And talking of personal vices, she had just walked in the door.

She was medium-height, slim and elegant. Her luxuriant blonde curls framed a face so angelic, yet so sensual, his heart skipped a beat as her eyes deliberately met his. After forty years his spouse could sense the rise of even one degree in his blood pressure. She followed his look then turned back to him with an acid frown. He looked away affecting disinterest, but his pulse was racing so fast he was concerned he might have a seizure. He had to have that woman. Woman? More girl. She couldn't be more than eighteen at the very most. With the make-up and the stylish clothes she could be even younger. The younger the better. In his vices it added an additional thrill to flirt with his own laws. He glanced again, but, like a mirage, she had gone.

What now? He couldn't just get up and follow her like a dog on heat. Over the years his wife had undoubtedly become aware of his little peccadilloes, but there had to be a pretence of decorum. A polite game of deceit. The girl had given him the look. The look of a professional even in one so young. Maybe she would return? Maybe she was staying in the hotel? As he agonized, turning his whisky glass round and round in his hand, a waiter approached bearing a telephone on a silver tray. Leaning down the man inserted the end of the telephone cord into a nearby socket in the wall, then straightened up and addressed him.

'Excuse me, judge. A telephone call for you.'

Both the judge and his wife frowned. Who would call him at this hour? He picked up the receiver. 'Judge Bennett Palmer.'

The voice on the other end sounded very near and very husky. 'Can you ditch the old broad?'

He glanced up quickly at his wife. His mouth had gone instantly dry. She looked at him, irritated at the interruption, though they hadn't exchanged a word in over five minutes. Looking towards the door he could just see her, standing at the hotel lobby desk, the telephone to her ear. She raised her hand and gave him a little wave. 'Er...yes. Yes...' He affected annoyance, the plan forming in his mind. 'Can't it wait? It's very inconvenient'

'I can't wait for you,' she replied softly. He could hear her soft breathing down the line. 'I have a cab waiting.'

'Very well. Very well. I'll be there,' he said gruffly. Putting down the receiver, he waved the waiter away.

His wife was looking at him suspiciously. 'Damned nuisance. Have to go. The mayor,' he explained. As he rose she raised her eyebrows. 'I'll be as quick as I can. If I'm not back start dinner without me.' With a brisk nod, he walked out of the bar, feeling his wife's eyes burrowing into his back.

The porter opened the front door for him. He could see the cab waiting at the curb, the rear door wide open. Ducking his head, he slipped inside, closing the door quickly behind him. The aroma of her perfume overwhelmed him momentarily. Close to she was even more beautiful than he'd thought. Her smile was at once innocent and inviting. 'Hi there,' she said.

Most 'johns' took their lead from her. She was, after all, the professional in the game. But Bennett Palmer was used to getting his own way and was constitutionally impatient. Seconds after the cab pulled out into the stream of traffic, his hands were all over her, trying to explore her graceful, slim legs sheathed in silk stockings. She seized both his hands in a surprisingly strong grip. At this precise moment she was suddenly thankful for all the years of hard work in the fields that had made her much stronger than she appeared. 'Wait, you naughty boy,' she said firmly. Outwardly calm and in control, inside May's heart was racing. The judge was the most powerful man she had ever met, used to controlling others. She had to take charge of the situation or she was in real danger.

The judge struggled to release his hands, then lunged for her face and neck instead, burrowing his lips into the hollow above her collarbone. Without relinquishing her grip on his hands May's mouth sought his ear. Her teeth closed around the fleshy lobe and bit down hard. The judge let out an astonished cry of pain and leapt backwards to the other side of the cab, holding his ear.

'You bit me!' he said in shock. He looked down at his fingers. 'You've drawn blood!'

'My older gentlemen generally like to take their time,' she replied, trying to keep the tremor from her voice. Taking a silk handkerchief from her sleeve, she leant towards him and gently pressed the silk to his ear, all the time looking deep into his eyes. 'I like men who take their time,' she said breathily. 'I can be a very, good girl for men who take their time. A *very,* good little girl...' She put her forefinger between her full, pink lips and gently sucked.

She could feel him trembling under the silk of her handkerchief. The poor man was desperate. A little boy in a man's clothes. Tenderly stroking his face with her fingertips, she cooed, 'It's all right. It's all right,' she said, speaking to the child inside. 'I'm going to show you such a good time.'

For the first time his stern, florid face relaxed into a grateful smile. May smiled in return. She had the beast under control.

Having done his research well, Eddie had chosen a more up-market hotel for the judge than the ones May generally used. Some rich and powerful men enjoyed the unaccustomed sensation of wallowing in low-life surroundings, but, among his many other vices, Judge Bennett Palmer was a snob and liked to take his illicit pleasures in comfort. This had made setting up the deal a little more tricky and expensive, but Eddie was sure it would be worth it.

May led the judge along the carpeted corridor and slipped a gold colored key into the lock of one of the doors. The door opened onto a well-appointed bedroom whose centerpiece was a spacious double bed. The judge followed her inside eagerly and closed the door. Throwing her fur wrap onto the bed, May turned to the judge and came so close he could smell her sweet breath on his face. She fingered his tie suggestively, then ran her fingers through his thick, silver hair. He was on her voraciously again, his mouth all over her face. She stopped him gently, fingertips pressed firmly against his lips. 'Don't want to muss your clothes,' she said softly.

She slipped her hands inside his jacket and slid it off his shoulders. Gliding to the double-door closet she opened one door, hung the jacket on a hanger inside and turned back to the room. The judge had already let his braces fall and was fumbling with the buttons of his flies. May crossed to him and took his hands in hers. 'There's no need to hurry, is there?' she asked.

'No, no,' he acquiesced meekly.

Letting her hands roam freely over his body, she felt the fleshy chest swell and his belly contract guiltily as her fingers explored. Beneath the material of his trousers she found that he was stiff and ready. Tracing his length with a lone finger, she sighed deeply, appreciatively. Moving to the bed, she stood with her back to him, and looked over one shoulder seductively. 'Unhook me,' she commanded.

Crossing to her he fumbled impatiently with the fasteners of her dress. Reaching behind to help, she let the dress fall at her feet. She turned to him, her hands held at her sides, allowing him the full view of her slender, shapely body, clothed only in a delicate cream silk shift with matching French knickers. He stood, mouth half open, panting heavily. 'You are so beautiful!' he gasped. 'So beautiful.'

May smiled an invitation. He embraced her, his hands roaming over her smooth back and buttocks. Releasing herself, May fell back on the bed in an abandoned pose. She groaned breathlessly, 'Take me. Now!'

Beside himself with lust, the judge fumbled furiously at his fly buttons, all fingers and thumbs. Wrenching his trousers to his knees he prepared to lunge forward onto his prize. At the same moment, there was a furious banging on the door and an irate man's voice shouting outside in the corridor.

'Open up! This is hotel security! Open up!'

The judge stopped, frozen in panic. May leapt up from the bed and grabbed her fallen dress to her.

The voice continued gruffly. 'This is a respectable hotel, not a whorehouse! You've got five seconds before I call the police!'

'The police!' the judge squeaked, frantically pulling up his trousers. 'I can't...'

May rushed to the closet, retrieved his jacket and helped him into it. Outside the door the man had started to count.

'One...Two...'

'Go!' May hissed. 'I'll stall him!'

'Three...'

Alarmed as he was, the judge had the instinct to feel inside his jacket to check his billfold. Reassured by its thickness, he made for the door. He looked back at May in desperate, abject disappointment.

'Go! Go!' she urged.

Wrenching open the door, the judge brushed hastily past the security man and hurried away down the corridor. The security man winked at May. She scowled in return. 'You cut that too damn fine!' she snapped, slamming the door in his face.

The closet door opened and Eddie emerged, grinning hugely. He waved a thick wad of bills in his hand and whistled. 'Boy, that guy has got real shitty fingers!'

Feeling exposed in front of him, May stepped into her dress and pulled it up. 'Here. Let me,' he said. She stood silently, feeling Eddie's fingers deftly fastening the dress at the back.

His hands rested gently on her shoulders. He laughed. 'Take me. Now,' he mimicked.

May laughed in return. 'It gets them really hot. They panic more,' she said, feeling a tinge of pride at her growing expertise.

It had been a sultry day and the evening was airless and heavy. All over the city people lounged lazily on steps outside their homes, or held noisy parties on the flat rooftops of the tenements. As the last of the daylight faded in the far west, a full moon rose and the smell of barbecued chicken and wood smoke hung in the air.

Inside the Blackbird Club the proprietor, Harry, was preparing ingredients for his famous club sandwich, a favorite of the post-theatre revelers, who would soon be thronging the club, wall to wall. For the few mid-evening customers the ceiling fans provided a welcome cool breeze from the oppressive heat outside, but when the place was full they wouldn't be able to cope. It would be a long, hot and sticky night.

Harry looked up as the door opened and a rush of hot air was sucked inside. It was Alice. She stood in the doorway, looking towards the empty booth at far end of the club where Eddie usually sat. Swaying slightly, as if in a breeze, she called to Harry, her voice a little slurred. 'Where's Eddie?'

'Out celebrating,' Harry replied. 'They had a big hit with the judge. Eddie said May was great.' He reached for a glass. 'The usual?'

Without reply, Alice turned, grim-faced, and walked out, leaving the door wide open. Harry shrugged, walked around the bar to close the door and shook his head. He'd seen it coming.

CHAPTER FIFTEEN

Eddie insisted on taking her home from the restaurant in his roadster. He was going on to the club, but May said she was too tired. It had been a momentous, but stressful day and all she wanted was to curl up in bed with Mick and go over the events of the evening till she fell happily asleep.

They had celebrated at Eddie's favorite Italian restaurant with the usual crowd, except Alice hadn't been there. No one knew where she was and May had felt a touch of concern. She knew Alice resented being ousted by Eddie, but told herself it was not her fault. Alice knew better than anyone that Eddie called the shots. They all had to go along with that.

As he pulled up outside her apartment block, he turned and beamed at her. 'You're quite an act, May, y'know that?' he said admiringly. 'We're gonna make a great team.'

May frowned. 'We? What about Alice?'

'She's losing it,' he said dismissively. 'Too fond of the sauce. From now on you work with me.'

'I'm flattered, Eddie. But Alice wouldn't like that.'

'So, let her take a hike.'

She was taken aback. 'But...you're gonna get married!'

Eddie gave a little laugh, his gold canine showing. 'She tell you that?'

May nodded. 'She showed me the ring.'

'She stole that from some broad. It's all a big fantasy in her head. Alice lives in cloud cuckoo land.' He saw her looking at him strangely. 'It's true. That was never the deal. I ain't the marrying type.'

It took a moment for his words to sink in. Could Eddie really be telling the truth? Was poor Alice deluding herself? It didn't matter. 'I still can't do that to her,' she insisted. 'Alice helped me. She taught me everything.'

He put a hand on her arm. 'You're better than she ever was, kid. You and me, the sky's the limit.'

'No, Eddie,' she said firmly. 'I'm sorry. Alice is my friend.'

Eddie gave a short, harsh laugh. 'Friend? Believe me, if the boot was on the other foot, she wouldn't think about you for one lousy minute.'

May knew she was taking a huge risk. Eddie was not used to being challenged, let alone refused point blank. But her tone was final. 'I'm sorry, Eddie. I can't do it.'

He looked at her hard, for a moment, then sighed and grinned. 'That's what I like about you, May. You're tough, but you've got feelings.'

Hugely relieved, May grinned in return. 'A sucker, huh?'

Eddie smiled and inclined his head. The jury was out on that one. Putting his hand inside his jacket he withdrew the judge's wad of dollar bills. He counted some out, then held them out to May. She looked surprised. It was much more than her usual percentage. 'Take it,' he said. 'You earned it.' He gave a wry grin. 'It was nice working with you.'

May was seated before her dressing table mirror, in her nightgown, languidly brushing her hair. She smiled at her reflection, thinking about the judge's disappointed face when he left. How much more disappointed would he be after finding the money in his pocket had been switched for a worthless wad of paper?

It was flattering that Eddie had suggested they work as a team. Eddie personally only scammed the high-rollers, the cream of the business world and the pickings were rich, as Alice's apartment testified. Though having a place like that was her dream, May was glad she had turned Eddie down. If Alice was really on the slide, she would be around to help. She'd be delighted to be able to return the friendship Alice had shown her.

The furious knocking on the door startled her out of her thoughts. Mick began to bark frantically. Fear gripped her. Who the hell could it be at this time? The angry voice answered the question.

'Open up!' Alice roared outside, still hammering on the door with both fists.

'Alice?!' Anxiously, May hurried to open the door.

Alice brushed past her into the room. 'Where is he?!' she yelled. 'Where is the rat?!'

May was bewildered, 'What? Who?'

'Eddie!' she screamed, wrenching open the closet door, with Mick yapping at her heels.

'Eddie's not here, Alice!' she protested.

'Liar! Come out, you rat!' Alice cried, flinging open the door to the tiny bathroom, then crouching to look under the bed.

'Alice, please,' said May trying to calm the situation by the tone of her voice. 'He's not here. I promise you.'

Panting heavily Alice stood in the centre of the room, glaring pure hatred at May. 'You dirty, lying, cheating whore!'

May felt like all the breath had been knocked out of her body. 'Alice! Alice, please...' she began tearfully.

Without warning, Alice flung herself at May, lashing out savagely with both fists. 'You stinking thieving Mick bitch! After all I've done for you! I'll kill you! I'll kill you!'

May tried to defend herself, but she was no match for Alice's drunken rage. As the blows rained down on her, she had a sudden image of her mother cowering beneath the fists of her drunken father.

'I'll kill you!' A stinging punch to her cheek floored May. As Alice began to kick out at her, she rolled up into a little ball, with Mick rushing round and round the two women, barking wildly.

'Alice, stop!' May cried, helplessly. 'Eddie's not here! He hasn't been! We're not together! Please!'

Alice stopped, exhausted by her own fury. She looked down at May still curled in a fetal position. 'Go near him again, you fucking Mick whore,' she gasped venomously, 'you're dead!'

Despite the painful assault May was determined to get through to her friend. 'Alice, please! Listen! Please!'

But Alice was storming out of the door, leaving it gaping open.

Holding her stinging cheek, May struggled up, her head swimming from the blows. She stumbled to the door, calling her name, but Alice had gone. Sinking to her knees in the doorway, May began to sob.

It was very late. A fine veil of rain had dampened the heat of the night and sent the revelers to their beds. Alone in the darkness the lights of the club glistened on the wet sidewalk. May stood outside shivering, a scarf covering her face. It wasn't cold. Her trembling came from the shock of the attack, and who had attacked her. She was deeply troubled. And there was no one else she knew to turn to for help.

The club was empty, except for Eddie holding forth to Harry and a couple of his cronies.

'I would have give a million,' he crowed, grinning widely, 'to see his face...' He stopped as the door opened. 'May!' he cried, delighted. 'Here she is! I was just telling the guys about the hit! What a star! You should have been an actress, May!'

May walked to the end of the bar, the scarf still hiding her face. 'Eddie,' she said in a quiet voice. 'Can we talk?'

Eddie looked at her, quizzically. 'Sure, doll. Hit us, Harry.' He followed May as she walked to a quiet corner and sat down in a booth. Sitting opposite her, he smiled, 'What gives, kid? You changed your mind, I hope?'

As May shook her head, the scarf slipped from her cheeks, revealing the vivid bruises below her reddened eyes. Eddie stared, shaken.

'May! Christ, babe! What happened?'

She covered her face again as Harry brought over their usual drinks, a martini for her, bourbon on the rocks for Eddie. He waited until Harry had returned to the bar.

'Doll,' he said, his voice a mixture of concern and rising anger, 'who did this?'

'Have you seen Alice?' she asked quietly.

He shook his head. 'She ain't been in...' He straightened up, looking at her, surprised. 'Alice did that?'

'She was drunk, Eddie,' she said quickly, wanting to take control of the conversation before his anger took over. 'She thought you were with me.'

His expression turned to an ugly scowl. 'The dumb stupid bitch!' he hissed. 'I'll kill her!'

May reached out and took hold of his arm, urgently. 'No, Eddie! She was right, in a way. You did ask me to take her place. She's frightened. She's hurting. I'm scared she might do something stupid.'

'If she touches you again -.'

'I meant to herself, Eddie,' she insisted. 'I'm scared she might try to hurt herself.'

'Never mind about her.' He put his hand on hers. 'You okay? Nothing broken? You should see a quack.'

She shook her head. 'I'm okay.'

'Come on,' he said briskly. 'I'll take you to my place and call my doctor.'

As he started to move, she grabbed his arm. 'No, Eddie. We gotta find her!'

He gave a tiny grimace. 'May...'

'Eddie, Alice is my friend! She needs help! You gotta help me find her!' she pleaded.

Eddie relaxed and sat back, staring at the violent red and blue bruises on May's face. The poor kid wouldn't be able to go back to work for some time. 'Okay. But you're in no state to go crawling round town. I'll get George to drop you home, then I'll go find her.'

She smiled gratefully. 'Thanks... And Eddie, you will be kind? You will tell her the truth, Eddie? That I'm not gonna work with you. Tell her I'm not stealing her place.'

'Sure, doll. Relax. I'll tell her the truth. Trust me. I'll put her straight,' he said, enigmatically.

After seeing May settled back in her apartment and giving her strict instructions not to open the door to anyone, Eddie trawled the drinking dives of the city looking for Alice. As pale violet and pink streaks seeped into the waning night sky, he found her in the Bronx.

It was a dive that Eddie had known when he was growing up in the area. A smoky, late-night watering hole for musicians, petty crooks and drug pushers. Eddie hated the emerging drugs racket. Cocaine had ruined some of his best girls. He suspected Alice had begun using some time ago, but had never caught her with it. But her mood swings had grown more wild and unpredictable. Her highs were often followed by deep, dark lows. It was a pain to live with, but he understood. The work was stressful and sometimes dangerous. A long prison sentence faced anyone caught plying her specialist trade. And prison was no picnic.

Alice had been his best girl for nearly four years. She had done well from it, and loved the high-life it brought, but the strain had begun to show, even before May came on the scene. He knew why Alice had made it her business to become May's best friend. It was the old Chinese saying, "Keep your friends close, but your enemies closer." Her woman's instinct had told her the moment May had walked in the door of the Blackbird, cold and alone, but fierily determined to get back the money he had stolen. Her instinct told Alice she had a rival. And she was right about that.

Peering through the blue-smoke haze, filtered by dancing bodies, he saw her slumped at a table in a dark corner of the crowded, noisy room. She looked up as he sat down, then bowed her head again. A trace of fine white powder glowed in the crack of the wooden table beneath her nose. 'I fucked up, didn't I?', she mumbled. 'You gonna beat me up, Eddie? Kill me?'

Eddie shook out a cigarette from his pack and pushed it under her face. 'Nah. You're doing that yourself, doll.'

She took the cigarette and glanced at him. 'Give me another chance, Eddie.'

'Can't take the risk, doll,' he said matter-of-factly, lighting her cigarette with his gold lighter. 'That stuff. Who knows what it'll make you do?'

Her blood-shot eyes were pleading. 'Please, Eddie! I'll give it up! I can! I will! I love you! I'll always be your girl, Eddie! I don't care what you do. Fuck the little Mick bitch if you want to, but don't me dump like a piece of trash!'

He looked around the smoke-hazed, seedy room and the customers who never wanted to allow daylight to break into their world. 'You've had a good run, Alice. Got yourself a nice place. Maybe it's time to find a sucker to help you hang onto it. Before it's too late.'

'Cocksucker!' She flung her fist at his head.

He caught her wrist in mid-air and held it in a grip he knew would hurt. The cigarette fell from her fingers. He squeezed harder to make her concentrate on his words. 'If you ever go near her again, you're dead,' he said without emotion. Dropping her arm to the table, he stood up and weaved his way briskly through the gyrating bodies to the door.

Alice put her forehead on the table, sobs wracking her shoulders.

CHAPTER SIXTEEN

The morning after the attack, Eddie came round, looking bright and alert despite having being up past dawn. In fact he'd skipped sleep entirely, freshening himself up in the Blackbird bathroom, and breakfasting on Harry's amazing ham and eggs washed down with thick black coffee.

May had also not slept a wink, and she looked wrecked. The vivid bruises contrasted starkly with the natural white of her face, made even paler by the shock of the night before. She had lain awake as the hours dragged by, turning the painful incident over and over in her mind. Why, she kept asking herself? Had she done something to provoke Alice's fury? She knew Eddie fancied her, but she took care never to encourage him, especially when Alice was around. Yet Alice had clearly believed that she had moved in on Eddie behind her back. That she was about to take over her position as Eddie's main girl. She fervently hoped that he had managed to find her, and that he could arrange a meeting to clear the air, so they could make up as friends.

'Not a sign,' he said, sitting down on the couch with a helpless shrug. 'I looked everywhere, doll. Nobody seen nothing of her. My guess is she skipped town till things cool down.'

May sat down beside him, tired and deflated. 'What are we going to do, Eddie?'

'What I'm going do is get my quack to come here and fix you up with something to calm you down, help you sleep. You look terrible, doll.' He looked at her crestfallen expression and

95

added, 'Hey, don't worry. Alice will show up and when she does we can all sit down and sort it out.'

'I hope so..'

'I know so,' he reassured.

'I'm sorry, Eddie,' she said wearily.

'What for?'

'Look at my face. I won't be able to work.'

'Doll, that's the last thing you should worry about. The johns will still be there with their dicks in their hands when you get fixed up. If they took a look at you now they'd jump in the river,' he said with a grin.

It hurt when she smiled in return.

'You just relax and get well. There's no rush. No rush at all.'

'Thank you,' she said. 'Thank you.'

His smile was wide and genuine. 'Hey, my pleasure.'

Eddie took to calling around late in the morning, each day, bringing her little gifts of flowers and candy, and anything she needed from the drugstore. He never stayed long. Just enough time to amuse her with gossip from the club. He was witty and charming, but that was as far as it went. There was never any suggestion he expected anything else but her company. May knew she was being singled out for special treatment, but she was determined to keep her feet on the ground. As far as she was concerned, Alice was still her friend. When she came back, as May hoped she soon would, she would find her place at the top of the tree was still waiting, unfilled.

Though it was the height of summer, May wore her scarf whenever she went outdoors. Early in the morning the heat was not so oppressive and that was the best time to take Mick for his walk. Back in Ireland the little dog had had the run of the fields, chasing rabbits and birds all day long. He'd had the best life of them all, being easily able to escape the flailing boot of her drunken father. May knew that third floor apartments were no place for a lively animal, so she took him out in the cool of the morning and at the end of the day when the heat had passed its peak. Likewise, cooped up in her tiny apartment, May was growing impatient to return to the club, to get back to her work, but she knew the bruises would take days to fade, and was resigned to killing time till her life began again.

Returning home from their morning walk via the drugstore, May collected a carton of milk and the cookies Mick liked best. On the second floor landing one of the residents' doors opened, a head popped out and, on seeing May, quickly ducked back inside again. She shrugged and continued up the stairs.

As a precaution, Eddie had arranged to have the lock of her apartment changed, but the first thing she saw when she reached the top of the staircase was the door hanging wide open. Mick barked and ran to the doorway. May followed cautiously, ready to run if the intruder was still there. Looking inside she felt a sickening blow in the pit of her stomach.

Her apartment had been utterly trashed. The curtains, cushions and sheets had been ripped to shreds, the ornaments shattered into little pieces, furniture over-turned and the mattress slashed with what looked like a knife. The pride of her life, her rosewood dressing table had been gouged with a sharp blade and the mirror smashed into jagged shards of glass. This was no frenzied raid, but a systematic attack designed to leave nothing undamaged. In the closet she found her clothes were hanging in rags. But inside she also found the one thing that had escaped the carnage. The full-length mirror on the back of the door was intact. Scrawled on it in her vivid red lipstick were words. Words she couldn't read, but which, Eddie told her later, read, "Dirty Mick Whore."

An hour later, on his daily call, Eddie found May sitting mutely on the ruined bed, twisting a fragment of the silk sheet in her hand.

'Oh, doll,' he said softly, sitting beside her on the bed. He took her gently in his arms and let her cry for a while, feeling her warm tears wet his shirt. He stroked her curls and smoothed his hand up and down her spine, comfortingly, like the father she never had. When the tears had dried up, he took her face in his hands and said with a smile, 'I'll fix it up, don't worry. Good as new. Better.'

She looked at him. 'No. I want to earn it, Eddie.'

'But, doll...' he began and stopped.

Her face was determined. He'd seen that look before, the first night in the club. May knew that the mayhem all around her was a message. A sign that the friendship had not been what she had thought and felt it to be. It hurt her to the bottom of her soul, but Eddie had been right to doubt Alice's motives. 'No. No handouts,' she insisted. 'I want to earn it, all on my own.'

'May...'

'I'll work with you, Eddie...'

A broad smile spread over his face. 'That's wonderful, doll!'

'But strictly business, understand? Strictly business.'

He shrugged. 'Whatever you say.'

CHAPTER SEVENTEEN

As the year turned from fall to winter, then headed towards the first spring of the new decade, May's beauty blossomed as she grew from girl into young woman. The bone structure of her face became more defined, her girlish figure developed rounded, womanly curves and her natural wit and intelligence was enriched by each new encounter with her 'johns'. Alice had taught her the basics of 'class' and May took that to a new level, encouraging young, emerging designers to create fashions exclusively for her. With her talented young brood in tow, she became a familiar face in the garment district, selecting fabrics for next season's wardrobe, and it was not unknown for established designers and magazines to take their lead from her instinctive sense of style. But, despite her notoriety in certain circles, she was very careful to keep herself out of the public eye. No newspaper ever published a photograph of stylish May Sharpe on their front page.

She no longer needed to take chances stealing from stores. For Alice that had been an addiction. A compulsion to beat the system, which May now realized was part of poor Alice's sickness. Teaming up with Eddie had made May the richest member of his entourage. As she had insisted, it was strictly business and, as Eddie had predicted, he and May made a great team, preying on the richest businessmen visiting town.

After the Judge Bennett Palmer episode, Eddie kept his role at a distance, leaving the cramped hours of closet hiding to his most trusted cohort, Charlie, who also acted as chauffeur and bodyguard for May. Setting up and managing each hit on these special 'johns' took meticulous care. They were not people you could trifle with. But for a small consideration office clerks and secretaries could be persuaded to reveal essential details, times, places, and, crucially, family background. Their prey had to be vulnerable in one vital aspect, they couldn't afford to have their peccadilloes exposed to the light of day. Any suspicion that an outraged 'john' would complain to the police, meant Eddie gave him a wide berth. There were plenty of mugs from all over America and Europe on business in the vibrant city of New York, who would leave poorer and wiser, but never tell the tale.

For her part May was reveling in her charmed life. By Thanksgiving she had moved to a spacious apartment in a more select district. She employed a black maid, who also took Mick for his daily walks, when May was too busy herself. By Christmas she had decorated and furnished her new home to create her own little paradise, a dream she could hardly dare to dream only a year ago. And all paid for from the billfolds of gullible men, whose companies and colleagues thought were the sharpest, most able men in their field. May had, at first, been amazed how easy it was to remove these men from their dollars. But, as she refined and perfected her technique, she came to realize that most men were boys beneath the sophisticated veneer they presented to the world. Boys she could twist around her little finger.

She still thought of Alice, asking everyone in the Blackbird clique to keep an eye out for her. But, if anyone ever heard, or saw, anything they never spoke, perhaps out of fear of Eddie, who wouldn't even allow the mention of her name. After the shock and sadness at Alice's betrayal of their friendship, May had slowly learnt to forgive. Alice was a damaged soul, as she herself was. Maybe she would also turn to uncontrollable violence if anyone tried to take from her what she had strived so hard for. Having nearly killed her father to save herself, she believed she was capable of murder if the circumstances arose.

In the meantime, life was good. More than good. She was on top of the world.

The jeweler laid out the tray for her inspection. She looked at Mick, sitting expectantly on the chair beside her, and grinned.

'Okay, Mick. Which do you want?'

The little dog barked in response. The old man put on his practiced jeweler's smile. He loved precious stones. They were a wonderful gift from nature. As a youth he had been taught how to lovingly fashion diamonds, emeralds, sapphires, rubies, to reveal their hidden, lustrous beauty. The fire burning at their heart. His own fire had died. Buried with his son lost fighting for freedom in The Great War. Freedom to what? Learning his trade in Vienna in the last century, he would never have dreamt that one day, while those who had fought 'the war to end all wars' were jobless and starving, he would be selling diamond encrusted collars for dogs.

As a child, May had often seen the fine ladies from the big house on the outskirts of the village riding across the fields on their thoroughbred horses. She formed the notion that to be a lady you had to be able to ride. When she was very small, she could remember that her father had once owned a horse. One of her earliest, most vivid memories was the day her mother had held her up in her arms so May could, with her heart in her mouth, stroke its velvet muzzle. But the animal had disappeared shortly afterwards. A casualty of her father's passion for gambling when drunk.

Over the peaty bog land that stretched as far as the eye could see away from her isolated home, groups of semi-wild ponies roamed. May became determined to ride. Maybe then, she thought, she could join the ladies of the manor on their outings, and start a new life away from the grinding poverty she had always known. On fine days when her father was away in the village getting drunk, she would wander out into the countryside, her pockets full of carrots dug from the small field she tended beside the lonely croft. It had taken several days coaxing to win over one of the shy creatures. She guessed this one, at some time, must have been someone's pet, or work animal, for it didn't bolt like the others when she approached. One rare hot summer's afternoon, she decided that this was to be the day. The day of her great adventure. The start of her new life. She knew the long day in the burning sun would have made the animals drowsy. There was no better time.

The pony was waiting for her, standing a little apart from the rest, idly flicking its creamy-white tail at the flies buzzing noisily around its flanks. May stroked the soft mane as she fed the carrots between its moist, fleshy lips. She talked to the animal quietly, reassuring.

'Would you like to take me for a little ride?' she asked into its ear. 'Sure I'm not very heavy, and you're such a fine strong animal. It'd be easy for you.'

The pony nuzzled its head gently against her. She took this as a sign. Stroking and talking all the while, she put her arms around the animal's neck, smelling the deep musk aroma that rose from its warm flesh. Raising herself up, she tried to sit her bottom sideways on the pony's broad, shiny back, as she had seen the ladies ride. The animal made a sudden move and she slipped off, landing with a bump on the earth. She stood up, brushing her skirt down. The pony was still standing calmly, looking at her with its big brown eyes.

'It's not easy that way, is it?' she said stroking the smooth muscles of its neck. 'Maybe I'll try like the men ride, should I? Till I get the hang of it.'

Taking hold of the thick mane, she jumped up, swung her right leg over the pony's back and then she was on, sitting upright, legs wrapped tightly around the firm belly. The pony took off immediately, and she clung onto its neck and mane for dear life. The other ponies scattered as they careered towards them across the peaty, uneven earth. It was all May could do to hold on. But hold on she did, determinedly. It was scary, but thrilling at the same time. She could feel the warm breeze rushing past her cheeks and the strong body of the pony jolting over the ground beneath her. She was riding!

The trees in Central Park were dressed in bright spring green as May rode the tall, grey mare along the bridle path. Unlike the other women out for their Sunday ride, she still rode like a man. Without a saddle she had never managed to sit sidesaddle on the pony's smooth, shiny back and so had never plucked up the courage to approach the fine ladies whenever she encountered them riding over the bog. It seemed to her a silly way to ride anyway.

She guided the horse under the dappling shadows of the trees with Mick trotting happily alongside. The sunlight breaking through the foliage in fits and starts lit up the diamonds on his collar like the twinkling lights on a Christmas tree. As they passed along the graveled path by the side of the lake, Mick was suddenly attracted by a movement in a dense thicket of bushes beside the pathway. Sniffing eagerly, he approached the edge of the bush. Scattered on the ground, just inside the first thin fringe of branches, were scraps of meat. Mick stuck his pointed nose into the bush, greedily devouring the food. As he gulped down the last morsel, a bony hand shot out and grasped his jeweled collar.

Riding alongside the lake, oblivious, May heard Mick's high-pitched yelp. Turning in her saddle, she saw the little dog beside the thicket, struggling and yelping in the grip of a ragged tramp.

'Mick!' she yelled. 'Stop!'

As she swung her horse around, the tramp wrenched the collar from the dog's neck and began to scurry away across the grass towards the cover of the trees. May spurred the mare forward, yelling as she rode. 'Stop thief! Stop thief!'

Clutching the precious collar, the tramp dove into the stand of trees, weaving desperately through the thin beech trunks. Unable to take her horse through the closely wooded copse, May drove the grey around the fringe, glimpsing the fleeing man as he ran through the strips of sun and shadow. Breaking out into the open, he raced for the sanctuary of densely packed bushes which stretched over a large area of the park. Once inside May knew he may be able to give her the slip. Driving the horse at full gallop she rapidly overhauled the thief. Hearing the thundering hooves approaching, the man turned his head to see the large grey horse bearing down on him. With a startled cry he stumbled and pitched forward headlong onto the grass. Reining in the horse, May sat towering above the fallen man. He looked up at her with desperate and terrified eyes. May stared down at him. Despite the grime on his face and the rags hanging to his lean body, May instantly recognized the tramp. Her eyes widened in shocked surprise.

'Henry?' she gasped, disbelievingly.

CHAPTER EIGHTEEN

May watched as Henry Rawl ravenously devoured a steaming bowl of chicken soup and demolished a hunk of crisp, fresh bread. After the shock of finding Henry living as a tramp, she had transported him to the Blackbird as quickly as she was able. The owner, Harry, had at first looked askance at the starved, ragged creature who followed May self-consciously into the club. But Sunday morning trade was always slack before noon and, provided May kept him out of sight in the far end booth, Harry was okay with helping out an ex-soldier down on his luck.

Henry had sat uncomfortably in the back of the limo with May, as Charlie drove them to the club. Haltingly, he explained to May how he had returned home to find that his parents had been turned off their farm by the bank which, in partnership with a local businessman, was keen to develop their land for new houses. The shock at having his whole life's work destroyed, at the stroke of a pen, had killed his father from a heart attack. His grieving, destitute mother had gone to live with her sister in Wyoming. Henry himself had returned to New York and found work in an iron factory until, three months ago, he was thrown out of work for trying to join a worker's union.

A thin trickle of soup ran down Henry's chin, unnoticed, as he tried to explain his present plight to her. A plight, he assured her, that was by no means unique to himself. 'There are no jobs, May,' he said with his mouth full. 'That's the truth. And what jobs there is, they're sacking proper workers and bringing in scab labor.'

May frowned, uncomprehendingly, 'Scab labor?'

105

'Folks so desperate they'll work for almost nothing. Unskilled. Foreigners mainly. Like yourself, from Europe.'

It was becoming clear to May that, over the past year or so, as she had been busy building her new life, she had never given a thought to the world outside her own narrow, charmed existence. If she had seen people sleeping in shop doorways and in shadowed alleys she hadn't really noticed. Now one of them was sitting right opposite her, stinking to high heaven.

'But how can they do that?' she asked naively. 'Throw people onto the streets. Why don't you protest?'

Henry gave a brief, hollow laugh. 'You think we haven't tried? We picketed the factories. Tried to stop the scabs getting in. The bosses just call us commies and set their hired thugs onto us. And the police don't lift a finger to stop 'em.'

'What are commies?' she asked.

'Communists. Y'now, Reds. Russians.' He paused at her blank look, his spoon halfway to his lips. 'Don't you read the newspapers?'

May shook her head. 'There wasn't much call for reading where I came from.'

Wiping his chin with his filthy sleeve, Henry looked at Mick sitting beside May. The diamond collar was back around the little dog's neck. 'You haven't done so badly for yourself, anyhow, May Sharpe,' he said without malice. 'Reading or not.'

It was May's turn to feel uncomfortable. She looked down and stroked Mick's head, surprised at herself for feeling embarrassed.

'I don't want to ask where you got your money.'

'Then don't!' she snapped.

Henry was immediately contrite. 'I didn't mean to sound like I was criticizing you, May. We all gotta do what we can to get along...' He continued after an awkward pause. 'What happened to your uncle in the Blue Mountains?'

'There never was an uncle,' she said a little sulkily. 'I just told you that so you'd help me.'

He smiled for the first time, showing the gaps in his discolored teeth. 'I'd have helped you anyway.'

May smiled in return. 'What would you have done if I told you I smacked my own father with a wooden pail and stole his money to buy a ticket on the ship?'

'I'd have said I guess he must have deserved it,' he said somberly, then added without thinking. 'Did he treat you real bad?' He immediately held up his hands in contrition. 'That ain't none of my business, May. Forget I asked.'

'I'm still a virgin, Henry.'

He looked at her, taken aback at her directness and the statement.

'Does that surprise you?'

'Well...Have to say it does, considering...' He looked about the plush décor of the club then back at May.

'I'm not saying I'm a saint,' she went on. 'I guess I'd have done that if I had to.' She smiled enigmatically. 'But there are more ways than one of skinning a cat.'

Henry shook his head, amused. 'I always knowed you do alright...You're real special, May.' His gaze sought hers briefly, then he looked down at his own ragged clothes, trying to hide the tears of shame in his eyes.

May looked at his grubby hands, lying trembling on the table. She reached out her white, gloved hand to touch his. He pulled his hand away instinctively, conscious of the contrast.

Behind her she heard Harry call. 'Hi, Eddie.'

'Harry,' Eddie responded. She turned as he walked up to their booth. He looked down at Henry with a frown. 'May?' There was a touch of edginess in his voice. 'What gives?'

'Remember the soldier I told you about, Eddie? The one who smuggled me off the boat in his kitbag?'

Eddie nodded at Henry. 'This him?'

'Henry Rawl meet Eddie Young,' she said smiling.

'Put it there, pal.' Eddie held out his hand. Henry wiped his own hand on his grimy sleeve, then shook Eddie's.

'Henry needs a job, Eddie.'

'Looks like it,' he said, sliding into the booth alongside May. 'No problem, pal. You got this sweetheart into the country. You deserve it.'

Henry looked at Eddie, taking in his expensive clothes, the diamond tie-pin holding his silk cravat, the Saks gloves despite the warmth of the day. He gave an embarrassed smile. 'Er...Look, no offence, Mr Young, but I don't do...you know, nothing illegal.'

'Except steal from dumb animals,' May said with a grin.

Eddie gave her a curious look. She waved the remark away with waft of her hand. He looked back at Henry. 'You drive, Henry?'

'Some,' Henry nodded. 'In the war...' He grinned,' My limo's in for repair though.'

May and Eddie chuckled. Despite his circumstances the guy still had a sense of humor.

'I got a trucking business. Strictly on the level,' he added fixing Henry with a look. 'Start tomorrow. Monday.' He handed Henry his business card. 'Six sharp.'

Henry could hardly believe his ears. 'Thanks. Thank you, Mr Young. I won't let you down.'

Eddie flipped a few coins across the table with a grin. 'And treat yourself to a bath, so you don't scare off my customers.'

May smiled happily across the table at Henry. Without him she would never have been where she was now, happy and successful with money in the bank. She would have never even have set foot in America, the land of opportunity, for some. Now she had repaid her debt to him. Ironically, though Henry had risked his life for his country, it was a poor illegal immigrant who had given him the break he had been denied by his fellow countrymen.

CHAPTER NINETEEN

Life for May was her work. Despite the Volstead Act, which had been passed in January to prohibit the sale and drinking of alcohol, the late nights at the Blackbird were still entertaining, with Eddie taking centre-stage. But May often excused herself early and went home to Mick and her elegant, but lonely apartment. Drinking till dawn, illegally or not, didn't mix with being bright-eyed and prepared for the next day's business.

Being naturally gregarious, she had made friends with other girls who worked for Eddie, and sometimes exchanged gossip over girlie lunches at the fashionable Algonquin, but, since the breakup with Alice, there was no one she felt she could truly confide in. Someone to share her hopes, dreams and her fears. Perhaps it was the betrayal of the trust she had given that had put May on her guard. Recalling the many happy hours they had spent together, she still found it hard to believe that Alice had merely been playing a game, keeping her under her wing, not for May's protection, but her own. For the moment, unable to feel close to anyone, she threw herself into being the best at her game. It was her protection in a tough, uncaring world.

Working with Eddie, fleecing the high-flyers visiting town, she invariably knew who her next 'john' would be. Alone at home she would pore over any information she had on the unsuspecting target. These men were confident and experienced, not as easily taken in as the rather desperate mid-American salesmen she had learnt her trade on. Skilled in employing the tricks of the business world for their own ends, her new clients had to be played cleverly, like fish on a line. They were big fish, and could bite.

Wearing his newly-pressed uniform, Joe Perski waited patiently outside the hotel. He was a patient man. He'd had to be to get his revenge. Though he didn't see it in that light. Revenge was personal, this was professional. He was a cop. A good cop. And he was going to prove it. It had taken him many months to work off the disgrace of losing his uniform to street urchins and shocking an old lady by swinging butt-naked from a fire-escape. In fact if the chief of his precinct hadn't died prematurely, and a new one appointed who had a soft spot for the young, conscientious cop, Joe might still be directing traffic on Broadway, or pounding the streets of the Bronx. He knew that his late father's reputation had been a great help. Joe Perski, Senior, was a legend among his former colleagues. Hard-working, generous, rigorously fair and honest, his dad was seen as the model cop. The archetype the press and public so loved to eulogize. Joe was proud that his father had been the myth made flesh, even if, ultimately, it had cost him his life. Today was his opportunity to live up to that reputation.

A cab was waiting at the opulent entrance, so he knew he had very little time to intervene when they came out of the hotel. May emerged looking stunning in a tailored day outfit. Her silver-haired companion holding her arm, was looking flushed and excited, like a naughty schoolboy, Joe thought grimly. As the porter opened the rear door of the taxi for them, Joe stepped forward and touched his cap to the man, politely. 'Excuse me, sir, may I have a word?'

The man looked at him frostily, but allowed himself to be taken aside by Joe. May watched surprised and a little apprehensive, as Joe talked quietly to her 'john'. After a moment the man turned to look in her direction, frowning angrily. May looked on, alarm growing, as the man took his wallet from his inside pocket and checked its contents. Relieved, he spoke quietly to Joe, then with a last fierce look at

May, he stormed back into the hotel. Joe walked back to May. Her emerald eyes were hard and cold as she glared at him. The cab door was still open. He waved his hand to usher May inside. 'If I was you, I'd be on my way.'

'Aren't you a little off your beat?' she said icily. 'I don't see any traffic.'

Joe gave her a cool smile. 'They put me on vice. You'll be seeing lot more of me.'

He touched his cap, sardonically, and held the cab door for her. May stepped inside, fuming. Joe closed the door and gave her a little wave as the cab pulled away.

Joe was as good as his word. During the next week, no matter which hotel she worked, he was outside, waiting to inform each of her clients about the real nature of her business. And every day May had to return empty-handed to the room where Charlie was confined in the closet and break the bad news. Eddie was beside himself, convinced someone had to be tipping Joe off. But the nightly interrogations of his acolytes got him nowhere. Privately, May was beginning to panic. She may be Eddie's best girl, but, if she could no longer bring in the money, she knew she could be on the streets and fast.

It was the Saturday before Thanksgiving and Eddie was untypically anxious. He had set up one of the biggest hits of his career and this rogue cop was about to screw it up. A senior executive from a long-established and highly respected English bank was in town. Known to have a penchant for younger girls, he would be carrying a very large wad to purchase his pleasure for the evening. May had heard that, because of Joe's harassment, Eddie had considered using one of the other girls, but he finally decided to stick with her. 'Don't worry, May,' he reassured. 'You're my best girl. I ain't about to dump you. Just do your business and let me take care of the cop.'

May felt a tiny ball of fear knot her stomach. 'What are you gonna do, Eddie?'

Eddie grinned. 'Hey, nothing drastic. Just create a little diversion for when you bring the john out the hotel. You'll be out and away before that fink cop notices.'

Despite Eddie's reassurance, May wasn't feeling at her best that evening. She was always nervous before a job, but it was a feeling she could contain, even use to enhance her performance like actors about to go onstage. The nerves she felt that evening were different. If Joe managed to intervene this time, with such a big hit, Eddie would have no choice but to turn to other girls in future for the high-rollers.

She took much more time than usual getting ready. After a long relaxing bath, which failed to totally relax her, she washed her hair, and toweled the curls dry sitting before the dressing table mirror. Propping herself up with pillows on the bed, she began to meticulously file and polish the nails on her toes and fingers. Under the warmth of her dressing gown she could feel her heart beating faster against her ribs. Sensing his mistress's mood Mick curled up beside her, his chin on her thigh, looking up at her with big, sad eyes.

Standing naked in the bathroom, she powdered her body and dabbed her most alluring perfume at her neck, wrists and behind the soft curve of her knees. In her slip, French knickers and stockings, she stood at the closet for an eternity, deliberating. Having filled out in her figure where it mattered to most men, she finally chose her most revealing dress, in a pale cream that matched her complexion. Completing the ensemble with her white mink fur, she was ready.

From first glance the banker was clearly impressed. As May sat down at a table in the hotel bar and slipped the mink from her shoulders he rose from his own seat, crossed the room and politely asked if she was alone. Finding that she was, he offered his company which May accepted, her eyes demurely cast down. When her club soda arrived, she raised the glass with a slightly trembling hand. She glanced up at the banker. His eyes were eager. Her genuine nervousness seemed to excite him even more. She felt like a little girl again, under the lustful eyes of her father.

The banker was completely hooked, but he was a difficult man to persuade away from his hotel. 'What's wrong with my suite?' he asked impatiently, over their second drink.

'This hotel's security is very strict,' she answered, looking about the spacious bar to give the impression that hidden eyes were watching them. 'Didn't you hear? Last month they threw out a big shot from Los Angeles for the same thing and he only just kept it out of the newspapers.'

Her lie finally settled the question. Now all it needed was to get her catch away from under the eyes of her resident cop. Feeling butterflies beating in her stomach, she led the banker out of the hotel entrance. A cab was waiting by the sidewalk. She felt herself holding her breath. Whatever diversion Eddie had planned didn't seem to be happening. Expecting a hand to land on her shoulders at any moment, she slipped into the cab, with her excited companion following behind. She gave the cabbie the location, and then they were away. May looked behind out of the rear window. People were walking the sidewalk, traffic choked the avenue. Everything seemed normal.

What had Eddie done to Joe? She realized, with surprise, that she suddenly felt anxious for the young cop's safety.

The hotel Eddie had chosen was small but exclusive, hidden in a side street leading away from the bustle of Park Avenue. The banker paid the fare and May led him through the lobby with just a brief nod to the receptionist behind his counter. The lift attendant let them out at the third floor. May produced a key from her silk clutch-bag and took her companion's arm with a bright smile that covered her immense relief. She had made it. Too late to worry about what Eddie had done to the cop now. She still had work to do. As they turned the corner into the corridor, May pulled up with a shock that made her gasp out loud. Lounging by the door of the room was a police officer. He turned and, with his handsome face breaking into a smile, addressed the banker. 'May I have a word with you, sir?'

The banker didn't wait to hear Joe out. Turning on his heel he almost sprinted around the corner and down the richly carpeted staircase leading to the lobby. Joe stood looking at May, a tiny smile of triumph playing around the corners of his mouth.

For a moment May was lost for words. Then she asked, almost resignedly. 'Why me? There are hundreds of girls working this racket, and worse.'

His voice was quiet and gentle. 'I guess I still remember that wide-eyed, innocent young girl I met at the docks, and figure she might still be savable.'

May's expression set hard. 'Save your breath!' She turned to go.

'In that case,' he said firmly,' I'll just have to put you out of business. Keep you out of jail that way, May Sharpe.'

She glared at him, fire burning in her eyes. 'And put me on the streets instead!' She swung away furiously down the corridor, amazed to think she had worried in case Eddie had done something to him.

'I can help,' he called out after her. But she was gone.

Standing alone in the brightly-lit corridor, Joe sighed. In vice you had a certain leeway to do things not strictly by the book. That was expected and hardly ever questioned. To catch devious and cunning criminals it helped if you could be devious and cunning yourself. In that respect that was what he was about. No one would argue with that. But he knew different. This was an obsession. It had started the minute he set eyes on May at the docks. At that moment, he'd felt his heart thump loudly and his face and neck get suddenly, uncomfortably hot. He'd had girlfriends before. He was young and attractive, with a kind and gentle personality. Women liked that. He was no saint, and had broken as many hearts as had broken his, but when he waved May off on the train to her fictitious relatives in Virginia, he had felt a sadness settle on him like a cold and heavy winter snow. He never expected to set eyes on her again and knew that something precious had gone out of his life for good.

His emotions had been in turmoil ever since he'd experienced the shock and surprise at catching her in New York stealing from one of the major department stores. Joy at finding her again was bound up with his dread at what she had become, and the company she was keeping. He was twenty-five years old and had been in the department since leaving school. In that time he had seen many pretty young girls whose lives had been ruined through crime. He'd found them drugged and dead in dark alleys, or watched them hauled off to spend the best years of their lives in a dreary, prison cell. It was always sad. A tragic waste. But it had never really touched him deep inside. Until now. Obsession or not, whatever it took, he was determined to save May from herself.

CHAPTER TWENTY

During many nights in the Blackbird, or over lunch with the girls at the Algonquin, she had heard all the stories about Eddie. Stories about a ruthlessness she didn't believe him capable of. She was certain they were just gossip, probably started by Eddie himself to enhance his gangster reputation.

But tonight she began to doubt herself. She had never seen Eddie look so murderous.

'The two-bit, badge-kissing punk!' he snarled, his face turned ugly with anger. 'I'll have him rubbed out!'

He and May were seated alone in a corner of the Italian restaurant, a couple of blocks from the Blackbird.

'No, Eddie,' she whispered in an anxious, insistent voice. 'You can't kill a cop. The whole city will come after you.'

'Let 'em,' he snapped. 'Nobody puts my best girl out of business and gets away with it. From tomorrow that guy is history.'

'Forget it, Eddie, please,' she pleaded. 'This is crazy. They'll send you to the chair.'

'No way, doll. He'll be an easy hit. Don't worry. He ain't gonna bother you no more.' He twisted his fork viciously in the spaghetti, as if it were Joe's guts, and shoved it into his mouth.

Despite her pleading, when Eddie dropped her off at her apartment he was still hell-bent on getting rid of Joe the next day. Unable to sleep, May lay wide awake and anxious, fearful that Eddie would carry out his threat. She told herself it wasn't really Joe she was concerned about. The cop was an irritant and

117

she wanted rid of him. But this was murder and murder carried the death penalty. Maybe for her as well as Eddie.

As the long night crawled into the early hours, she tossed and turned restlessly, her mind spinning, searching for an answer. Disturbed, Mick left his usual place at her side and grumpily went to sleep on the floor at the foot of the bed. Sometimes she guessed murder could be justified. If your life was in danger. That was self-defense. Joe was threatening her work, her future, in some ways you could say her life. How could she defend herself and prevent Eddie bringing them both down?

Grey dawn light was bleaching the eastern sky when it came to her. She turned on the bedside lamp, pulled on her dressing gown and hurried to the telephone. The phone in Eddie's apartment rang several times. She waited, hoping she wasn't too late. At last a bleary voice answered.

'Yeah?'

'Eddie, I got a solution.'

His mind was still fogged with sleep. 'Solution? What solution?'

'I've got an idea for a real big hit, without killing the cop.'

'No way.' His voice sounded irritable. 'You can't move with that fink sitting on your fanny all the time.'

'So we go somewhere he ain't.'

'Like?'

'Chicago.'

'What's in Chicago?' he asked, confused.

'Cops that don't know us.'

It wasn't easy to convince him at first. He was the boss, used to making all the decisions. Now this upstart young broad was trying to tell him what to do.

'Eddie, you told me many times I'm the best.'

'You are, doll,' he insisted. 'The very best. Never been anyone like you.'

'When you said we got a great future together, you really mean that?'

'Absolutely. One hundred per cent,' he said earnestly. 'You and me, we got it made.'

May waited until Harry had refilled her cup with black, steaming coffee and returned to the bar. They were his first customers that morning. 'So let's go somewhere I can do my thing,' she said. 'Without taking the risk of killing cops.'

Eddie shuffled the scrambled egg around his plate distractedly, his face screwed into a petulant frown. 'Chicago. I don't know. I'm a hometown boy, May. From New York. I know this place. I know all the angles.'

'Chicago's just another city, Eddie. We hit it big and get out.'

His fork stopped shuffling around the plate. He looked up at her. 'You got something cooking, doll?'

'Oh yes,' she grinned mischievously at him.

'How big?'

May sat back and relaxed. She had planned it all out on the way over to the Blackbird and become more and more excited as the details slipped perfectly into place in her brain. 'Very, very big.'

In December Chicago lived up to its nickname 'The Windy City'. They had arrived by train, under leaden skies which threatened snow. Icy gusts of wind, straight from the freezing shores of Lake Michigan, whipped around their ears as they hurried from the cab into the warm, sanctuary of the hotel.

'You got a two-bed suite booked in the name of Franklin McDonald,' Eddie informed the reception clerk.

'Two-bed suite?' May asked as they waited for the elevator.

'Sure,' Eddie replied casually. 'Charlie can sleep in the other room.'

May was silent on the way up to their floor. Inside the suite, the porter was arranging their luggage.

'No,' she said, as he made to take Charlie's suitcase into the adjoining bedroom. 'This one.' She pointed to her own large alligator leather case.

Eddie looked at her. The porter nodded and took her case into the other room. May checked the door. The key was in the lock. She took it out and put it into the pocket of her fur.

'What gives, doll?' said Eddie, with a frown.

'"Strictly business", Eddie,' she said calmly. 'Remember?'

'May, it's not what you think. You're not just another broad. You're special,' he said pleadingly. 'I knew that the first time I saw you. Why do you think I stole your purse? I knew you'd come looking for it.'

She smiled at him, confidently. 'Then you know I mean what I say, don't you?'

Eddie had been slightly sulky as they went through May's plan again over dinner. She wondered if one of the reasons he had finally agreed to her idea was the thought of spending a few days alone with her in a hotel bedroom. That's what he had clearly planned. It had surprised and, secretly, delighted her. So far, in their relationship, Eddie had always been the perfect gentleman. When the dust had settled after Alice's disappearance, there had been a little suggestive banter and some booze-fueled flirting late at night in the Blackbird, but he had always allowed her to take the lead. Now he had finally made his move, but she was still in control.

Since arriving in New York wide-eyed and innocent, May had learnt a great deal about men. They had a drive, a need, that was alien to most women she knew. Her father had been no different. In retrospect she was surprised that she almost felt sorry for him. Men just couldn't help themselves.

She had no doubt that Eddie fancied her. Not just in a casual way, as a man used to having his pick of female companions, but with a growing passion that went far beyond flirtation. The feeling was mutual. She had never met a man with such magnetism. Such an aura of being a man among lesser men. Both men and women acknowledged the charming, wise-cracking con-man as a natural leader. If the men resented it, they never dared show it. Among the women, not one of them would have hesitated a second if he had given them the come-on. But May had turned him down and she believed, in a strange way, Eddie respected that. She had the key in her pocket. When she chose, she had let Eddie know, she would unlock the door.

The next day the snow arrived. Braving the foul weather, Eddie went researching the options for their hit, while May spent the morning in her bedroom, making her meticulous preparations. By mid-afternoon Eddie had found what he wanted and returned to the hotel, chilled by the biting wind, though excited at what he had seen.

May was not in her room. He called reception, but she hadn't left any message. He was about to pour himself a bourbon, from the stash he always carried, when the phone rang. It was the reception clerk.

'There's someone to see you in the lobby, Mr McDonald.'

'Who is it?'

'The party wouldn't say, sir.'

Eddie paused. He didn't know anyone in Chicago, but someone must have heard he was in town. As far as he knew he didn't have any enemies in the city, but it was prudent to meet whoever it was in the public lobby rather than alone in his room. 'I'll be right down,' he said guardedly.

Pouring a shot of bourbon into a tumbler, he drank it down in one. Striding down the corridor he entered the elevator, which carried him down to the ground floor. As he'd hoped, the lobby and reception were busy. Looking around he saw no familiar faces. He was making his way to the reception desk when a high-pitched voice with an aristocratic English accent called out behind him.

'Are you looking for company, big boy?'

He wheeled around sharply and frowned, puzzled. The speaker was an old dowager seated alone in an armchair, with a woolen shawl draped over her knees. The woman was probably in her late eighties, with a grey complexion and heavily wrinkled skin. Her silver hair was tied in a severe bun topped by a tiny black hat.

'Pardon me?' he said warily.

The old woman smiled, displaying irregular, discolored teeth. 'I haven't had the pleasure of a handsome man like you for many years.'

Eddie looked around the lobby, perplexed. People were going about their business as normal. Was this really happening? An ancient English broad hitting on him in public?

'Come,' she ordered, holding out her black gloved hand like someone used to giving orders which were never disobeyed. 'Take my hand.'

He was in two minds. His instinct was to turn around and scoot. But who knew what kind of fuss this mad old woman would make if he did, and he didn't want to draw attention to himself right now. Taking a self-conscious look about him, Eddie took a step nearer and gingerly took the proffered hand. The fingers closed around his in a grip that made him wince.

'Ah, sorry, was that a little too hard for you, Eddie?' said the woman, reverting to the Irish lilt that Eddie had grown so fond of.

'May?!' he said in total surprise.

The ugly mouth grinned up at him.

CHAPTER TWENTY ONE

The following day the snow clouds had given way to a bright, diamond-blue sky and a biting wind which whistled through the streets of Chicago. On the ground floor of the art deco Mallers Building in Wabash, Harvey Sachs raised the metal grill of his shop window and hurried thankfully inside out of the numbing cold. Taking off his thick tweed overcoat and gloves, he went through to his workshop, rubbing his hands, to brew his first cup of coffee of the day. Tolkowsky's book lay on the workbench where he had left it the night before. While waiting for the coffee to brew, he leafed through the pages. To his mind Marcel Tolkowsky was a genius. The 'round brilliant diamond cut' the Belgian master jeweler had recently perfected was as brilliant as its name. The many tiny facets of the cut allowed the light to penetrate to the very heart of the stone revealing its hidden fire in a way never before seen. It was the talk of the diamond trade, and the rich and famous were queuing up to be among to the first to own this new marvel. And he, Harvey Sachs, was one of the first of the Belgian's disciples to master it.

Across the city in the hotel suite the group ran through their individual roles for the last time over breakfast. The fourth member, Connie, had arrived from New York the previous evening. She was one of the Algonquin luncheon girls May had personally selected for the assignment.

'Good god, May,' she gasped, on seeing May's transformation. 'Even your own mother wouldn't know you.'

'And no one would ever believe you wearing an outfit like that,' laughed May.

The group left the hotel using the service elevator, and found Charlie waiting for them at the rear of the hotel with the hired limousine. They drove through the city in an edgy silence, each with their own thoughts and quickening pulses. No matter how many times you had made a hit, May had come to learn, each one was different. Each held its own unique thrill and danger. The fusion of fear and excitement rushed the adrenalin round in the blood. And this one was the most exhilarating of them all. It was her own idea. Would it be a triumph or a disaster?

Harvey Sachs watched the dowager being lifted from the limousine into the folding wicker wheelchair. The nun in attendance wrapped a thick blanket around the old woman's knees and the young priest wheeled the chair towards the door of his shop. Harvey skipped around the counter to let the grand lady and her small entourage enter.

It was the first time he had served a member of the English aristocracy and he was impressed. The old duchess clearly knew her way around diamonds and the four C's - carat, clarity, color and cut. 'Has your Ladyship ever encountered the "round brilliant diamond cut"?' he asked self-importantly. 'A recent invention of Marcel Tolkowsky?'

'I have heard of its existence, most certainly,' she replied in her strange, high aristocratic voice, 'but have never yet seen an example, I am sorry to say. I am told it is the most exquisite thing.'

'Then you were told the absolute truth, my lady,' he responded, his excitement mounting. 'May I have the honor of being the first person to present you with an example?'

'You have one here?' she asked, matching his excitement in her voice.

Harvey smiled conceitedly. 'Not just one, your Ladyship. If you will allow me.' Giving a slight bow of his head, he hurried through the archway into the small room beyond. May, Eddie and Connie exchanged looks and waited expectantly. The jeweler returned, a little breathlessly, clutching a small, black velvet bag with a draw-string. Opening the bag he tipped five large, perfectly cut, diamonds into his hand and presented them to the dowager with a triumphant flourish. 'The round brilliant diamond cut!'

May let out a little gasp of wonder, and held out her gloved hand. Harvey put the diamonds into her palm one by one.

On the icy street outside, the street urchin couldn't believe his luck. In the summertime, living on the streets hustling for nickels and dimes, wasn't a bad way of life. People were happier with the warm sun on their backs. And when they were happy they were more generous. But, in the depths of a Chicago winter their hearts turned as cold and as hard as the frozen sidewalks. The few people who braved the sub-zero air hurried by, huddled to the ears and unseeing. He hadn't eaten for two days.

The man in the big car and the uniform had called him over and told him what to do.

'Five dollars!' the boy yelped. He didn't think he'd held that much in his hand ever before. The man even gave him the brick.

'Your Ladyship will see how each perfect facet individually releases the fire within the stone,' Harvey was saying, pretentiously, an instant before the shop window shattered into a thousand pieces. For a brief moment there was pandemonium in the jeweler's tiny shop. The priest and nun were yelling, the duchess screamed. Recovering himself quickly, Harvey swept up the stones from the old woman's lap and stuffed them into the safety of their bag. Glancing through the wrecked window, he saw the chauffeur leap from his vehicle and give chase to the culprit down the road.

Inside the shop the dowager slumped down in her wheelchair, groaning and gasping on the verge of collapse, white foam bubbling from her lips.

'A hospital!' the priest cried. 'We've got to get her to a hospital!'

As Charlie guided the limousine smoothly through the city traffic, Eddie and Connie tore off their disguises in the back of the car, yelling and whooping with glee.

'We did it! We did it!' yelled Connie, whipping off her nun's wimple and shaking her long hair free.

May was seated between them on the rear seat, deep in thought. Eddie caught her look and became serious. 'You alright, May?' For a moment May didn't respond. An awful thought struck him. 'You did switch the stones?'

Connie froze and looked at May. In the driver's seat, Charlie's eyes were fixed on the rear mirror looking anxiously at May's face. In reply May opened her gloved hand and rolled the five sparkling gems in her palm. She smiled. 'You see how each perfect facet individually releases the fire within the stone,' she said, mimicking Harvey's Chicago twang.

The yelling and hooting began again, only this time May joined in.

It was only twenty-four hours later that Harvey Sachs discovered the loss of his treasured 'Tolkowsky cut' diamonds. He gave a detailed description of the duchess and her gang to the police, who found the hired limousine abandoned two days later in a disused garage. Despite the detective's reassurance that stones with such a rare cut would be easy to trace, Harvey knew in his heart that they were gone for good. In time, they would be adorning the necks or hands of society beauties in the watering holes of the wealthy around the world. And the rich never gave up their secrets.

CHAPTER TWENTY TWO

In the early 1920's the McAllister Hotel on Biscayne Boulevard was the tallest building in Miami. From its roof you could look out across the flat, sun-baked landscape of empty, arrow-straight new roads enclosing vacant building plots, to a limitless horizon. Everywhere the lush mangrove forests which had once been home to a myriad species of plants, birds and animals, were being torn up and burnt to make way for the rapidly expanding holiday and gambling resort. After the somber years of the Great War, the good times were arriving in aces.

Twelve floors below, in the deliciously cool water of the hotel pool, May was having her first swimming lesson. She and Eddie had travelled the exhausting sixteen hundred mile journey from snow-bound Chicago in a special two-carriage train reserved solely for the elite. As soon as they stepped down onto the platform the heat enveloped them like a hot, damp blanket. By the time the taxi had conveyed them to the hotel their clothes were sticking uncomfortably, and the first thing they did, on reaching their separate rooms, was take a cold, invigorating shower. Eddie, who'd had a hard time sleeping on the train, then crashed out naked on the bed, beneath the rapidly whirling ceiling fan. Unable to rouse him by knocking on his door, May had gone off to explore on her own, too excited to sleep.

She ran the images of the diamond hit over and over again in her head, like a movie. It had gone so perfectly that for a few hours afterwards she feared that something must go wrong. It wasn't until they were on the train heading away from the white-topped buildings of Chicago, that she realized that they had made it. She had made it. She had masterminded the biggest hit anyone in her New York crowd had ever achieved and she was rich. Now she was going to take some time to enjoy it.

May had never seen a swimming pool before. The brilliant blue clear water sparkling in the sun took her breath away. Bending down to feel it's refreshing coolness running through her fingers, she knew she had to go in, as soon as she could buy a costume. When Eddie emerged, three hours later, he found May up to her waist in the water being coached by a sun-tanned, athletic young man.

On seeing Eddie's dark expression, May waded up the pool steps and stood dripping beside him. 'Hi. Have a good sleep?' she asked lightly.

'What gives?' he answered gruffly, nodding towards the man standing in the water.

'Oh, Mario's the hotel swimming coach,' she explained. 'Have you ever swum, Eddie? It's brilliant!'

'Swimming's for fishes,' he replied, looking her up and down stonily. She had chosen the new 'tank' swimming costume which was designed for real swimmers, as well as being the most daring on the market. 'Go get some clothes on. You're not decent.'

May looked at him, taken aback. 'I beg your pardon? You're not my husband.'

'You're showing everything you've got,' he said, sounding more prim than he intended.

Her amused smile did nothing to lighten his mood. 'You've no trouble with it when it's a john in a hotel.'

'That's different. That's business.'

'And this,' she said defiantly, 'is pleasure. My pleasure, Eddie, which I've earned, don't you think?' Turning abruptly on her heels she waded back into the water. "Now show me again, Mario,' she called.

Eddie stood scowling for a moment, aware the other bathers were giving him sidelong looks. Striding to a wicker sun-bed, covered with a candy-striped cushion, he sat down firmly and glared suspiciously across the water at Mario.

'Don't worry about him,' May reassured the young man, who was taking wary glances at Eddie. 'We're just business partners.'

Encouraged, Mario resumed his coaching. He was good and May was a natural swimmer. After her first few attempts, when she swallowed so much water that Mario jokingly suggested they may have to refill the pool, she relaxed and swam her first few strokes.

'Look at me, Eddie,' she cried out like a excited child, 'I'm swimming!'

In an hour she was swimming across the width of the pool, exhausted, but elated. After thanking Mario, and arranging another lesson for the next day, she came to sit on a lounger beside Eddie. He was reading a newspaper that a waiter had brought him.

'I did it, Eddie!'?

He held out the newspaper to her. 'You sure did, doll.'

May looked eagerly at the front page. Prominent was a blurred photograph of the abandoned limousine, alongside a close-up of a diamond. 'What's it say? What's it say?'

Eddie read from the article beneath the photograph. '"Chicago Police Department have set up one of their biggest ever criminal investigations after the discovery of the theft of diamonds valued in their millions."'

'Millions!? Is that what they're worth?' said May astonished.

'They're worth what we can get for 'em.' Seeing her puzzled expression, he added by way of explanation. 'You don't get the real value for hot stones, doll.'

She frowned. 'So how much?'

'Leave it to me. Hey, get this,' he said, reading on. '"Chief suspect in the daring robbery is...an ageing English duchess."'

'They didn't know it was a disguise?' she laughed. 'They're not even looking for us, Eddie!'

Eddie shrugged and grinned. A waiter was hovering by the pool holding a silver tray. Eddie beckoned him over and said quietly. 'I hear before prohibition this joint had the best champagne cellar on the coast.'

'That's true, sir.'

Producing a fifty-dollar bill from his pocket, he said in an even softer voice. 'A bottle of your best in the lady's room.'

'The Laurent-Perrier Grand Siecle?' the waiter enquired.

'The one that costs the most dough,' Eddie snapped in response.

'Very good, sir.' The waiter took the proffered bill, inclined his head and moved smoothly away into the hotel.

When May emerged from the shower in her room, the world-famous champagne was standing in a silver ice bucket on the terrace. Eddie waved his hand at the bottle. 'They say there's a lot of dough to be made out of this prohibition game.'

'It's too dangerous, Eddie. People are getting killed.'

He shrugged. 'Yeah, maybe you're right. Let's just enjoy drinking it, doll.' Opening the bottle with a flourish, Eddie poured out two glasses and handed one to May. He raised his glass, the bubbles sparkling in the sunlight. 'Here's to you, May Sharpe!'

'No, Eddie.' May said. He looked at her enquiringly. She raised her glass. 'Here's to...Chicago May!'

'I like it!' he grinned and saluted her with his glass. 'Chicago May!'

That evening they ate a candlelight dinner on the hotel terrace, under a millions stars. Looking at the full moon casting a shimmering, silver path over the waves, May thought of the last time she had seen that ocean. She had come so far. To a world she could not even have imagined. How her mother would have smiled to see her now. She hoped that somewhere she was looking down. She sighed deeply. Eddie looked up from his crayfish dinner.

'What's up, doll?'

May shook her head, her eyes brimming with tears. 'Is this me, Eddie? Am I really sitting here? Or is it just a dream?'

He smiled and reached across the table to put his hand on hers. 'It's no dream,' he said softly. 'Paradise maybe. But it's real.'

Later, as they returned from the casino, where she had amused the other gamblers by jumping up and down with delight at winning twenty dollars at the wheel, they passed hotel staff decorating a tree in the foyer.

'Let's stay here for Christmas, Eddie,' she urged, hugging his arm. 'It's snowing in New York.'

He flashed his winning smile. 'Whatever you say.'

On the top floor, they stopped outside her room. He leant forward and kissed her lightly on the cheek. 'Night, doll,' he said fondly.

May took his hand as he turned to leave. She had been thinking about it for a long time. Alice had begun her education and the girls at the Algonquin had added their experience, amazed that she had somehow escaped so long. Suddenly, she felt naked and vulnerable. She was about to enter a new world, crossing from childhood to womanhood. But it was a journey she was aching to make. Looking deep into his eyes, she heard herself say, 'Do you want to open your present now?'

CHAPTER TWENTY THREE

During the next week, May swam every afternoon under the watchful eye of Eddie, who never let her out of his sight when she was in the pool being coached by Mario. After the first night together, when he had surprisingly been so gentle and considerate, their passion became obsessive, stretching towards each dawn before they fell asleep happy and replete in each others' arms. At last May felt complete. She found that her body responded to love-making as she responded to life, with passion and fearlessness. Eddie was possessed. In his young life he'd taken the virginity of many girls, but May was different. She was a free spirit, giving and taking as naturally and easily as she breathed.

As they lay watching that first dawn together, he stroked her curls tenderly and asked, 'Why now, May? After all this time?'

She turned her head to look up at him and smiled. 'Don't you know, Eddie..? I wanted it to be so right. The first time...I needed it to be equal. I needed to be somebody in my own right. As good as you. Now I am...I'm Chicago May'

They took to rising after midday, taking a leisurely breakfast on the terrace of their suite, which they had transferred to after that first night. Around three each afternoon, watched by an admiring Eddie, May pulled her swimming costume over her naked, lissome form and spent an hour carving an ever-more stylish path up and down the sparkling waters of the pool. Eddie's eyes never left her. Even when the fence arrived to trade for the diamonds, on the mid-afternoon train all the way from New York, he was made to wait until May had finished her swim and was safely back in their suite.

'Mario says I could swim in the next Olympics,' she announced proudly to them both.

'Yeah? How much does it pay?' Eddie asked with a cynical grin.

The fence looked up from examining the diamonds under his glass. 'Not as much as you'll get for these babies,' he said.

A week after the deal was done, for the first time, Eddie was not in his usual place beside the pool. Mario was curious.

'He's out looking at real estate,' explained May. 'He says this place is hot. Gonna be boomtown.'

'That your business, real estate?'

'In a manner of speaking,' said May enigmatically, and set off in a graceful crawl up the pool's length.

Mario watched the beautiful young woman turn at the top and swim back to him with stylish ease. Wiping the water from her eyes with her hands, May noticed him looking at her strangely.

'What?' she asked.

'You like to swim in real water?'

Each day a crowd gathered where the waves met the golden sand. Though holidaying by the sea was becoming a regular pastime for Americans, it was still unusual to see a woman swimming with such power and grace in the ocean, and May had gained quite a following. Eddie had grudgingly accompanied her and Mario on their first trip to the beach, after arguing vehemently against the whole idea.

'There's things out there that eat people,' he warned. It was true. Since sea-bathing had grown in popularity over the years there had been occasional reports of shark attacks up and down the East Coast.

'They know better than to try and eat Chicago May,' she replied flippantly.

Mario had been right. Ocean swimming was something else. The first thing May found was that staying afloat in salt water was much easier than in the pool. 'You can't even drown out there,' she told Eddie after her first experience. 'You gotta try it, Eddie!'

Eddie was unconvinced and, after a few days, went back to hunting real estate, leaving May and Mario alone to swim among the long rolling waves. Alone except for May's growing fan club on the shoreline, and the hired boats that became a growing nuisance and a hazard.

'You know he's having you watched every day, don't you?' said Mario as they were toweling down, prior to returning up the beach to the hotel.

May looked along the sand at the groups of holidaymakers playing games and sunbathing. 'Watched? How do you know? There are dozens of people here.'

'The little boy by the steps,' he said with a flip of his head to indicate the direction. 'He follows us home every day. Then reports to your business partner.'

Wrapping the towel around her body, May looked sheepishly at him. 'He isn't my business partner anymore.'

'Oh?' Mario looked surprised and pleased in equal measure.

'He's my lover,' she said.

Mario's face fell. He shrugged his tanned, broad shoulders. 'No wonder he has you watched. So would I.'

The following evening, seated on the terrace of their suite, May watched the sun slipping towards the horizon. She was sipping a fresh orange juice and reliving her wonderful afternoon, when Eddie entered with a face like thunder. 'Where the fuck have you been!?' he demanded.

May was shaken by his tone. 'What do you mean?'

'Where did you go this afternoon?'

'Swimming with Mario, like I always do,' she replied.

'Yeah? Well, let's see how he likes swimming wearing a fucking concrete necktie!'

'What?' She was alarmed, suddenly reminded of Eddie's rage at the interfering young cop, Joe Perski.

'You went on a boat!' His face was turning purple with fury. 'You were seen!'

'Oh, you mean your little spy?' she responded, trying to keep the mood light.

He stood over her, his questions coming like bullets from a tommy-gun. 'Where did the fucking spick take you? Why did you need a boat? What did the little fuck do to you? Tell me!'

May rose, and put both her hands soothingly on the front of his cotton shirt. 'I was going to tell you, Eddie. I've been waiting here for you. Dying to tell you.'

His eyes narrowed suspiciously. 'What?'

Moving her hands to rest gently around his neck, she said, 'We went diving.'

'Diving?'

She went on, her eyes shining, the words tumbling out as she tried to enthuse him with her own excitement. 'There's a wreck out there. It's two hundred years old or something. It's only just under the water. On like a sandbar. You can swim down to it easy. And the fish, Eddie. The fish! Like you've never seen! Blue and yellow and purple and striped and millions of them..! Oh, Eddie, you should have been there!'

Eddie turned away from her, grimly, wanting to believe. But he was a natural competitor, a predator, and in his world it was dog eat dog. Any man like Mario was his rival.

'You do believe me, Eddie?' she asked quietly.

He remained staring at the wall of the room. 'The last two months you spent more time with that human shark than you have with me!' he said sulkily.

May crossed to him. She put her hands around his waist from behind and pressed her cheek to the cool cotton on his back. His heart was beating rapidly beneath her fingers. 'Oh, Eddie. Eddie. I don't want Mario.'

'No?' There was still disbelief in his voice.

'No...' With her arms still locked around his waist, she moved to face him and looked into his eyes. 'Eddie, please try to understand. I love it here. I love the sun on my face. I love the feel of the water on my skin. The freedom of being out in the ocean, feeling the waves move beneath me...And most of all I love us, being together...Oh, Eddie, if you knew how I used to lie awake at night as a kid and dream of this. Not that I knew a paradise like this existed...I'm living my dream, Eddie. Please, don't wake me up...' Reaching up she kissed him tenderly on the mouth.

His expression softened a little. 'Yeah, well, we have to get back.'

'Back?'

'To New York.' He saw her frown and shrugged. 'We need the dough, doll.'

The frown on her face deepened. 'But the money from the diamonds..?'

'I've been buying real estate,' he said defensively. 'I told you. It's a goldmine here.'

'It's all gone?' she asked incredulously.

Again the familiar guilty shrug. 'Don't worry, we're gonna be millionaires down the line.'

It was May's turn to move away. She stood, her arms folded across her chest. 'But I don't want to go back, Eddie. I want to stay here.'

'I like it here too, doll,' he said sympathetically. 'But we need to earn some dough.'

'So, we earn it here.'

'Here? How?'

She turned back to him, decisively. 'The same way we always do. There's high-rollers from out of town crowding the casinos every night, ain't there? And we know for certain they've got dough in their wallets.'

Three days later, after Charlie arrived from New York to make up the team, they got back to earning their living. May was right. In the casinos the 'johns' with lots of dollars to burn were easy to spot. But coaxing them away from the tables when they were on a winning streak was not so simple, and when they were losing it could be harder still. It was frustrating watching the money that could be theirs being handed back to the tables. Nevertheless, with May blossoming into one of the most desirable women on the planet, they began to have some success. A new life in the sunshine of Florida stretched ahead of them.

The morning after their third successful hit, May and Eddie were taking breakfast on their terrace when the door-buzzer sounded in the suite. Still in his dark-blue, silk dressing gown, Eddie answered the door. Outside, in uniform, was the portly figure of the Dade County Sheriff himself. He strode inside without being asked.

Despite the heat of the morning, May wrapped her peignoir around her, feeling a sudden icy chill. The Sheriff touched the brim of his hat in her direction. 'Ma'am.'

'Sheriff,' Eddie said, with false smile. 'What can I do for you?'

'Be on the next train out of town,' the Sheriff replied matter-of-factly.

The smile froze on Eddie's face. 'Pardon me?'

'We heard you're a big shot in New York. That's where you belong.'

May had left the terrace and entered the room to stand beside Eddie. 'Is there a problem, Sheriff?' she asked mildly.

'No, ma'am, I'm sure they ain't gonna be,' he said smugly. 'Now I don't give a swamp-toad's ass if some wide-eyed old boy from the boondocks loses his money at the tables, or on some cute young lady's bed.' He tucked his thumbs into his broad leather belt and went on. 'But there are some important folks around here who might take exception to their customers being frightened off frequenting their establishments for fear of being robbed with their pants down, so to speak...Am I making myself clear?'

Eddie looked at the sheriff, coolly. 'You got any specific evidence, sheriff? Someone complain about being robbed?'

The sheriff shook his head and looked Eddie straight in the eyes. 'No, sir. Same way as there wouldn't be any 'specific evidence' about a boating accident involving a pretty, young lady at sea. Or an unfortunate automobile crash late at night on a dark country road.'

Eddie looked at May, concerned. She had never seen him look helpless before. 'Thank you for your advice, sheriff,' May said coldly. 'We were just about to pack for home.'

CHAPTER TWENTY FOUR

The New York winter had been bitterly cold and interminable, and still hadn't allowed spring to wrestle the year from its icy grasp. Over the long frozen months not a day went by that Joe Perski didn't think about May. Shortly before Christmas, she and Eddie had disappeared from the scene and he was concerned about where they were and, more importantly, what was happening to her. After five years in the force he wasn't a naïve rookie, but since working on vice his eyes had really been opened to the greed, depravity and corruption that pervaded that particular slice of the city's underworld. He knew that even some of his own superiors and colleagues had dirty hands, and that many politicians, both local and national, wouldn't stand scrutiny into their private lives. Sex, power and money went hand in hand. But, in his experience, it was the girls who finally paid the price.

Standing over the deathly-white, naked body stretched out on the stone mortuary slab he tried to erase the image that this was her lying there, lifeless and ice-cold to the touch. The timing was very fortuitous. He had heard that Eddie's right-hand man, Charlie, had recently left town and reappeared in Miami. Liaison with the Dade County Sheriff's Office confirmed that a man and woman matching Joe's descriptions were staying in one of the premier hotels. It was then that he had made his move.

Acting on Joe's advice, the local sheriff ordered round-the-clock surveillance on the couple and their accomplice, Charlie. He soon discovered that May and Eddie were no longer just holidaymakers, but had set up a Miami branch of their former

New York business. It wasn't a welcome development. He
could have let the new casino owners deal with the situation
themselves, but dead bodies could be messy. Unless they were
fastidiously disposed of, they had a nasty habit of reappearing
and causing awkward questions to be asked. And the elections
for sheriff were coming up. So, let New York handle the
problem. In fact, the officer there had seemed extremely
anxious to do that himself. Who knows, perhaps the broad was
his sister, or maybe he was just sweet on the girl? Whatever,
when his new friends in the expanding casino business heard
how discreetly he'd handled it all, he was sure they'd be pretty
grateful.

A cloud of steam from the engine shrouded them as they
stepped down from the train. When it cleared they saw him
standing on the platform, waiting for them. 'Welcome back to
New York,' he said sardonically.

'What gives, badge-kisser!' Eddie snarled.

Ignoring Eddie, Joe addressed May. If anything she was
looking more beautiful than ever. She looked fit, tanned and
healthy, and much more a woman than the girl who had left
only a few months ago. 'I'd like you to come with me,' he said
seriously.

'What's the charge?' snapped Eddie.

'There's no charge,' Joe replied. 'I want you to see
something important.'

'I'm kinda tired for games just now,' May replied
dismissively.

'This isn't a game, I'm afraid. It's on the way to your
apartment. I can give you a ride.'

Eddie laughed loudly, a short, harsh bray. 'Hey, the New
York cops are offering free cab rides now!'

Joe still kept his eyes intently on May. 'It's something you really ought to see.'

May was suddenly curious. His expression was one of sadness rather than aggression. She shrugged.

On that cold, grey winter morning, the New York City Mortuary was as grim as its name suggested. Eddie had not wanted to take up the invitation but May sensed that, as Joe had said, this was important, and at the moment Eddie generally deferred to the new love in his life. Besides, what had they got to lose? When they turned into the gates of the mortuary he began to have second thoughts.

'What is this place?' May asked him. They were seated in the back of the car, with Joe in the passenger seat in front.

'City morgue,' Eddie replied stonily. He was no stranger to the place. In his world he had grown to accept that violent death often went hand in hand with making a buck.

As they stood silently in the bleak empty room, the mortuary attendant wheeled in the metal trolley bearing a body covered by a grey-white sheet. May had a momentary, incongruous, flashback to the breakfast trolley that had been wheeled into their Miami suite each morning. Joe nodded to the man. As he pulled back the sheet from the face and upper torso, May gasped in shock and turned away, hands clasped to her mouth. The marks of violence showed up vividly on Alice's pale body.

'They dragged her out of the East River,' Joe said quietly. 'She'd been beaten and strangled with a necktie.'

Eddie's expression was compassionless. 'So?'

'You should look,' Joe said to May.

She didn't turn back, and could not conceal the tremor in her voice. 'I looked, damn you!'

'Is this how you want to wind up, May?'

'What's it to you?!' she snapped, fighting back her tears.

'Just my job,' he said resignedly. He nodded to the attendant who covered up the lifeless body.

'Take me home, Eddie,' she pleaded.

'I won't go easy on you again,' Joe warned.

Eddie wheeled round to confront him. 'Listen, punk..!'

'No, Eddie,' she cried. 'Leave it. Take me home.'

She had been silent in the cab all the way back to her apartment. But Eddie had not stopped talking, railing against Joe. How had he got the nerve? Who the fuck did he think he was? Why was he picking on May? He was going to have a word with his chief, to get the punk off their backs. Either that or he'd do it himself. 'There's plenty more room in the East River,' he snarled insensitively.

'Eddie!' May snapped.

He looked contrite. 'Sorry, princess.'

When they entered her apartment he was still in full flow, on a different tack. 'I don't trust that cop. I reckon he's sweet on you.'

Without reply, May rushed towards the bathroom, clutching her mouth. Eddie listened unhappily to the sounds of May throwing up. They had been having such a great time. Now that junky Alice and that frigging cop had combined to spoil it. He poured himself a bourbon and savored its heavy, rich taste, looking out at the flakes of snow drifting past the window.

In the bathroom, May rinsed her face in cold water. As she dried herself on a soft, thick towel, she remembered the first time she had felt such luxury, in Alice's apartment. She looked at her reflection in the mirror. The shock had temporarily drained the tan from her skin. The face looking back at her was as pale as poor, dead Alice.

Going into the adjoining bedroom, she opened her suitcase and started to unpack. Eddie came to the open door, a glass in each hand. 'You need a drink, princess.'

She continued unpacking automatically without response. He put her drink on the dressing table and put his hand on her arm, causing her to stop and look at him. 'I was going to save this till the right time, but I want you to move in with me.'

May shook her head. 'No, Eddie. I want a place of my own. That no one can kick me out of.'

Taking her firmly by the shoulders, he turned her to face him. 'It will be yours,' he said with a smile. 'When you're Mrs Eddie Young.'

Her eyes widened in surprise and her lips moved, but no sound came out. He kept his grip on her shoulders.

'Listen at me. 'Society' Eddie Young, proposing.' He shook his head, amused. 'Never thought I'd see the day.'

Taking his hands from her shoulders, she moved away and picked up her glass. She took a sip and said, 'Is that what you told Alice?'

Eddie groaned audibly and shook his head, in frustration this time. 'I told you, doll. That was all in her head. She - '

May didn't let him finish. 'We killed her, Eddie!' she cried.

'What? That's crap!'

'Between us we killed her! We killed her!' The tears came at last, streaming down her face as she stood trembling with grief in the middle of the room.

Moving to her, he put his arms around her, so she couldn't move away this time. 'May, this is crazy talk. Forget it.'

She looked at him, her voice incredulous. 'Forget it?'

His tone became as sympathetic as he could make it. 'I mean, look. It's sad, but it's over...Alice was a junky. We're not to blame. We can't bring her back...We've got to look to the future. You and me...' His arms tightened around her and he continued over her sobbing. 'Marry me, May, and I promise you you'll never have to work again. You'll never want for nothing. You can have anything you want.'

For a long moment, she didn't speak. She stood with her face pressed against his chest. He could feel her warm breath through the fabric of his shirt. 'Anything you want,' he repeated gently.

Finally the tears subsided. She sniffed loudly and looked up at him. When she spoke her voice had become firm and resolute. "I want...a headstone.'

Bayview Cemetery, Jersey City, stood on a vast sloping hill, with a view of New York's constantly-growing skyline in the distance. Alice had told May she been born only a few blocks away, and it seemed fitting that she be laid to rest near where she had spent the happiest years of her young life, before her mother passed away.

May had designed the headstone herself, with the help of one of her young clothes designers sketching her ideas. It was an expensive and elaborate commission and, so, was given to the company's top stone-mason, who was thrilled to be able to finally stretch his craft to its limit. As a young apprentice he had once bought a postcard photograph of Bernini's 'The Ecstasy of St Theresa' and had marveled at how the master Renaissance sculptor had carved those richly fluid, flowing folds from such an unyielding material as marble. This headstone was to be his masterpiece. His homage to Bernini.

Eddie waited in the limousine, sheltering from the chill North-Easterly breeze, as May knelt beside the grave to lay a bouquet of pink and white lilies at the base of the statue.

The carved inscription was simple.

> 'Alice S. Rayner
> 1895-1921
> Beloved Daughter
> and Dearest Friend.'

Bathed in the weak spring sunshine, the white marble angel was smiling.

CHAPTER TWENTY FIVE

During the month while Alice's headstone was being so lovingly carved, Joe kept close surveillance on May, both on duty, when he could, but mostly in his own time. He'd found a flat rooftop with some shelter, that commanded a good view of her apartment block and, generally, he didn't leave until he knew she was safely tucked up in bed. Thankfully the nights were getting warmer, but the lonely vigils were beginning to take their toll. He was growing increasingly tired and irritable, and for no reward.

Having worked out the details of his plan, to his frustration May did nothing apart from walk her dog, and make occasional visits to the Blackbird, or Eddie's apartment. She hardly ever slept over. Eddie spent more nights at her place. Joe convinced himself that his main target was the racketeer, Eddie Young, whose empire built on cheating and thieving was rapidly growing. He believed that if he could trap May and arrest her, she might be persuaded to cut a deal to save herself from a long prison sentence and put Eddie behind bars where he belonged. His justification for this was an unshakeable instinct that somewhere inside May there was an innate goodness that was crying out to be set free. His colleagues would have just called him crazy.

Unaware of Joe's close attention, May spent her days making plans for her future. Seeing poor Alice lying naked and abused on the mortuary slab had deeply affected her. She was determined that, having escaped her father's tyranny, she would never again be at the mercy of any other man. Even Eddie. His proposal of marriage had been quite genuine, she was sure of that. If that interfering cop hadn't shocked her with the image of Alice's tragic, lonely death, she might have accepted and become Mrs Eddie Young. But that would have made her vulnerable again. And that prospect still frightened her and kept her awake at night.

The previous year America had voted for female suffrage. May wasn't interested in politics, but she was aware that more and more courageous women were making lives of their own, independent of both fathers, husbands or boyfriends. It was a battle she was resolved to take part in, and to win. But how? How could she make a living when, every move she made, Joe Perski was there to frustrate her? Crime was the only thing she knew. It had given her the trappings of the good life that she was reluctant to give up by becoming a shop-girl, or waitress, which was all she could hope for in the normal, honest world. Eddie was right. That was for mugs. She needed to find a way of making a regular income from crime.

The imposing Metropolitan Opera House was built in 1883 on the Corner of Broadway and 39th Street. Financed by a group of wealthy businessmen, keen to make their money reflect their status in high society, the Met, with its policy of high salaries for star performers, soon became one of the premier opera venues in the world. It was the board's proud boast that from his debut in 1903 until his untimely death in 1921, the famous Italian tenor Enrico Caruso appeared at the Met more times than in all the other opera houses combined.

Eddie Young had heard of Caruso, just. But that was the extent of his knowledge, or interest, in what is considered by many to be the premier art form. 'Go to the opera?!' he exclaimed when May first broached the subject. 'What the fuck for?

'Why not?' May countered. 'You're called "Society" Eddie, aren't you? So take me into Society.'

Joe watched from across the street as the richly-attired opera-goers gathered in front of the brightly-lit building. It was the first time May had gone anywhere other than the Blackbird or Eddie's place since his surveillance had begun, and he was intrigued. He'd followed them in a cab the short distance from May's apartment and had been very surprised when he saw them disappear into the crowded entrance of the Met. Since when had Eddie or May become opera lovers? Something was going on.

Heads of both sexes turned among the chattering throng in the foyer as May drifted regally through their midst, stunning in a white silk gown and matching mink wrap, with diamonds sparkling at her throat. Eddie followed behind, feeling uncomfortable and exposed in white tie and tails. This was not his environment. These were not his people. They were the kind of people he conned and stole from. Wouldn't they spot him as an impostor? Any moment he would feel a heavy hand descend on his shoulder. Sensing his discomfort, May turned and took his arm. 'Can you smell it, Eddie?' she whispered, leaning so close to his ear he could feel her warm breath. 'Real money.'

Eddie forced a smile at the watching crowd and spoke from the side of his mouth. 'You ain't said what the game is yet.'

'All in good time,' she replied. 'Let's enjoy the show.'

Richard Wagner's opera 'Parsifal', loosely based on a medieval epic poem about the search by an Arthurian Knight for the Holy Grail, has a running time of about five hours. By the time of the first interval Eddie's legendary impatience had reached boiling point. He was the first into the foyer when the interval arrived. 'Thank Christ that's over!' he hissed to May alongside him. 'Let's go get lammed.'

'It's not over, Eddie,' she said sweetly. 'It's just the first interval.'

Eddie looked stunned. 'You mean there's more of that crap?' he asked disbelievingly. 'No. Shoot me. I ain't going back in there.'

'Maybe you won't have to,' May said enigmatically. She took his arm and squeezed it gently, looking in the direction of a distinguished middle-aged man standing on the fringe of an animated group who had just emerged from the auditorium.

'What?'

'Keep moving,' she instructed, steering him through the noisy, enthusiastic crowd. Over her shoulder May noticed the distinguished man move away from the group to follow them.

'Where are we going?' said Eddie, stopping in his tracks.

'Come on,' she urged.

'What is this, cat and mouse?'

'Exactly,' she purred. Eddie allowed himself to be led through the crowd to the top of the grand staircase leading from the circle. At the edge of the stairs May checked the man was still following, then dropped her lace handkerchief. They had not taken two steps down when the man swooped and called after her.

'Excuse me, madam, I believe you dropped this.'

May turned to him and took the proffered handkerchief from his hand. 'Thank you, sir. How kind.'

As their fingers touched May, surreptitiously, slipped a gold-edged card into his palm with an inviting smile. His fingers quickly closed round the card. He returned the smile with a slight nod of his head. May took Eddie's arm and glided gracefully away down the red-carpeted staircase.

Eddie had seen the sleight of hand with the card. 'I don't get it,' he said.

'Do you see any interfering cops?' she asked.

May hadn't answered any of his questions as they drove to the Blackbird to round off the evening. Intensely relieved to have been spared the last two acts of the opera, Eddie didn't press her too hard. She had a scheme in mind. That was enough. She'd dreamt up and pulled off the diamond heist, hadn't she? But when the man telephoned May the next morning and she suggested a quiet dinner in her apartment, Eddie went wild.

'What the hell are you thinking, May? Inviting him to your apartment! This is crazy!' They were having a light lunch at the Blackbird. He stabbed a pickle viciously with his fork and waved it around like a vital piece of evidence. 'You can't rob the guy if he knows where you live!'

'I'm not going to rob him,' she replied calmly. 'Until I know how big a fish I've landed.'

CHAPTER TWENTY SIX

Despite Eddie's protests, May stubbornly resisted his demands that she call the arrangement off. He was adamant he didn't want her dining alone with a strange man, no matter what she had planned. The bottom line was he was jealous and freely admitted it. If he was that concerned, May replied with a mischievous grin, he could hide in the bedroom closet, but she wouldn't be handing the man's jacket in for him to rifle through his wallet. Using the bedroom was not in her plan. Eddie speculated that she was concocting an elaborate scheme to get access to the man's bank account.

'In a manner of speaking,' she had replied, infuriatingly, without revealing the details he was seeking.

She had left him fuming impotently to go back to prepare her apartment and herself for the evening, having first called into her favorite 5th Avenue caterers to choose a Cordon Bleu menu to impress her guest. Alaskan salmon croquettes with lemon and chive marinade, wild duck breasts with pears, and their specialty desert, 'Pets de Nonnes' served with apricot sauce, all to be delivered and prepared in her kitchen from eight onwards.

The dress she chose was her most elegant and modest, a sea-green chiffon with delicate, miniature pearl beadwork. She smiled to herself as she assessed her image in the full-length mirror. Alice would have approved.

As soon as her guest arrived, promptly at eight-thirty, she said to him, 'Please don't think I am one of these free-thinking women agitators. I merely suggested my apartment in case the situation could create unwanted complications for you.'

'Thank you,' he replied. 'That was most thoughtful.'

During dinner May charmed him with fictitious stories of her past life in Ireland and her new life in the New World. Probing his life in return, she was delighted to learn that Hugh Forbes-Carlton was exactly what she had gone to the opera to find. A minor British aristocrat working in the New York Consulate, with an English wife and three beautiful children living upstate, away from the hustle and bustle of the city. A man with serious complications.

When the caterers had left, they sat together over the candle-lit table, with the twinkling lights of the city outside.

'I never knew the Donegal Sharpe's had a daughter,' he said, gazing deeply into her eyes.

May dipped her head and looked at him through lowered lashes, 'I am the family secret...You understand?'

'I see...And, your mother?' he enquired tentatively.

'I'm afraid that has to remain a secret...even from you,' she added, reaching over the table to lay her hand on his apologetically.

He put his other hand on hers and gently stroked her fingers. 'Such little hands. So soft.' He smiled mischievously, 'I can safely say that you have never done a day's work in your life, May Sharpe.'

Smiling at the memory of the years of drudgery at her father's beck and call, she said, 'My family keep me well provided for. So long as I am not an embarrassment to them.'

'How could such a delightful creature ever be an embarrassment to anyone!' he gushed. 'If I were Bertie Sharpe–'

She stopped him with a squeeze of his hand. 'Please', she said, her voice catching with sadness, 'No more of my family...It still hurts. Being rejected.' To empathize her emotion, she took a handkerchief from her sleeve and dabbed lightly at her eyes.

Leaning across the table he stroked her cheek with his fingertips. 'Rest assured. I will never reject you, May.'

With a heavy sigh, she said, 'How easily those words trip off a man's tongue.' She sniffed and raised the handkerchief to her nose.

'I mean every word,' he responded earnestly. Rising from his seat he raised his arms to caress her. 'May,' he said huskily.

She held him off gently, but firmly, then rose and stooped to pick up Mick who had been lying contentedly asleep in his basket. Holding the pet to her cheek, she moved away towards the window. The street lights below bathed her in a pale, ethereal light. 'I'm sorry...' she said softly, gazing out into the night. With another sigh she went on, 'After what happened to my poor mother...' She let the sentence die in the flickering candlelight. Somewhere across the city a dog howled. Mick whimpered, sleepily. She shushed him with her lips close to his ear. 'Sshh, little one.'

He stood looking across at her solemnly. 'May', he said at last. 'I would never, never do anything to harm you...' His breathing was audible now. 'You are the most wonderful creature...' He took a step towards her then stopped, uncertain. 'I don't know how to express my feelings for you.'

May turned to him and shyly smiled, 'Then tell me, in beautiful words.' Crossing to a bureau, she picked up a slim, leather-bound book and held it out to him.

'Love poems,' he said, reading the cover, then opening the book.

'I read them often, when I'm alone...Read them to me' she asked, almost pleading. 'Please...so I can pretend.' With the dog still in her arms, she reclined decoratively on a chaise-lounge.

Leafing through the pages, he selected a sonnet, cleared his throat softly, and began to read. 'How do I love thee? Let me count the ways...'

May put her mouth to Mick's warm fur and smiled a secret smile.

A week later, after two more ardent, but chaste, meetings with her new beau, May arrived early at Eddie's apartment and pressed the bell excitedly. Roused from sleep he wandered from his bedroom, yawning, to answer the doorbell, wrapping his robe around him as he went.

'Okay, okay!' he called irritably as the bell chimed again. He checked through the spy-hole in the centre of the door. May was standing outside with Mick under one arm and a package in the other hand.

As soon as he opened the door, May thrust the package into his hands excitedly. 'It's from him! It's from him! What does it say?'

'Hey, good morning, May.'

'What does it say, Eddie!' she repeated urgently, stepping inside and closing the door behind her.

With May standing eagerly by his side, Eddie took a slim book from the wrapping and read the title. 'Shakespeare's sonnets.' He looked at her quizzically. 'So what?'

'Look inside,' she said, breathless with impatience. 'There's writing inside.'

He read the handwritten inscription on the frontispiece. ''To my beautiful Irish secret, with all my heart, H'' He's got a nerve,' he said testily.

'It's from him! Hugh!'

'Yeah? And I repeat, so what?' He was not accustomed to being woken at such an early hour, and mention of May's secret admirer did nothing to improve his mood.

May took a sheet of notepaper from her pocket, unfolded it and handed it to him. 'There,' she said emphatically. 'That came with it.'

He looked at the crest at the top of the letter. 'The British Embassy.'

'Read it. I want to know what he says.'

'My dearest, darling May,' he began, scowling as he read. 'My own humble words are too feeble to express my undying devotion to you.' Hey, where does this guy get off!' he snapped.

'Go on, Eddie, go on!' she urged.

With a grunt, he continued, 'Please accept this gift of 'beautiful words'. Read them when you're alone, think of me and know that you will never again have to pretend that you are deeply, passionately loved. Your adoring, devoted slave –'

May snatched the letter from him with a squeal of delight. 'Yes!' she cried triumphantly. Dancing round the room with Mick in her arms, she yelled, 'We've got him, Eddie! We've got him!'

Eddie was looking at her, concerned. 'May –' he began.

'We've got him, Eddie,' she repeated in a breathless voice.

He crossed the room and took her by the shoulders. 'Listen to me, May, and listen good,' he said seriously. 'In this state they throw the key away for blackmailers.'

'But the British Embassy, Eddie! It's wonderful!' she exclaimed. 'A chance to get one back for the old country!'

'A chance to spend the rest of your life looking at three walls and a set of bars for a door!' He was angry now. Angry about the whole situation and deeply concerned for her.

'Eddie,' she said, as if talking to a young child. 'He has a wife and three kids. He's got an important job as a diplomat - '

'Which is why they'll lock you up forever if they catch you! The bigger the guy the worse it'll be for you.'

'But he won't say anything, Eddie,' she continued, half-patronizing, half-pleading. 'He's got too much to lose.'

Eddie turned away, abruptly and started to pace, then spun round to face her again. 'I ain't gonna let you do this, May.'

'I've got to make a living, Eddie.' She was surprised and irritated that he wasn't sharing her excitement. 'That fink cop is on my back. You know that. I can't do the old stuff anymore!'

'I told you,' he said gruffly. 'Marry me. You don't have to work no more.'

May heaved a huge sigh. 'Eddie, please don't think I ain't flattered -'

'To hell with flattered! Marry me, doll! I don't want to spend the rest of my life visiting you in jail.'

She smiled, amused. 'Would you do that, really?'

'May, please, be serious -'

'I am serious, Eddie. I need to earn my own living. Nobody is ever going to own me again.'

The look on her face told him he was wasting his breath. He knew how stubborn and independent May could be and she had dug her heels in once more. Eddie shook his head wearily. 'Count me out, doll. Blackmail ain't my racket.' There was sadness mixed with the frustration in his voice. 'If you're really gonna do this. You do it on your own.'

May looked at him, a petulant expression marring her pretty face. She had really thought that Eddie would be as delighted as she was. It was another clever scheme, like the diamond heist, and it was working perfectly. There was no way the diplomat would refuse her request. His whole career and family life was on the line. What she was going to ask was a small price to pay.

She shrugged and folded the letter safely inside the book. 'Come on, Mick,' she said determinedly, making for the door.

As she opened it, Eddie called to her. 'I'll have Charlie look out for you, in case the guy turns rough.'

She left without a word, leaving the door wide open.

CHAPTER TWENTY SEVEN

When the phone call came, it was easier than even she had expected. Hugh called to ask her feelings about the book and the letter, and she told him what the price would be for her silence. She could hear over the phone line that he was shocked and deeply hurt. He had seriously thought it was a genuine relationship, he said. What saddened him the most, he went on, was that he had invested so much of his emotions into it. She had seemed to be the woman he had been searching for all his life, and he had allowed himself to dream that theirs would be a long and beautiful liaison. She had, he confessed, broken his heart.

May felt a twinge of pity for him. He was a genuinely nice person, and had never done her any harm. Yet he was cheating on his wife and risking his career and family. She remained resolute and, finally, he agreed to her terms. The money wasn't really important, he added. His deepest regret was for what might have been. In a way, he said, he understood and didn't really blame her. Single women had a difficult time in society, he knew. She was only asserting her own right, as the suffragettes were doing in his country. As they had successfully done in America. So she was one of those 'free-thinking agitators' after all, he had added wryly.

Jacob W. Weismann, attorney at law, telephoned her early the next day. He informed her that his client, Mr Forbes-Carlton, was too distressed to face seeing her again and had asked him to handle the delicate matter. Would she call into his office where he would complete the transaction? May was a little uneasy about this development. She hadn't expected Hugh to tell anyone about his very personal predicament. But top lawyers were involved in shady dealings every day, she guessed, and were party to all kinds of secrets that they were duty bound never to reveal. She agreed to call in at noon.

The cab stopped outside a stylish, recently completed, art deco building in Madison Avenue. May paid the driver and got out. She looked up at the tall building towering above her and, despite the warmth of the sun, suddenly felt a cold shiver.

For a moment she thought of turning round and going back. Of calling him and saying it was all a joke. That she didn't want his money. Maybe they could still be friends? She wouldn't object to the occasional present, of course, the more expensive the better. But he would expect something in return and Eddie wouldn't stand for that. Nor would she. Despite her fierce determination to be independent, she still felt that she and Eddie were an item, and that long term they belonged together. Everyone else thought that too. They knew May was the main girl and behaved to her with the respect that rank demanded. But that position kept her at a distance from the others, and she was lonely. After proving to Eddie that she could manage on her own, she would then let him be the boss again, satisfied she had made her point in the relationship.

She looked at the brass plaque on the entrance to the building. This was the place. Looking down at the bag in her hand, she thought of its dangerous contents and clutched it more firmly to her. Taking a deep breath, she pushed open the heavy oak door and entered the shadowed lobby.

The waiting room of attorney, J.A. Weismann, reflected the wealth and importance of his clients. Handmade designer furniture in the latest style, paintings and objet d'art tastefully displayed around the large reception area, bright drapes and carpets in the spirit of the new jazz age, all announcing that you were about to enter the presence of an extremely successful, trendy New York lawyer. Who was likely to keep you waiting.

May was sitting alone with the bag held tightly on her lap. She wished she had brought Mick along to keep her company, but felt that would have appeared somehow frivolous, and she wanted them to know she was not someone to be messed with. At the far end of the room a secretary was absorbed touch-typing in a businesslike fashion, reading from a document and never once glancing at the keys. May wondered what living a normal kind of life was like. Nine hours a day in the same room, doing the same things day in day out. Boring, she guessed, no matter how elegant the surroundings or important your employer. There was nothing normal or boring about sitting with your heart racing and your mouth dry, feeling the excitement as you were about to make a hit. You felt truly alive.

Jacob Weismann himself came out of his private office to apologize for keeping her waiting. He was younger than she had expected. Slight, with an olive complexion and slicked back hair. When he held out his hand to shake hers, she smelt the expensive eau de cologne that Eddie sometimes wore. It surprised her. She had never thought of two such different men having the same taste. But maybe lawyers and conmen weren't so different in reality.

He showed her politely into his room and invited her to sit in one of the large leather armchairs facing his outsized black-wood desk. As she took a seat, May vaguely wondered if the desk was painted or made of some strange exotic wood she had never seen before. She reminded herself that she must tell Eddie about it. He would love it.

Weismann seated himself behind the desk. He reached forward and offered her a long, filtered cigarette from an ebony box. 'Cigarette, Miss Sharpe?' he said evenly.

'Thank you.' Taking one she noticed the monogram 'JAWS' in gold letters on the white paper of the cigarette. She looked up at him.

He smiled, showing even white teeth. 'A little joke of mine. My initials.'

May felt another sudden chill. It felt like he was playing with her. She shook the thought away and looked at him confidently as she had learned to do even when she was quaking inside. 'I believe you have something for me, Mr Weismann, ' she said businesslike.

'You have the documents?' His tone was cool.

With a brief nod, May opened her bag, took out the book of sonnets and handed it across the desk to him. He opened it and glanced cursorily at the inscription inside.

'And the letter?' he asked mildly. 'I believe there was a letter?'

She leaned back against the cool leather of the chair. 'No offence, Mr Weismann, but I'd like a little evidence of good faith...The money?'

He looked at her with only a trace of mild disgust. In his business he'd seen much worse. Unlocking the top drawer to his right he withdrew a large brown paper envelope, which he handed to May. She opened the flap. Inside was a large quantity of hundred dollar bills. 'I'm sure you'd like to count it. Take your time.'

Expertly May riffled through the money. It was all there. Satisfied, she took the letter from her bag and held it out to him.

He looked at her with steely grey eyes, but made no effort to take the letter. She held it out further towards him.

'Take it,' she said, puzzled. 'It's genuine.'

The corners of his mouth lifted, revealing the tips of his even teeth. 'Okay!' he said loudly.

Before May could move, an inner door in the office opened and Joe Perski emerged, followed by a uniformed colleague. May's mouth dropped open in disbelief. She looked at Weismann who was grinning broadly now.

'Here's my 'beautiful words' to you, May Sharpe,' said Joe. 'You're under arrest.'

CHAPTER TWENTY EIGHT

Harlem Courthouse and Women's Prison, on 121st Street between Lexington and Third avenues, was an architectural contradiction. The elegant courthouse interior included among its treasures a richly-worked, wrought iron and marble staircase in black and gold which would have graced any Venetian palace, while the adjoining prison with its bleak metal stairways and narrow, cockroach-infested corridors would have not have been out of place in a Victorian horror novel.

May had spent the night alone in a cold, austere cell trying vainly to block out the anguished cries and crazy ramblings of other inmates that echoed throughout the five-tiered cell block. The previous afternoon, Joe and the other officer had brought her there and, after having been processed, she had been hustled up three flights of clanging metal stairs and thrown into a tiny cell with, as Eddie had predicted, 'three walls and set of bars for a door.'

She had not been able to send any word to Eddie. It might be days before he learned where she was. And, when he did find out, would he bother to visit her after she had so pig-headedly ignored his warnings?

During the long hours of the night, she lay awake on the hard, unyielding bunk wracking her brains to understand how she had come to be here. How had she misread Hugh Forbes-Carlton so badly? The court-case would be sensational. The press would be crawling all over May's colorful past, and he would be dragged down into the morass with her. Why had he destroyed his career, and no doubt his family life, for the sake of a few thousand dollars? Was it revenge for her leading him on with her lies and faked affection? Had she created a romantic dream so real and vivid to him that its shattering had driven him mad with rage? He had told her over the telephone that she had broken his heart. Now he seemed intent on breaking hers through long, relentless years of captivity. For she had no illusions that the establishment would make a very public example of her and her youthful beauty would be long gone by the time she was free again. As daylight filtered through the small, grimy window high above her head, she finally cried herself into a fitful, dream-troubled sleep.

The gruel they served her for breakfast through the bars of the cell door was inedible. Even back home in the croft, poor though the family had been for most of her life, there had always been a few vegetables and herbs to make a palatable stew. If she had to survive on prison food she would waste away. That might be the best option, she thought despondently. For years cooped up in this hell-hole would drive her crazy. The rattling of the warder's stick on the bars startled her out of her gloomy thoughts.

'Got a visitor, Sharpe.'

May looked up from where she was half-lying on her bunk. Joe was standing at the bars looking smart in a dark suit and tie. He carried a grey homburg in his hand. She swung her legs over the bunk and put her feet on the bare stone floor.

'You didn't need to put on your Sunday suit to visit me,' she said caustically.

'Better get used to seeing me in civvies. They're gonna promote me to detective.' He smiled broadly. 'I got my badge, thanks to you.'

'Congratulations. I'm sure your dad would be very proud,' she replied, sourly. 'But you're still a fink,' she added.

'How they treating you in here?' The question seemed genuine.

'Hey, like royalty. Five star.'

He gave a little grimace and shuffled his feet. 'It's bad, ain't it? Sorry about that. I hate to put you through this.'

'Then you should have thought twice about pulling me in.'

'You gave me no choice, May.'

'It's Miss Sharpe to you, fink!' she snapped. 'So you got what you wanted. You've seen me rotting in here. Now get lost!' She turned away to face the wall, feeling suddenly vulnerable under his gaze.

His voice was gentle in reply. 'I can help you, May. Miss Sharpe,' he corrected. 'If you'll let me.'

She responded fierily, her face still to the wall, ' I don't need your help. Just tell that English aristo-rat I can still spill the works. And I will unless I get out of here. To his wife, his Embassy. If I go down, so does he!'

Joe smiled. 'You don't understand, do you? It was a set-up. He's not a diplomat. He's not even married. He's an actor, just like you.'

For a moment May didn't reply. She sat letting his words sink in, her mind turning them over and over. Then she turned to examine his face, hoping to see the lie, if that's what it was. 'I don't believe you. You're lying. You couldn't have set me up. You're not that smart. You're just a dumb fink cop.'

He shrugged. 'It doesn't matter either way. Who'll the jury believe? A distinguished British diplomat or a notorious, two-bit, bog-Irish swindler?'

'Fuck you!' she yelled, her voice ringing through the landing.

Joe saw the warder at the end of the corridor start to move towards the cell. He waved him away and turned back to her.

'May,' he began and, this time, didn't correct himself, 'you're gonna rot in here...D'you hear me.?'

This time her voice was quieter, more resigned. 'Go to hell.'

'Imagine...that beautiful hair crawling with lice. Your skin -'

'Shuttup! Shuttup, damn you!' Her fury was back, but this time with a note of despair.

He let the thought linger in her mind before continuing. 'It doesn't have to be that way...Let me help you, May. Please. It may hurt your pride, but you're not the big fish we want. I didn't set you up to put you away.'

She suddenly stood up and grabbed the bar with both hands, glaring fiercely into his face. 'If you think I'm ratting on Eddie, save your breath!'

'He can't help you now.' His expression was pleading, not triumphant. 'Only you can. Please, save yourself.'

'You gonna watch me rot?' she said bitterly. 'That make you happy?'

He shook his head vigorously. 'No, May. No. That's the last thing...I don't...I...' He shrugged helplessly, uncomfortable. 'He's not worth it. He's just a cheap rotten punk...Please. Think about it.'

She stuck her middle finger in his face defiantly. 'Think about this!'

In contrast to the fetid prison air, the morning smelt fresh as Joe stepped through the solid entrance gate into the sunlight. He turned back to stare at the grim wall of the prison. With a sad shake of his head, he moved off towards the Lexington Avenue elevation to await his train. It was a bright sunny day and he should have been feeling elated. His plan had worked to perfection. His chief had been very impressed.

'Real detective material,' he said, when Joe gave him the details of the plot and May's arrest.

The idea had come to Joe while idly reading a review of a play at a downtown repertory theatre which had failed after half a dozen performances. The plot involved a husband trapping his wife in a lie by using an actor masquerading as a psychiatrist. The work of some poor dramatist jumping on the fashionable Freudian bandwagon and falling off again. Joe's problem catching May with a regular victim was that the men she chose to steal from would never testify in court. A British bit-part actor living in his apartment block, while waiting for his big break on Broadway, was the ideal solution.

Joe had been staking out May for nearly a month when he was lucky enough to catch her on the unexpected trip to the opera. Thanks to the German composer's prolixity, he just had time to fetch the actor from his apartment and slip him into the foyer dressed like a toff as the audience emerged for the first interval.

May's invitation to Hugh to dine at her apartment had been a total surprise. Joe had expected his 'bait' to be taken to a hotel where he could have arrested May and her accomplice in the act. This new development was worrying. Blackmail was one of the first scenarios to come to his mind. He hoped he was wrong because, if things didn't go the way he planned, the penalty for May would be much more severe. Nevertheless, he instructed his actor accomplice to go and play along.

It had worked like a dream. May had fallen into the trap with such unexpected ease that Joe wondered if Eddie had really been involved. That didn't matter. His job now was to convince May to testify against Eddie's rackets in return for a light sentence. And he had failed at the first hurdle. Maybe the time she would have to endure in that grim place before the trial would change her mind. He hoped so, but he waited for his train with a heavy heart. So he had made it. Detective. He would visit his father's grave later to tell him the news.

CHAPTER TWENTY NINE

It was four long and lonely days before Eddie finally came to see her. She didn't know if he had found out sooner and left her to sweat it out, thinking that she'd been abandoned. She didn't care. Seeing a friendly face was an intense relief. To her surprise he didn't chastise her for ignoring his warning. He was kind and sympathetic, and brought her a parcel of decent food which he knew she would need.

'Got to keep you looking good for the judge,' he said, as she tucked ravenously into a pastrami sandwich on rye, with extra pickle. He told her he had hired the best attorney and not to worry. 'We're gonna beat this rap together, doll,' he assured her.

Over the days leading to the trial she had many visitors from The Blackbird, all echoing Eddie's sentiments. He came daily with more food and cigarettes than she could use. 'What you don't want give to the guards,' he advised. 'They'll treat you better.' It was good advice as most of the guards were randomly vicious, picking on any inmate who happened to be in reach of their sticks or boots.

Joe Perski took to coming to see her every few days, standing outside the bars of her cell, pleading with her to change her mind. Though she cursed or ignored him in turn, she began to look forward to his visits. Every time he brought her a little gift of food or cigarettes, which she refused to accept, but he'd leave them just the same. Out of loyalty to Eddie she gave them straight to the guards without opening them, and rapidly became their favorite prisoner.

After a few visits Joe changed tack and started to tell her about himself and the funny, or sometimes tragic, events that made up the everyday life of a cop. She pretended not to listen, lying on her bunk staring at the ceiling and never once responding. He had a captive audience and he talked. Stories about his father, who was a legend in the force, and his mother who had abandoned him and who he still missed. Gradually, she stopped cursing him and just listened. He was amusing and told good stories. Sometimes it was an effort for her not to smile or to laugh out loud. She told herself it passed the time. But every visit ended with her 'Fuck you!' when he concluded by asking her to reconsider his request to save herself.

For some reason May couldn't quite explain, throughout all the time she was imprisoned awaiting trial, she never once told Eddie about Joe's visits, and his pressure to get her to turn evidence against him. She guessed she was concerned that Eddie would do something foolish without her to restrain him, and make it worse for them both. Most nights she had nightmares about being locked up forever, and woke up many times in the dead of night soaked in sweat. Though in her heart she had abandoned the church as a child, every day she prayed that somehow Eddie would be able to work a miracle and get her freed. She felt like a caged bird, desperate to fly again. There was no way she could survive being locked away for years.

On the morning of the trial, May dressed carefully in the modest, girlish dress Eddie had bought for her. The lawyer had advised him that the younger May looked the better. The previous day at visits, Eddie had shoved a brown paper package across the table to her. May looked up at the guard standing by the door. He turned away, disinterested. As well as the dress, the package contained her powder, lipstick, nail varnish and perfume.

'Judges are only human,' he'd said. 'What guy in his right mind is gonna send a pretty young girl down till she rots?'

'Do you want me to look like a young girl or a hooker?' she'd asked, managing a smile.

In the event, when she entered the crowded courtroom, she had reached a compromise, modestly dressed, but with her prison pallor artfully enhanced to make the most of her natural beauty. Probably due to her generosity to the guards, she had been allowed to wash her hair and had shaped the curls into a more demure style. Now, standing beside her attorney with all eyes on her, she suddenly felt like another person. Someone she couldn't recognize. A girl so frail and insubstantial that she thought that at any moment she might float away, up to the elaborate fresco on the plastered ceiling, where angels adorned the crests of towering white clouds.

As she waited, with the rest of the court, for the arrival of the judge, she glanced around her surreptitiously with lowered head. There wasn't an empty seat in the room. The public gallery was packed with people who'd read about the case and were desperate to get a first glimpse of the notorious young con-woman, for the press had acted as judge and jury long before the trial began. The twelve men of the jury sat in two rows, acutely aware of the public gaze and keen to look suitably serious and grave. A posse of friends from the Blackbird were seated around Eddie, who was looking immaculate in three-piece tailored suit with cravat held by an ostentatious diamond pin. There was no sign of Officer Joe Perski. She guessed that was because he would be called as a primary witness.

Despite the whirring ceiling fans the room felt uncomfortably hot. But she knew that was probably because of what she was about to be put through. The court usher cleared his throat and announced, 'All rise for his honor, Judge Bennett Palmer.'

May's blood ran cold. Surely she had misheard? It was just an aberration of her feverish imagination? Then he entered, looking taller and more imposing in his flowing black gown. She stared in disbelief and horror. As he took his seat, she was unable to drag her gaze away. Their eyes met and she saw that he recognized her instantly. She turned to look at Eddie, panic written all over her face. He shrugged, impassively. In an instant, she felt all hope draining away from her body, as if someone had just opened all her veins. She swayed slightly, feeling faint, and her attorney held her arm to steady her. If she remained loyal to Eddie, she knew she would never see freedom again.

CHAPTER THIRTY

Judge Bennett Palmer was a bitterly disappointed man. Having studiously courted the Democratic candidate for the Presidential election, and been promised a seat in the Supreme Court for his support, his hopes had been cruelly dashed when the Republicans won the race to the White House instead. He could not imagine how anyone in their right minds had voted for that nonentity Harding. But there it was. If Harding lasted the full term, he would be nearly eighty when his own chance for high office came again.

In the meantime he would have to soldier on performing a duty he had long since grown bored with. Dispensing wisdom and justice from on high had once given him a thrill. As a younger, virile man he had been delighted to find that with power came all manner of easy rewards and privileges denied to lesser men. Over the years, despite his wife's glowering presence, he had been able to indulge his hedonistic impulses to the full with a string of adoring, enthusiastic women. But a surfeit of anything can pall, and lately he found himself increasingly drawn to the less mature of the female sex. Those pretty young creatures who could land him in jail for a very long time. Not unlike the one who was seated before him right now.

He listened with interest to the prosecution's watertight case. From the witness stand, in finely modulated tones, the actor May had known as the diplomat, Hugh Forbes Carlton, gave an eloquent account of how Officer Perski, a friend of his, had enlisted his help to entrap a prolific swindler and thief, now turned blackmailer. The girl seated before them, he said, pointing out May dramatically. Who, he added for the court's

175

information, bore no resemblance to the elegant, sophisticated woman he had first encountered at the opera. This was his biggest audience since arriving in the land of opportunity, and he took his chance in grand style, describing in minute and fascinating detail Joe's plot, his own romantic dinners with May, the purchase of the book of sonnets, and Joe's dictation of the incriminating letter. He closed by declaring his delight at having provided a performance to match that of the accused, and so bring a habitual criminal to justice. Judge Bennett Palmer cut short the applause that began at the end of his statement, reminding the audience that this was a court of law not a theatre.

After the lawyer Weisman had taken the stand and succinctly described his role in the operation, it was Joe's turn. Sitting in the witness box, he looked pale and nervous in his dark blue suit and light grey tie. Since entering the court he had not once looked in May's direction, though he felt her eyes burning into him. On his last visit to May, the day before, he had hoped that she would have finally come to her senses. But as every other time, she had given him the same two word answer. Now he was about to play his part in condemning the young woman he was infatuated with to a lengthy prison sentence.

The prosecutor obliged him to go through his account of the plan to snare May, which he did, still unable to look her in the eye. Several times Joe tried to steer the topic away from May to focus on Eddie, but each time the judge intervened to remind him who was the accused in the case. As he came to the end of his evidence Joe became more and more agitated and distressed.

'And what did you do after you had seen the accused at Mr Weismann's office, in possession of the letter and attempting to extort a great deal of money for its return?' asked the prosecutor calmly. This case was so easy he was almost bored. If it hadn't attracted so much pre-trial notoriety, he wouldn't have taken it.

'I arrested her and took her into custody,' Joe replied, then rushed on. 'But, your honor, May Sharpe is not the real criminal here. She won't admit it but she was working for –'

'I have warned you already, Detective Perski,' said the judge cutting across him, sternly, 'to confine yourself to the question. Anymore and I will have you removed and fined for contempt of court. The fact of the matter is, did you, or did you not, catch the accused in the act of blackmail?'

Joe looked down at his hands. They were shaking. 'Yes, your honor,' he mumbled.

'Speak up!' Bennett Palmer commanded. 'The court can't hear.'

'Yes,' said Joe miserably.

'The witness is excused,' the prosecutor said.

Joe stood up and felt his legs shaking. As he stumbled from the room, he finally took a glance at May. She was glaring hatred at him.

May sat alone in her cell, calmly waiting for lights out. She had no knife, nor rope, but the modest dress she had worn for her court appearance was a thin summer material and would easily tear. It was lucky that she was shorter than the barred door of her cell. She could attach the noose to the top of the door and that would be enough. Not to break her neck, the drop was far too short, but at least to choke the life from her body.

When the lights were turned out in the cellblock, May set to work. By the light of a full moon, which cast a shaft of ghostly, diffused light from the tiny window above her head, she tore the dress into strips, using her teeth to make the first tear.

Plaiting the strips together, as she had many times sat by the hearth watching her mother do with her long, brown hair, she fashioned a strong, thin rope. Forming a noose at one end, she pulled hard to check that the knot would slip to tighten it. It was not as smooth as a professional hangman would achieve, but it would do. Then she sat with the noose on her lap, thinking about the events of her short life.

She remembered the happy times when she was a small child, before the mood of the house turned as dark and gloomy as the rain clouds that seemed to permanently hang low over the tiny croft. Playing games with her mother before the peat fire while her father was out, firstly looking for work, then later getting drunk. She relived riding the wild pony across the bog, in imitation of the fine ladies from the manor. Wouldn't they have been surprised to have seen her riding like one of them through Central Park? On reflection it had not been a bad life. She had crossed the sea on a liner. She had dressed and lived like a lady. She had swum in the ocean and made love under the moonlight and stars. Better to go with those memories than suffer years of soul-drowning imprisonment, which would finally swamp those happy times as she sank deeper and deeper down to the bottom.

The one scrap of consolation was that she had seen how miserable, how distressed, Joe Perski had been giving his evidence against her. And it had made her glad. It was his fault she was here. It would be his fault when she died. She fervently hoped that her ghost would haunt him for the rest of his life.

No tears came as she sat there. She felt strangely calm. But when she stood, her legs were trembling. She listened, aware of an unusual sensation. Silence. For once the prison was quiet. No cries of anguish, or screams of madness. It was as if it knew. Why not? The bricks and mortar had known many such moments over the years. Perhaps those sad ghosts were there tonight, imposing a silent vigil on the rest?

Reaching up she tied the end of the rope tightly to the top bar of the door. The rope was too long. Patiently, she untied the rope and re-knotted it, leaving the noose just below the knot. With an effort she pulled herself up on the bars. She pushed her head through the noose and felt the twisted rope against her skin. Taking a deep breath, she let go. As the noose tightened, the blood rushed to her head like a blow. The muscles in her neck fought against the tightening rope as her fingers instinctively went to their aid. She could hear her breath strangling in her throat and felt her tongue swelling in her mouth. She felt her legs thrashing wildly, and her bare feet striking hard against the metal bars. The drumming of the blood in her ears was deafening. Then the air drained from her lungs in a strangled cry, and she was falling, falling.

CHAPTER THIRTY ONE

Joe entered the crowded, noisy courtroom and stood against the back wall. As he expected, every seat was full with chattering people. He had not wanted to come to the trial today. Sitting in the witness box the day before, sealing May's fate with every word he uttered, he had felt that he was the one on trial and he felt deeply ashamed. The tangible excitement of the watching public had magnified that feeling and disgusted him. Outside the courtroom people he had never met came up to him with warm congratulations and firm handshakes, wanting to be part of the action, probing him for minute details of the case. The press, of course, were the worst. His picture appeared on the morning front pages, along with a fuzzy snapshot of May that didn't do her justice. He was the hero, she the villain. Somehow, in the bright light of day, it didn't feel that way.

He was a cop. A good one. Like his father before him, he didn't take bribes or turn a blind eye to his colleague's petty misdemeanors. Not that he reported them to his superiors. That would have been crossing the line. But he let them know how he felt whenever something occurred. Their job was to prevent crime not to participate, he'd say. That didn't make him the most popular guy in the precinct, but he sensed there was a grudging respect for his stance nonetheless. And this case had raised his status to the roof. It was a brilliant sting, he'd been told a hundred times. Fooling the trickster. Using their own methods against them. A masterstroke. Except he hadn't been after May. He had been after saving her.

In his heart, he didn't want to be there to watch the final sad ritual. Whatever the defense said the trial was already over. The only question now was how long a sentence the 'hanging judge' would pass down? As an ambitious young officer, he had set this whole sordid process in motion. Now it was Detective Joe Perski's responsibility to be there, to share the fateful moment with his victim, May Sharpe.

But where was she? The crowded room was becoming restless. By the large clock hanging on the side wall, the starting time had already passed. People were standing up, looking about them, enquiring of their neighbors. Joe craned his neck to see over them, a kernel of anxiety beginning to form in the pit of his stomach. Then, suddenly, she was there walking with head bowed, looking frail, her attorney by her side. As May took her place behind the defense table, Joe noticed she was wearing a different dress. A very plain, out-of-date fashion, with a high collar. Not at all her style. She looked pale, older than her years, and, he noted with deep regret, she looked defeated.

The court rose at the command, 'All rise for Justice Bennett Palmer!' As she stood, May sneaked a glance behind at the audience. That's what she felt they were. An audience coming to watch a drama. But unlike the theatre, this one was free and for real, and she was the sacrificial lamb. She put her hand to her throat. It was hot and sore where the rope had burned her skin as she had struggled to die.

'We always keep a special watch on some folks,' the guard had said who cut her down. 'You get to tell 'em after a while. Mostly the quiet ones. Till last night, you ain't bin quiet since you bin in here,' she had added, with a relieved grin, as she watched some color return to May's cheeks.

Looking at the crowd, May felt a stab of alarm. Eddie was not in his usual place in the centre of the Blackbird group. What had happened? Had he given up on her, knowing she was a lost cause? She couldn't blame him if he had. She'd been stupid and naïve. It wouldn't do his reputation any good to be associated with someone like that.

Bennett Palmer settled himself and looked around the room imperiously, before letting his eyes rest on her attorney. 'Is the defense ready to present its case?' he asked.

The attorney rose beside May and cleared his throat. 'Your honor, the defendant declines to speak on her own behalf.' There was an audible groan of disappointment from the gallery before he went on. 'Instead the defense would like to call a character witness at this point.'

Prosecution counsel was on his feet in an instant. 'Objection! Your honor, it's not the defendant's character that's on trial here.'

'Over-ruled,' Bennett Palmer replied abruptly. 'Continue.'

'The defense would like to call Mr Edward Theodore Young the Third.'

May looked up at her lawyer. Her voice was hoarse when she asked, in disbelief, 'Eddie?'

All eyes turned as the doors at the rear of the courtroom opened and Eddie strode in like an emperor entering his throne room. He was immaculately dressed, as usual, in three-piece suit, cravat, and holding a homburg in his gloved hands. But today there was something extra special about him. At first, May couldn't work it out, as she watched him take his place in the witness-box. Then as the court usher handed him the bible and he raised his right hand to say the oath, she realized what it was. No-one who didn't know Eddie intimately could have noticed, but she did. She had traced every inch of his face many times with her fingertips. She knew his square jaw, his full lips, the straight line of his nose, the arch of his eyebrows. Eddie was wearing makeup. Not the crude makeup that prevented an actor's features from disappearing completely under the glare of the stage-lights, but a subtle application that highlighted and defined every feature to its maximum potential. May's heart began to beat more quickly, and her spirit, so long crushed almost to dust, began to rise. Eddie Young had arrived to give a performance.

Her attorney rose and walked to stand by the witness box. 'Can you please state your full name for the court,' he asked.

'My name is Edward Theodore Young the Third,' Eddie replied, casting a confident eye over the room.

'And what is the nature of your business?'

'I'm what the French call an entray-prenewer,' he said in his thick Bronx accent.

The attorney turned to address the jury. 'The sort of man that makes this great country tick.'

Eddie smiled apologetically. 'I try and do my bit, gentlemen,' he said modestly. 'I love America. As did my father and his father before him.'

'Mr Young, can you describe to the court your relationship to the accused, May Sharpe?'

'Gladly.' He looked across at May and held her gaze. 'She is my dearest friend and companion.'

Eddie and the attorney had worked through the night on their presentation to the court. The gallery listened intently as Eddie unfolded the romanticized story of his first meeting and subsequent relationship with May. In turn he portrayed himself as the Good Samaritan, the kind and generous uncle, the warm close friend and, finally, as the audience listened with open mouths, the ardent lover of the young girl barely above the age of consent.

Joe watched, jealously, but with a grudging admiration of Eddie's expertise as a storyteller. It was an absorbing, almost totally fictional tale, and he could see that the jury was as hooked as the public. At last, on cue, the attorney turned to the judge.

'No further questions, your honor.'

Before the prosecutor could rise, Eddie turned to face the jury, a look of deep concern on his handsome, suntanned face. 'Look at this young girl, gentlemen of the jury! Look at her..!' He paused to let the jury take in May, sitting head bowed, hands folded in her lap awaiting her punishment. 'She's only a child. A little girl brung up in an Irish hovel in the middle of nowhere. Her mother died when May was just five years old. A little girl who had to watch her darling mother being beaten to an early grave by a brutal, sadistic husband.'

The prosecution attorney was on his feet. 'Objection! The accused's past is irrelevant, your honor!'

'Over-ruled. Continue, Mr Young,' said Bennett Palmer calmly.

'Thank you, your honor,' Eddie said with a humble nod of the head to him. Turning back to the jury he went on urgently, 'After her poor dear mother died, her brutal father turned his anger on his little daughter, the girl sitting there, May Sharpe...He beat her. Beat her everyday of her life. Beat her, gentlemen of the jury...' He paused for emphasis 'And worse...'

Responding genuinely to the memory, May gave a little sob. Her attorney handed her a large, white handkerchief which she pressed to her mouth. Eddie waited, letting the little tableau play. Seizing his chance, the prosecutor rose to make his way to cross-question Eddie.

'Look at her, gentlemen,' Eddie hurried on. 'May Sharpe is not evil.'

The prosecutor paused and looked at the judge. Bennett Palmer studiously ignored his gaze.

Eddie pressed home his advantage. 'When she arrived here May Sharpe was a lonely child. A little girl alone in a foreign land. She had no money. Couldn't get a job. She had no friends. She was desperate. She's a right to eat, ain't she? Everybody's got a right to eat...What's them words on our glorious Statue of Liberty? "Give me your poor –'

The prosecutor was still on his feet. 'Objection!'

'Over-ruled,' repeated Bennett Palmer.

'Gentlemen,' said Eddie, turning to look pointedly at the prosecutor, 'unlike some people, I'm proud to be an American. I believe those words on that great statue of ours. That Statue of Liberty. I wanna give that young girl, May Sharpe, a chance. A chance we lucky Americans take for granted. A chance given to all our dear womenfolk by our forefathers. The chance to grow up like every decent American girl. To become a loving wife, a gentle, caring mother, a credit to the country she fled to, hoping to save her life. The country she entered with nothing but the clothes on her back. The country that took her in, then left her to starve...Your honor, gentlemen of the jury, give me the chance to make an honest woman of her. I want to marry May Sharpe...'

There were gasps of astonishment around the court. At the back of the room Joe scowled, angrily. Seated in front, in full view of everyone, May burst into tears. The prosecutor looked at the judge with an open mouth, confused.

'Over-ruled,' said Bennett Palmer, before the man could speak.

'Gentlemen,' Eddie went on, addressing the jury directly, 'if you will release May Sharpe to me, I undertake to marry her, to take care of her, and to bring her up to become a decent, law-abiding American citizen. A credit to this great country of ours.' He wound up with a theatrical flourish. 'Gentlemen of the jury, will you give her that chance? The chance she has risked so much for? Will you give May Sharpe her liberty?'

As one, the gallery rose with cheers and wild applause.

CHAPTER THIRTY TWO

Later that day, Judge Bennett Palmer stepped from the cab and entered the hotel. There was no porter to open the door, it wasn't that kind of establishment. Without a glance at the receptionist he crossed the small lobby, walked into the waiting elevator and pressed the button for the fourth floor. The doors closed and he waited impatiently as the elevator ground slowly upwards. It had been a hectic, but successful day. He had presided magisterially over a controversial case, which the press would sensationalize. As a man who had learnt to keep his ear tuned to the seismic shifts of public opinion, he was certain his stock would rise. Now he needed some relaxation.

He left the elevator and strode quickly along the short corridor to the end room. Taking a key from his pocket, he inserted it into the lock and opened the door. The room was comfortable though not luxurious. Looking at the large bed he saw that it was occupied. Breathing heavily, he crossed eagerly to the bed and pulled back the cover. As requested, the three young girls were naked.

There had been pandemonium both inside, then outside the courthouse when the verdict was announced. After the two attorney's had made their closing submissions to them, and the judge had summed up very succinctly, the jury had retired for the briefest of time to debate their verdict. The facts spoke for themselves, said the foreman, a mild man in his late fifties. The unfortunate young girl was guilty of blackmail.

'To hell with facts.' The speaker was a bullish man in his mid-thirties. 'You heard the guy. What chance did the poor kid have? With that kind of life? With that kind of father? You heard what he did to her! Are we Americans, or what? Do we kick a dog when it's down?'

'But why did she need to blackmail?' said another. 'That entre-guy -'

'Entrepreneur,' injected the studious-looking young man at the end of the table, helpfully.

'Yeah, whatever,' said the man, irritably. He hadn't liked that smart-ass kid as soon as he'd laid eyes on him. 'He was her lover. He's loaded. She didn't need the money.'

'What do we know?' the bullish man replied. 'What do we know about other people's lives? What do you know about me? Or him, or him,' he said pointing at jury members at random. 'Only what we get told. We don't know why she did it. Who cares? The fact is it was a set-up anyway. The cops were out to get the broad. The guy she tried to stiff was a limey, fag actor. The money was returned. So tell me, who got hurt?'

'I tell you who will get hurt, if we come up with the wrong verdict.' The man who spoke was a small, grey-haired old man. So far he had said very little to anyone, keeping himself to himself during the recesses, reading a book on metaphysics. 'Did you see that mob out there? We come up with the wrong answer', he said prophetically, 'we get lynched.'

Eddie popped the cork and sprayed champagne over the onlookers packed into his spacious apartment. The Blackbird regulars 'whooped' in celebration as the chilled liquid splashed their smiling faces. Alongside him, wearing Eddie's new present, a figure-hugging, red velvet dress, May was grinning broadly. At her throat was a matching chiffon scarf, concealing the red wheal on her skin. She told Eddie she had fallen on the metal steps in the jail, but she didn't know if he believed her.

'Ladies and gentlemen!' Eddie cried, raising his hands. As the noise subsided, he went on, 'What am I saying? Enough of speeches! Friends, I give you a toast! To the future Mrs May Theodore Young!'

'The Third!' cried May.

Eddie grinned. 'Hey, I ain't never bin married before!' He went on, as the laughter from the assembled group died down, 'Make yourselves at home. There's booze, all you can eat. Tonight nobody leaves till sun-up!' He turned to the trio of black men standing in the corner of the room. 'Play the music!'

As the band struck up a lively ragtime tune, Eddie took May in his arms. 'Happy, princess?'

'Oh, Eddie,' she gushed. 'You don't know how much!'

He grinned. 'Hey, what did you think of the speech?'

'Who needs Shakespeare?'

Eddie laughed and hugged her. 'Some performance, huh? Maybe I should go out to Hollywood. You know, get into those new movie things.'

'They don't do no talking.'

'Yeah, you're right. So Broadway, huh?'

Taking his hand, she led him out onto the terrace overlooking the lights of the city. Inside the band was playing 'Ain't We got Fun.' She breathed in the warm summer air deeply and sighed. 'You know, Eddie, I thought I'd never get to smell fresh air again.'

He held her close, nuzzling his face into her neck, smelling her exotic perfume. With his lips on her skin, his voice was fuzzy, 'You wouldn't have done if that guard hadn't cut you down.'

She pulled away and looked at him. He shrugged. 'I slipped 'em a few bucks to keep me in the picture...Why'd you do that to me, princess? Didn't you trust me to make it right? I told you we'd beat it, didn't I?'

The muted trumpet wailed as the band segued into Gershwin's hit, 'Somebody Loves Me'. She stroked his lapel with one hand, putting the other to her throat. 'I was scared...I didn't think...I thought the judge was out to get me, Eddie. To get his revenge.'

Eddie grinned, the lights of the city reflecting in his eyes. 'Judges are human. They got their needs like everyone else. Their little fantasies.'

Her voice showed her surprise. 'You got to Bennett Palmer?'

'Everybody has their price, babe. He wanted you.'

'What?!' she gasped.

He pulled her tightly to him. 'But I traded him, three for one.'

She thought for a moment. 'What if he hadn't accepted?'

'I'd have made it a round half dozen. Nobody gets you, princess.' Over her shoulder he saw that the door to the apartment was open. One of his 'associates' was outside talking to one of the Blackbird clan. 'S'cuse me a minute, doll,' he said.

She watched him weave through the dancers and open the door wider to go outside. In the hallway, she caught a glimpse of a familiar figure. It was Henry Rawl, looking bloodied and distressed.

CHAPTER THIRTY THREE

After the 'war to end all wars' was over, there had been a great surge of optimism and hope for the future. A feeling that the world had changed forever. The slaughter of millions on the battlefields of Europe had brought the rulers of men to their senses, or so it seemed. Having lost countless friends and endured unimaginable horrors in the mud of France, it was time now for the common man to get his due reward. A fair deal and a stake in his own country.

When Henry Rawl left May on the dockside he'd headed home with a light heart, glad to be alive and ready to make a fresh start on his parent's farm. What he found blew his dreams to pieces like the mortars that for months had showered him with mud and tiny fragments of human remains, as he lay wet and shivering in one shell-hole after another. As in the war, there had been no redress. With the bank's withdrawal of the mortgage his father's heart gave out. After the funeral, having seen his mother off on the train to their distant relatives, Henry headed to the city to find work.

The conditions and wages at the iron foundry were poor. Now the demand for tanks, ships and all the trappings of war had ceased the employers' profits had shrunk. Their solution? Cheaper labor. Faced with near starvation wages or being thrown out on the streets, many men were turning to the example of the Russian workers, who had taken control of their destiny and their workplaces. Returning ex-soldiers, determined to get what they had fought so bravely for, rallied to fight again. This time at home.

As one of the more vocal agitators for union membership, Henry Rawl was one of the first to be sacked. If May had not found him that day in Central Park, he would probably had died from hunger and exposure on the streets, or wound up in prison. Now, he was thinking, maybe it would have been just as well.

Waiting inside the cab of the lorry, he could hear the quiet chatter of the others hidden in the rear of the canvas-sided truck. He wiped the sweat from his brow with his sleeve and checked for the tenth time, with a trembling hand, that the pick-axe handle was on the floor by his side.

May closed the apartment door, leaving the sounds of the party inside. In the hallway Henry and another man were in earnest conversation with Eddie. Henry's clothes were torn and his face was bruised and stained with blood.

'There was just too many of 'em, Mr Young,' Henry was explaining apologetically. 'We was outnumbered.'

'Henry?' she exclaimed, shocked at the state of him.

They all turned to face her. 'It's alright, doll,' Eddie said brusquely. 'I can handle it. Go back to the party.' He took her by the arm and steered her back towards the door.

Determined not to be shrugged off like a little child, she pulled herself from his grip and confronted him. 'Never mind the party, Eddie. What's going on? Henry, what happened to you?'

'Leave it, May,' warned Eddie.

'Henry?'

Henry looked down at his scuffed boots, shamefacedly. He had not wanted to come, but Eddie's lieutenant had insisted.

Her tone was resolute. 'Henry. I want an answer.'

Eddie shrugged. 'Henry's bin doing a little job for me,' he said patronizingly. 'Some people objected.'

'What kind of job?' she asked, her stomach starting to clench like a tiny fist.

Henry was squirming now, shifting from one foot to the other.

'I thought you said you'd never do anything illegal, Henry,' she reminded him.

Eddie interrupted impatiently. 'Strike-breaking ain't illegal! Them fucking commies are the ones breaking the law!'

May felt for a moment that she had misheard. She looked from Eddie to Henry, incredulous. 'Strike-breaking?...You've been breaking strikes, Henry?'

'No!' he protested. He took a quick, fearful glance at Eddie. 'I was only supposed to be driving!'

'Driving! Driving thugs to beat up strikers?'

'May, it's nothing,' Eddie insisted. He was irritated now. 'It's not your concern. Butt out.'

Ignoring him, May focused on Henry, her dismay turning to anger. 'How could you? Beating up innocent folks just for fighting for their rights! How could you, Henry? You was one of them before I dragged you out the gutter, remember?!'

'Hey, lay off the guy!' As Eddie's raised his voice, ironically, the band inside broke into a ragtime version of the Paul Whiteman hit 'Sweet Lady.' He had busted a gut to save May from prison and here she was sticking her nose into stuff that didn't concern her. 'He was just following my orders! Lay off him!'

May turned to face him. The scarf had slipped from her throat revealing the crimson burn turning now to brown. 'No, Eddie, you lay off the commies! Or we're through!'

She strode angrily away towards the elevator and pressed the button.

Eddie called after her, exasperatedly. 'May!'

The elevator bell chimed, the doors opened. Eddie made to follow her. 'May,' he said, trying to sound more reasonable than he felt.

'Don't follow me, Eddie!' she warned. 'If you follow me, I'll throw myself in the river and finish the job properly!'

It had started with little things. On his legitimate lorry runs, delivering goods from the docks to wholesalers' warehouses, one of Eddie's 'lieutenants' began to ask him to stop at various anonymous addresses to drop off little packages for a relative or friends. At first he had thought nothing of it. But as the drops became more frequent, Henry became uneasy. He voiced his concern quietly when Eddie visited the lorry depot in the Bronx.

'I said I wouldn't do nothing illegal,' Henry told him.

Eddie laughed loudly, the sound echoing around the large hanger that housed his fleet of vehicles. The two bodyguards, that he had taken to going around with recently, joined in. Henry looked perplexed.

'You dummy,' said Eddie, when he had stopped laughing. 'What do you think you've bin delivering in them barrels all this time?'

'They told me it was cooking oil!' he said defensively. Suddenly, even to himself, his answer sounded lame. He had accepted what he'd been told. How could he know what was in the sealed metal drums that were hauled from the ships' holds and loaded onto his lorry?

'How about premium scotch whisky?' said Eddie with a grin. 'Watered down two to one it still tastes better than the crap they make over here.'

Henry was crestfallen. 'No...Well, I won't do it again,' he heard himself say in a thin voice.

'Pardon me?' In contrast, Eddie's voice was hard.

'I told you, I don't want to do anything illegal,' he repeated, trying not to feel the stony eyes of the two brutal-looking bodyguards boring into him.

'But you have been, Henry. Very illegal.'

'Well, I'll just leave then,' he said, trying to make it seem like a calm and reasonable proposition.

Eddie glanced at the two thugs at his side. 'Leave? And do what? Go to the feds? Cop a plea for ratting on me?'

'No. I won't say nothing, I swear.' He was sweating now. Since his ordeal in the war any threat of violence brought him out in sweats and palpitations. 'Shell-shock' some medical people called it. 'Cowardice' was the word the generals used. All he knew was, that now, physical violence scared him so much it made him wet his pants.

'How can I be sure of that?' Eddie asked. It wasn't a question. Eddie put a hand on his shoulder. Henry could smell the new leather of the gloves Eddie had taken to wearing, even in the summer. 'Henry, you're either with us, or you're against us...Now which is it gonna be?'

May stared down into the dark water, where the lights from the other side of the river broke into shimmering fragments, endlessly changing shape. Water calmed her, and she needed calming now. She was intensely grateful to Eddie for saving her from prison. Looking back she was grateful to him for giving her a life and showing her the many good times she would never have had on her own. She had no problem that he was a career criminal. So was she. People had to make a living and, if you had a particular talent, as she and Eddie had, you should use it.

Stealing from the rich was one thing. Most of the money came from the backs of the poor anyway and, ever since she had met Henry Rawl living as a tramp, she gave to beggars and street urchins as a matter of course. Not to salve her own conscience. Because it helped them get through another day. But making money from trampling on ordinary people's rights. That she couldn't bear. And if it meant losing Eddie and all that went with him, she had no choice. Years of being trampled on had left wounds that had never really healed.

'Sounds crazy, but I'm really glad you got away with it.'

The familiar voice behind her made her jump. She turned. Joe was standing a few feet away. His car was parked at the curb. May turned away sharply and continued staring into the water.

'I just keep turning up, like a bad nickel, huh?' he said lightly.

Her face like stone, she rounded on him fiercely. 'What is it you want! You wanna save me? Well, I'm telling you, I've had enough of being saved! I was brought up in a land full of saviors. I've been saved by the best of them! By priests who gave me ten Hail Mary's if I forgot to say my prayers when I'd fallen into bed deadbeat from working all day and night. From saviors in long black robes who tried to put their hands up the frock of a little five year old girl, and would have done God knows what, if her mother hadn't caught them. By priests who stood by and didn't lift a finger while my father beat that same mother to an early grave!'

Joe shifted his feet, uncomfortably. 'I'm sorry.'

'Save your sympathy for the fishes! Go fucking drown yourself!'

May stormed away, furious at having her solitude disturbed. Joe opened his mouth to call after her, but thought better of it.

He had said what he wanted her to hear. To let her know his relief at the verdict. For the moment, he could do no more.

The party was finally over. Eddie went around the room turning off the lamps, allowing the grey light of dawn to take over in the room. 'Thought they'd never leave,' he said, uncomfortably.

May was seated on the sofa, a drink in her hand, gazing out of the window at the lights of the city being extinguished one by one. She didn't respond.

'Listen, princess,' he began hesitantly, 'about tonight. That little business -'

'Henry Rawl was out of a job when he came to you,' she said sadly, without turning her gaze from the view. 'He was a good, honest, decent man, and you've turned him against his own people.'

'What people?' he responded, stung. 'They're bums.'

'Like me when I arrived, Eddie. Like you said today in court. With no job. No food. No friends. Am I a bum too?

'Hell no, you're different, princess.'

She turned to face him in the dim light of the apartment. 'No, I'm not, Eddie. I'm a criminal. I rob people. I cheat 'em and take their money. But I don't kick a man when he's down. I don't set the dogs on a man who's fighting for his rights, for his job, for his family...'

Eddie shrugged. 'Business is business. It's nothing personal.'

She raised her voice. ' Are you listening to me, Eddie? *I won't have it..!* I'd rather rot in jail than marry a...a...I don't know what the word is for it. Maybe they haven't got one. Maybe it's just too rotten to have a name.'

'Okay, okay, princess. Amp down. Amp down...' He came and sat on the sofa beside her. 'Did you mean that? You'll really marry me?'

'I thought that was the deal.'

'Forget the deal,' he said, gesturing the notion away with a wave of his hand. 'That was just to help Bennett Palmer get off the hook. To give him something to work with, to persuade the jury. I'm not going hold nobody to that. It's too important... You got to want to marry me, May. Like I want to marry you.'

She was silent, her gaze shifting back to the awakening city.

'May,' he began, his voice catching. 'I ain't never felt like this about anyone else, never...You're special. One of a kind... I don't need that dirty game. I was just doing it as a favor anyhow.'

May turned back to him, looking deep into his eyes. The early morning sun sent a golden shaft of light onto the wall behind them. 'You mean that, Eddie?' she asked. 'No more strike-breaking?'

He took her hand and placed it over his heart. 'Word of honor...Now, will you marry me?'

She squeezed his hand and smiled. 'Of course, eejit!'

CHAPTER THIRTY FOUR

Despite the fact that his own high-profile case had ended in failure, Joe was genuinely glad that the jury had acquitted May. Surprised, but very relieved. He had explained to her many times, as she lay gazing disinterestedly at the grey ceiling of her tiny cell, that he was after Eddie not her. How badly he had misjudged her, he was now only too aware. As the trial approached, he spent many sleepless nights pacing the floor of his tiny apartment trying to think of an angle that would convince May to save herself by giving him the goods on Eddie. Finally, complaints from his neighbors below forced him to take to his bed, where he would lie wide awake wracking his brains until dawn.

After drawing a blank with his initial approach to May, he had changed his method, using his uninvited visits to try and draw her out by talking about himself. Whether she had listened he didn't know. She had never responded nor revealed anything about herself. If she had told him some the events of her childhood, he might have realized much earlier that she was a fiercely stubborn and loyal young woman, and that he was wasting his breath. That belated realization only emphasized that Eddie was a very lucky and, in his eyes, unworthy guy.

It was obvious that Eddie had put in a fix at the trial. Regardless of his impressive, patriotic speech to the jury, there was no way they would have dared acquit May without Judge Bennett Palmer's summing up. It had been a travesty of the judicial system. But Joe was used to such charades. He'd been in the force long enough to become jaundiced about his country's proud boasts about justice. Justice was for rich people. People with influence. Bennett Palmer had given the ordinary men of the jury carte blanche to ride roughshod over the evidence and set May free. What his reward was Joe didn't know and didn't care. He'd heard rumors of the judge's sexual preferences and Eddie was ideally placed to provide for them. The fact was that May had escaped many grinding years in prison, but only fallen deeper into Eddie's clutches. Joe was jealous, of that he had no illusions, but his whole instinct told him that Eddie would eventually do May harm. And, now, with the date of the marriage announced, he seemed powerless to prevent it.

Eddie was surprised when May insisted on a civil ceremony. No white gown, no maids of honor, no choirboys, and definitely no church.

'But this is your chance to shine, doll,' he urged. 'You'll be the toast of New York!'

As much as anything he wanted to show the city, the world, what a fabulous young woman had agreed to be his wife. Little Eddie Youngman, the snotty-nosed kid from the Bronx, with the most beautiful girl in the city walking down the aisle on his arm, while the whole world and its dog watched. For despite the trappings of his success, Eddie had never been able to shake off a secret, inner feeling that somehow, in some way, he was a bum. On the surface, he knew that was crap. He had a fancy apartment, a swanky limousine, a chauffeur, a maid, money in the bank and friends in high places who would do him favors. So why did he still feel the surges of murderous rage, like the ones he'd felt as a kid, cowering beneath his father's legs as the belt lashed down, ripping the shirt on his back? He'd shaken that off, hadn't he? He'd seen his father buried and wept on his grave, while at the same time cursing his memory. But all that was hidden in the past. He was a changed man, Edward Theodore Young the Third, master of his world and, yet, still the little boy so desperate for love and praise. And lethal with anger.

'I'm not going anywhere near a church or anything frigging like,' May said adamantly. 'I've had priests up to here,' she added, touching the single string pearl necklace resting on the creamy skin of her neck.

'I thought you'd want to show off. You was never shy before.'

'If you make me go to church the wedding's off, Eddie.'

'You're that serious?'

'Deadly.'

He had come to know the expression on her face well. He shrugged, disappointed. The world and its dog would miss his moment of vindication, but he still had May.

She saw the little boy hurt look on his face. 'That doesn't mean we can't have the best party this city's ever seen,' she said, going to him with a radiant smile. She put her arms around his waist and kissed him firmly on the lips. 'Does it?'

That's how it was reported in all the newspapers. A contact at the New York Registry Office had informed the vice squad about the date of the wedding, so they could put in an appearance. Such public occasions were useful for the police to gain knowledge of which hoodlums were associating with each other. But this event, amazingly, wasn't going to be public. Knowing nothing about May's intense hatred of all things religious, Joe was surprised to learn that the couple had opted for a low profile civil ceremony, with a glamorous reception for a hundred guests to be held in a private function room at the Algonquin. He had expected the ceremony itself to be a lavish occasion, perhaps held in the city's premier church, St. Patrick's cathedral on the east side of Fifth Avenue. And he wanted to be there. In a perverse way he wanted to be a witness. To see May looking wonderful, as he was sure she would, gliding down the soaring nave of the mock-Gothic church on her special day.

Joe day-dreamed about standing up at the back of the congregation and voicing his protest when the priest asked if anyone knew of any just cause why the couple should not be joined together in holy matrimony. Yes, *he* did, he'd cry! Because he, Joe Perski, truly loved May and Eddie was evil. He'd even begun to wonder, with a mixture of excitement and trepidation, whether, when the time came, he would really do it. If he did, what would it do to his career? And if it destroyed it, would he care? His fantasizing took him to a future where May and he lived far away in a small town, bringing up a couple of kids in a clapboard house with a white picket fence. Happily ever after.

As it turned out, Eddie arranged to change the timing of the civil ceremony at the last minute to evade the prying eyes of the police. So the only view Joe got of the marriage was a Daily News photograph of Eddie and May holding hands standing outside the registry office. With regret, he saw that May looked stunning in a tailored Japanese silk suit. That evening, while the revels were in full swing at the Algonquin, he got very drunk at home, alone.

CHAPTER THIRTY FIVE

'The French Riviera?' exclaimed May. 'Are you crazy?'

They were sitting together eating a Caesar salad lunch in a little family restaurant overlooking the East River. Instead of his usual bourbon on the rocks, Eddie had chosen an aromatic Chablis to accompany the meal. He was determined that as a newly married couple they should be seen to have 'class'. Beside the water the city's summer heat was tempered by a light breeze blowing off the shining river. It was two weeks before the wedding and they were discussing their honeymoon.

'It's the place to go. Kings and Queens, princesses, and all sorts of classy people hang out there.'

'Are you suggesting we go there and work the joint?'

'Hell no.' He speared a plump green pitted olive on his fork and offered it to her. As her lips closed around it, he went on. 'I want you to have the best, princess. You're class. You'd knock all those frigging princesses dead.'

May chewed the olive and swallowed. 'It's a lovely thought, Eddie. But remember I'm not legal in this country. If I leave, they might not let me back in.'

'I can fix that. Besides you'll be Mrs Edward Theodore Young. My wife. That's legal.'

She shook her head, the yellow curls dancing in the sunlight. 'I'd be nervous all the time. I wouldn't enjoy it.'

Eddie dug his fork into a crisp lettuce leaf and stuffed it into his mouth, feeling a twinge of irritation. Women could be awkward. This one in particular. But he guessed that was why he wanted to marry her. He'd had, and could still have, any number of compliant, submissive girls, if he wanted. But they

202

were no challenge. Was that what May was? A challenge? Maybe they were locked in a competition that he was ultimately determined to win? And to begin the contest, he wanted to show her off on the most exclusive resort on the planet.

'Besides,' she went on, reaching across the table to take his hand, 'there are so many wonderful places to go here. We could go back to Miami.'

He dismissed that with a wave of his linen napkin. 'They'd lock us up or dump us in a ditch.'

May looked out across the glittering river. 'I love the water, Eddie. Maybe because I never saw it as a kid.' She squeezed his hand. 'Let's charter a boat,' she said urgently. 'Take off, on our own.'

'A boat? I can't swim.'

She grinned. 'I can. If we sink, I'll save you.'

Eddie shrugged. Round one to May. It was a small thing.

The forty-five foot cruiser slipped through the calm waters of Long Island Sound, the engine gently throbbing. Out of the city, the late summer had been kind to them. Sunny days and balmy nights under the stars, with the sound of waves caressing the wooden hull as the boat lay anchored overnight in one of the many coves and bays along the shoreline. After a long day cruising in the sun, dinners on board at sunset consisted mainly of seafood and champagne. Local oysters were their favorite. An aphrodisiac Eddie had read somewhere, and whatever the scientific truth, it worked for the newly married couple. Towards the end of the first day, which was filled with Eddie's curses at other boats and wayward tides, he had gratefully handed over the controls to May. She proved to be a natural and loved it, navigating the sandbanks and the commercial shipping, as Eddie admiringly said 'like an old seadog'.

The Sound was over a hundred miles long and some twelve miles across at its widest, so after a week they had still not explored it all. On the final day, May had regretfully turned the boat for home. She lounged lazily at the wheel in the mahogany-paneled wheelhouse, as Eddie emerged from the cabin with two glasses of champagne, looking tanned and handsome in cream linen shirt and matching slacks. He handed a glass to May and they clinked glasses.

'To us, princess. And fuck the rest of them.'

May grimaced a little at the toast and put down her glass, holding it to prevent it falling as, with her other hand, she deftly steered the bow into the breaking wake of a passing steamer headed for nearby Port Chester. When the rocking of the boat gently eased, she took a sip of her drink. 'I could do this for the rest of my life,' she said wistfully.

Eddie settled beside her, his arm around her waist. 'Why not? You don't have to work no more. You're a respectable married woman now.'

She turned to him, looking a little surprised. 'Respectable? Is that what I am, Eddie..? D'you know, I think that's what I've always wanted. Way back. When I used to dream...Not money, not being famous...Just to be respectable. Somebody I could feel proud of...Someone my ma wanted me to be.'

'You got it, princess, and no one can take it away,' he said, planting a kiss on her warm cheek. 'So where are we?'

'Here,' she replied, indicating a point on the chart with the tip of her red-painted nail.

They were approaching a low headland jutting from the otherwise flat landscape. 'I want to show you something,' he said with a mischievous twinkle. 'Hang a right.'

'You mean go to starboard,' she corrected, grinning.

'Whatever.'

As the boat nosed around the headland a wide picturesque bay came into view, its shore fringed with several palatial houses set against a lush green backdrop of beech and sycamore trees.

May sighed. 'It's beautiful.

'Great place to live, huh? And so close to the city.'

'Wonderful,' she agreed, drinking in the view.

Eddie pointed to a white clapboard mansion standing in a large manicured garden beside the bay. 'Hows 'bout that one?'

May nodded. 'Perfect.'

Eddie put his hand in the pocket of his slacks and drew out a set of shiny house keys, which he dangled before May's eyes. She looked at him, puzzled.

He grinned. 'Shall we go and see if they fit?'

She sat up straight beside him, her eyes widening in surprise.

Eddie shrugged. 'What the hell. Wedding present.'

CHAPTER THIRTY SIX

The months leading up to Christmas were a busy time for May. Eddie completed the purchase of the old colonial house at the beginning of the fall, but before they moved in, May set about transforming it to her own modern taste. Determined to supervise the work herself, she often slept over amidst the clutter of the smallest bedroom, with only Mick for company, as Eddie was busy in town. Besides, she told him, she didn't want him in the way. The walls separating the lounge, dining and kitchen areas were ripped down to create a large flowing open space, decorated in fashionable Art Deco colours. Built in wardrobes replaced free standing furniture and a new window seat, running the full length of the wide bay window, allowed the sitter to relax, looking out at the ever-changing waters of the Sound. New bathrooms in vibrant contrasting colours were created in place of the traditional white originals. But the piece de resistance for May were the bookshelves, built along an entire lounge wall, which she filled with books of all shapes and sizes bought in job lots at auction.

'Looks like a frigging library,' said Eddie when he saw the finished effect. 'And you can't even read.'

'I intend to learn,' said May firmly. 'You don't want an ignorant wife, do you?'

'I ain't got one,' he replied, wrapping her in his arms and lifting her off her feet. 'Let's go see what you've done with our bedroom.'

Joe had spent the late summer and the fall immersing himself in work, trying and failing to forget about May. After the wedding, she had vacated her apartment and moved in with Eddie. But, Joe noted when on surveillance duty, she was seldom around The Blackbird. Through his contacts, he heard about the mansion out towards Port Chester. With difficulty, on his day off, he resisted the temptation to take the trip out of town to see the place she was going to live. He tried to keep his focus on Eddie and his widening circle of hoods, convinced that one day he would be able to put him behind bars for a long time. Telling himself it wasn't just revenge for stealing the woman he loved.

Thieving from gullible johns and prostitution were difficult to get convictions for. The road never led back to Eddie and locking the foot soldiers away for a few months, to try and hurt his business, was a waste of time and energy. Joe knew about the strike-breaking, but the strong-arm tactics Eddie's thugs used against the striking workers were universally praised by both the press and public, rather than being seen as illegal.

On the Tuesday before Thanksgiving he pulled in some of Eddie's men for questioning, trying to apply pressure to get a lead. One of them, Henry Rawl was clearly on edge, like something big was being planned, which the guy wasn't very happy about.

'You're sweating, Henry,' Joe said.

They were in the cramped, dark, windowless room used exclusively for interviewing suspects. Rawl was seated in the middle of the room with a bright desk lamp shining full in his eyes. The three detectives crowded around him were just shadows lurking in the darkness.

'It's hot in here,' Henry responded lamely, wiping away a shiny bead of sweat running from his forehead into his eyes.

'It's winter, Henry. I'm freezing my nuts off in here...I'll ask you again. Who's your grass in the unions?'

Henry shook his head. 'I don't know what you're talking about.'

Joe pressed on. 'We know you drive the truck packed with those big palookas. What's your snitch telling you, Henry? Names, addresses? You planning on going visiting?'

'I wanna see a lawyer,' said Henry, trying to sound calm and confident.

'What you need a lawyer for, Henry, if you ain't done nothing illegal?'

'I ain't done nothing illegal!' Henry protested. 'I said I wouldn't - !' He stopped himself, and looked down at his feet. Joe's colleague took a handful of Henry's hair and yanked his head up to the light again. Henry winced. The man didn't release his grip.

Joe put his face close to Henry's. 'Who did you say that to, Henry..? Eddie Young..? What did Eddie want you to do?'

'I wanna see a lawyer,' Henry whimpered.

After the interview, Joe confided to his chief that another session with Rawl might cause the guy to crack. The chief hauled his feet onto his desk, unimpressed.

'He's small beer, Joe,' he said, stretching his beefy arms skyward. 'Forget him.''

'But I think we may get something from this guy, chief,' Joe protested. 'Something big's going down and Rawl knows what it is.'

The chief straightened up in his chair, put his feet back on the floor and leaned forward. 'Like I said, Perski, he's small beer. Believe me, Eddie Young wouldn't confide nothing big to him.' He leant both his ham-sized forearms onto his desk and looked Joe straight in the eyes. 'Listen to me good, Perski. Forget Rawl. Keep your eyes on Eddie.'

On the day before he questioned Henry Rawl, Joe had got his first glimpse of May for several weeks.

By the time the builders, decorators, plumbers, electricians and landscape gardeners had packed away their tools and left, Thanksgiving was almost upon them, and the lawn leading down from the house to the shore was a carpet of crisp white snow. On a bright blue November's day, May had driven into town in her new Oldsmobile Roadster, top down, wrapped in her furs, with Mick snuggled in the passenger seat beside her. This was the first time she would be entertaining in her own house and she wanted to select all the foodstuffs and booze herself, as well as buy a present for Eddie.

She had lunched with some of the old crowd at The Blackbird and spent the afternoon catching up with gossip, not having seen them for a while. On leaving the club, with Mick under her arm, she caught sight of a black car parked across the road with two men inside. She recognised Joe immediately. He was staring out of the window straight at her. Then he waved.

For a moment she almost found herself waving back. She felt good, happy, healthy, rich and glamorous. Life was treating her well. She was a respectable married woman looking forward to entertaining friends for Thanksgiving, and then for her first Christmas in her new home. Why not be charitable? She raised her free hand and extended the middle finger skywards. And instantly felt bad.

The sun was setting behind violet-blue clouds as she drove along the narrow, hedge-fringed road towards the house. The threat of rain hung in the air, but for the moment the last of the day's light bathed the house and the surrounding snow in a golden glow. On the drive home from the city, she had shaken off the troubled feeling that had descended after her crude gesture to Joe. It was a mean act, and she no longer had cause to feel bitter or vengeful. Her life had changed. She was living her dream.

A canvas-sided truck she recognised was standing on the gravel drive beside the front door. She parked behind it, and was getting the shopping from the back seat when she heard the raised voices coming from the lounge.

'No, sir,' she heard Henry say, 'I won't be a party to that!'

'You back out now, you punk, you're finished!' Eddie's voice was thick with anger. 'I made you, remember! I can break you just as easy!'

The raised voices drowned the sound of May entering the house. She put down the shopping in the hall and entered the lounge. Eddie and Henry Rawl stopped their argument immediately.

'Hey, May!' said Eddie beaming. 'Look who's just dropped in!' He clapped Henry on the shoulder, harder than he had intended.

'Hi, Henry,' she said probingly.

Henry looked down at the carpet, cowed. 'Hi, Mrs Young.'

May frowned. 'What's with the Mrs Young?' she asked. 'It's May...Are you staying for dinner? I've got fresh clams.'

'Er, no...Thanks...' he replied, shifting uncomfortably on his feet. 'I've got things -'

'Yeah, run along, Henry,' Eddie said, affecting a casual, friendly tone. 'We'll talk some more. Don't worry, it'll be fine.'

Relieved to get away, Henry hurried past May into the hall and retrieved his hat. 'Goodbye, Mrs Young,' he said almost tripping over the doorstep in his haste to leave the house.

As the front door closed, May turned to Eddie with a stern expression. 'What's going on, Eddie? Why were you threatening Henry?'

Eddie shrugged expansively. 'What threatening? You know Henry. He goes off the handle sometimes.'

May was not to be put off. Her whole feeling of well-being had been changed in an instant. Suddenly she felt afraid. 'What about this time?'

'May,' he sighed patronizingly, moving to her with open arms.

She waved him away and moved across to the bay window. Outside the sunlight had been replaced by a brooding, grey darkness as the rain began to fall. Eddie crossed to the drinks cabinet and poured himself a bourbon. He held up the bottle to May. She shook her head. He poured a second drink anyway and topped both glasses with cubes from the silver ice-bucket.

'I wanted him to help out with some of the girls, is all. But you know what he's like. Principles. Nice when you can afford 'em...Tell you something, I think he's just chicken.'

He moved to her, the drinks clinking in his hands. 'How's about them clams with champagne?' He put his arms around her waist, still holding the drinks, and grinned. 'Remember the first time?'

May faked a smile in return. Deep inside she felt hollow.

CHAPTER THIRTY SEVEN

Joe raised himself on one elbow and looked at the luminous dial on the watch that lay on the wooden chair beside his bed. It was 3am and he was wide awake and anxious. Outside, somewhere nearby, a drunk was singing the Marion Harris hit, 'I Ain't Got Nobody.' He knew the feeling. Lying on his back, with his hands behind his head, he surveyed the dim grey shapes of the cramped single room he called home. A table, two chairs, a closet, dresser and the bed on which he was lying, alone. Thanksgiving was coming, but he had no plans for a celebration. All over America people were preparing to make trips to loved ones to give thanks with friends and family for what the Good Lord had seen fit to give them. The reward for their hard work pursuing the American Dream. He was nearly twenty-eight years old and he had been pursuing that same dream since he was a boy. So far, as his present circumstances showed, it had eluded him.

As long as he could remember he had wanted to follow in his father's footsteps and become a cop. His dad had encouraged him further. 'Get off the beat as soon as you can, son,' he advised. 'Get your gold badge. Detective work is where it's at.'

His father had been gunned down long before his son achieved the ambition he had set for him. Shot in mysterious circumstances that had been glossed over and covered up in the press, and never talked about by his colleagues in the precinct. A punk thief caught in the act had blasted his dad at point blank range. The thief had never been traced and Joe sometimes wondered if he ever existed. His father was a man of principle and, in the NYPD, principles sometimes got in the way. As his father's son, Joe had inherited the same set of beliefs and lived by them. Was the same fate waiting for him around the next corner, in the next alley? All he knew was that earlier today his chief had deliberately got in the way of his investigation. After weeks of surveillance he felt he had finally made a breakthrough with Henry Rawl. But he had been steered away, warned off. Had Eddie's long arm reached as far as the chief? If so, by his questioning, Joe might just have signed Henry's death warrant. Whatever the cost to his career, or to himself, he had to warn him.

May had waited impatiently at home all day. She knew that Henry Rawl would be out delivering in his truck and wouldn't be home until the late afternoon. Unable to concentrate on anything to distract her thoughts, the hours dragged by. Since confronting Eddie about the argument she had interrupted late yesterday afternoon, she had been desperate to know the truth. She knew Eddie had lied about wanting Henry's help with the girls. It was obvious from Henry's discomfort with her that it was something much more serious than that.

She had been dismayed at how rapidly one's life and feelings could change. Driving home from the city, in the golden winter sunlight, she had been on top of the world. Now she felt as if she was teetering on the brink of a deep dark hole. That life with Eddie would always be like living on the edge she knew when she agreed to marry him. Eddie was a career criminal, and she accepted he would never change. She had hoped that, as his wife, she would be able to rein in his worst excesses, but Henry's manner the previous evening made her believe that she had failed. When she found out the truth, she knew she may have to confront Eddie with an ultimatum. And, though that thought scared her, she was determined to see it through.

Eddie had still not arrived home when she set off once again for the city. She hoped she wouldn't meet him driving along the narrow roads leading to their house and have to explain where she was going so late in the day. When she reached the open road, she breathed a sigh of relief and put her foot down to the floor. The howl of the racing engine matched the adrenalin surging around her body. If Henry wasn't in, she would just have to have it out with Eddie cold. Accusing him of lying. She was going to do that anyway, but she wanted the facts to back her up. At the same time, in the pit of her stomach, she didn't want to know. She wanted to believe her instinct was way off line and that, for once, Eddie had not been treating her like an irritating child.

Henry Rawl had been trembling all the way home from the 5th precinct station. That morning two detectives had picked him up as he left his apartment block for work and he had spent the day alternatively being grilled by Detective Perski, under a bright light which pierced his eyes like a needle, or being left alone in a windowless cell at minus two degrees below. He didn't know if the trembling was from the cold or his fear of the questioning. Both he guessed.

He hoped he'd managed to convince them he knew nothing. That he was just a small, insignificant little cog in a very big machine. But he had never been good at lying. That wasn't the way his parent's had brought him up. Own up and tell the truth, was his father's motto. Much good it had done him, Henry thought bitterly, wrapping his arms around himself against the icy wind blowing through the subway. He shivered again. Pray God he'd convinced them.

Dusk was creeping over the city as he reached the brownstone tenement which housed his apartment. He looked nervously about him as he climbed the stone steps to the front door. Letting himself into the gloomy hallway, he was about to mount the staircase when a voice from the shadows made him jump in alarm.

'Henry.'

Peering into the dimly-lit alcove at the side of the stairs, he said in surprise, 'Mrs Young? What are you doing here?'

May moved into the light. 'I want to know why all of a sudden I'm "Mrs Young". '

Henry looked about him again, like a small animal caught in headlights. 'Mrs Young, please -'

'Henry, you're going to tell me if I have to stand here all night.'

He let out a heavy sigh and shook his head.

'I dragged you out of the gutter, Henry. You owe me.'

'I got you off the ship,' he responded defensively. 'We're even, I figure.'

In the gloom of the lobby May's smile was like a sunbeam. 'If it hadn't have been you, it would have been one of the others, Henry.'

He looked at her in surprise. 'But...you didn't know about Ellis Island till I told you...Did you?'

'You didn't think I'd go through all that. Stealing from my Da, travelling all that way across the sea, if I thought I wouldn't be able to get off at the other end, did you?' she lied.

'So you chose me as the mug?' he said, dismayed.

May's voice was warm in reply. 'I chose you because I liked you, Henry. Because I could see you was a good person. Because you was honest...Honest enough not to do what Eddie wanted you to do...What was that, Henry?'

Her eyes bored into him. He turned away, shoulders drooped, and started to climb the stairs. After the last twenty-four hours, first with Eddie and then the cops, he was shaken and beaten. May followed, her heels ringing on the tiled stairway. At the top of the first flight, Henry paused by a brown-painted door and inserted a key. The door creaked as they entered.

'It's not much, I'm afraid,' Henry mumbled, apologetically.

May looked around the cheaply furnished room. A thin-mattress bed, tiny cooker, a thick ceramic sink, table and a chair. The pattern on the carpet was almost invisible through years of wear. 'Not what you fought a war for.'

'I've nothing in to drink, I'm afraid,' he said, taking off his hat and spinning it around between his fingers, nervously. 'I still don't.'

'Henry, I'm not here on a date.'

He indicated the single chair. 'You wanna sit down?'

May didn't move. 'I'm waiting. I don't want to be late home.'

Henry moved about the tiny space, not looking at her. He cleared his throat. 'There's this union guy...' he began at last, and stopped to look at her questioningly. 'You know 'bout trade unions?'

'I can't read,' she said, 'but I do have ears.'

'Well,' he went on uncomfortably, 'There's this union guy. His name's Flaherty.. A Mick troublemaker.'

'Like me,' said May, without humour.

'I didn't mean - ' he stuttered.

'Go on,' she said impatiently. 'I've been called much worse.' The mention of unions was starting to ring distant alarm bells. She'd heard a lot of bar-room talk about 'commies' trying to destroy America. It didn't look that way to her.

'Seems like he's been leading a lot of strikes. Whipping people up -'

She interrupted again, anxious to be reassured that what was forming in her mind was way off beam. 'Wait a minute, Henry. What's this got to do with Eddie?'

He looked at her confused. 'Well, he, er...I...thought you knew.'

'Knew what?' Her voice was brittle now.

'I just thought...' He stopped, feeling himself sinking deeper into the morass. His head was spinning. All the questions that had been thrown at him since the morning were knotting together like a log-jam in his brain. He was scared what the consequences of them all would be for him.

Speaking very slowly and precisely, as if the manner of her question would alter the answer in her favour, May asked, 'Are you trying to tell me that Eddie is still strike-breaking?'

Henry stood, shoulders slumped. 'I really thought you knew...' He looked at her, knowing his answer had struck her like a fist.

May was rooted in the centre of the threadbare carpet. In her peripheral vision, she was vaguely aware of the once-vibrant floral pattern, which had faded much more slowly than her dream. She didn't want to ask the next question. 'This Mick troublemaker...' she began and let the unfinished question hang in the air.

'Patrick Flaherty,' Henry said. 'Eddie...Mr Young...' he continued guiltily. 'Wants him...out of the way.'

CHAPTER THIRTY EIGHT

May's car must have found its way home by itself, for she had no recollection of driving herself there. She could remember walking unsteadily down the gloomy stairway from Henry's room, feeling the cold metal banister slide through her fingers, and hearing the sound of her own heels rasping on the stairs. But by the time she reached the car, her whirling mind had slipped into automatic pilot. Under her urgent questioning Henry had expanded on his answer, and she had been left in no doubt what Eddie was planning. She couldn't believe it, but Henry Rawl was not a liar. He had told her about the police interrogation and was clearly very scared about being dragged into something he wanted no part of.

'I told 'em nothing, Mrs Young! Believe me,' he said, his eyes imploring her. 'I didn't say nothing to the cops about Eddie. Nothing at all.'

'I believe you, Henry,' she said, numbly, still stunned by what she had just heard.

'You wanna a coffee or something? You look sorta pale.'

May shook her head slowly, only half hearing him. She found herself wandering to the door. Putting her hand on the handle, she turned back to him. 'Thank you, Henry,' she said quietly. 'Thank you for being so honest.'

'I had to tell you, Mrs Young. I'm sorry.'

'It's May, Henry,' she said. 'Please.'

'I had to tell you...May,' he replied, with a shy half smile.

Taking the few steps that brought her to him, she put her hand on his shoulder. 'You're a good man, Henry Rawl.'

He shrugged, embarrassed. 'That's the way my folks brung me up to be. Always tried to be a credit to them.'

Opening her purse, she took out all the bills inside and held them out to him. He looked at her puzzled.

'Hell, I don't want paying.'

She shook her head gently. 'I'm sorry, Henry. I have to have it out with Eddie. I won't drag you into it, I promise, but I have to stop this madness before it's too late.'

'But he'll know who told you,' he said, turning as white as May had earlier. 'He'll know it was me.'

'That's why I want you to have this,' she replied, holding out the bills. 'There should be enough to see you through for a while. After you've left town and settled some place, send me a wire where I can send you some more.'

As Henry took the bills their fingers touched. May put her arms around him and hugged him. He could smell her skin next to his. She smelt like peaches. 'God bless you, Henry Rawl,' she said and planted a kiss on his cheek.

'You too, May Sharpe,' he said, the words catching in his throat.

Driving home, with tears streaming down her cheeks, she tried to remember the times when Eddie had lost his temper. He had a notoriously short fuse and would threaten people with all kinds of dire consequences if they crossed him, but, though there were rumours, she had never known him carry out any of his threats. When it came to it, she didn't believe Eddie was, or could be, a killer. If she had believed that she could never have married him. But what pressure was he under? Maybe whoever was pulling the strings was the sort of person you didn't say 'no' to? For she was convinced that Eddie was only a link in a chain. One that led all the way up to the top of big business.

They were the ones with everything to gain by smashing the unions. Not Eddie. She had to make him see that.

As she drove she prayed aloud that she could, for, despite her childhood experience with the clergy, she still believed that someone was looking out for her. After all, someone had led her away from her misery and shown her happiness. Surely they wouldn't let her whole world crumble around her, now she had come so far?

The chandelier in their living room was shining out like a beacon in the surrounding darkness, as her tyres scrunched on the gravel leading up to the front door. Eddie had not yet drawn the curtains and, through the French windows, she saw him entering the brightly-lit room with a drink in his hand. She pulled on the handbrake, killed the headlights and let the engine die. Then she sat waiting for her courage to come back to her.

With trembling hands, Henry packed his few belongings into the cheap cardboard suitcase. The nearness of violence had started the tremors again, and twice during packing he had to leave off to go down the hall to the communal bathroom. After he closed the suitcase, he stood in the centre of the tiny, bleak room, frozen like a statue. Memories flooding back.

The screams. The mud and blood mingled together in the trenches. The deep black nights illuminated by the vivid flashes of enemy shells bursting along the line, shattering bodies and dreams alike. Faces of friends who hadn't come back. Then the long sea journey home, suddenly enlivened when he literally bumped into the beautiful young girl with the strawberry blonde curls and the startling green eyes. From the very beginning there had been something mysterious about her.

'Are you emigrating, Miss Sharpe?' he asked. They were standing at the rail together looking out at the vast, calm ocean stretching away to the ruler-drawn horizon.

The girl looked at him, uncomprehendingly. 'Pardon?'

'Are you emigrating? Going to live in America?'

'Oh, yes. Yes. I'm emigrating,' she said proudly, pronouncing the word for the first time.

'All by yourself?'

She hesitated only for a second, 'Ah, no. I have relatives there. My Uncle Pat...He's very rich.'

'That's nice. Where does he live?' he asked, reaching out to pat the head of the little dog that was cradled in her arms.

'America,' she replied.

He smiled. 'But where? America's a big country.'

'He lives...by the mountains,' she replied, avoiding his gaze.

Her answer and tone made him curious. 'Which mountains? The Appalachians? The Rockies? The Blue Ridge Mountains?'

'Yes. The Blue Ridge,' she said, hastily, as if fastening onto the prettiest sounding name. 'The Blue Ridge Mountains.'

'What does he do there?' He hoped he was not sounding too much like an interrogator, but there was something about the girl that didn't add up, and he wanted to know what.

'He digs...for oil,' she replied firmly.

'In Virginia? Ain't no oil in Virginia, last I heard.'

She turned to face him, a frosty expression on her pretty face. 'Well, he's digging, isn't he? And he should know! I didn't know Americans were so nosey.' She hefted the tiny dog in her arms. 'Come on, Mick!'

'Miss, I didn't mean anything...' he called after her as she strode away along the deck. She never looked back.

He had won her round by collecting the unfinished meals from his seasick comrades and taking the meat and bones to her cabin for the dog.

'I'm sorry I was out of line,' he said, when she answered his knock the first time.

'Out of line?'

'Yeah. Out of order. Asking questions that are none of my business,' he explained.

'Ah no. That's all right. Quite all right...' She waved her hand around the cabin. 'Will you sit down?'

'Thanks.' He sat down on the only chair. She perched on the edge of the bed, watching Mick eagerly devouring the scraps on the floor.

'I love that Irish accent.'

'I'm afraid, I've nothing to offer you to drink,' she said, opening her hands as if to demonstrate she had nothing in them.

'That's okay. I don't drink.'

'Me neither.'

There was an awkward silence. They sat, both acutely aware of Mick's noisy gobbling. Then they both spoke at once.

'Perhaps-' she began.

'I guess-' he said simultaneously.

'Sorry,' she said, smiling shyly.

'No, you go on. Please,' he insisted.

'I was going to say...' As she looked at him he wondered if he had ever seen such eyes, like bright, emerald windows to her young soul. 'I wondered if perhaps you could teach me some American? As I'm going to be living there. I don't want to be standing out like an eejit.'

'I'd be glad to, Miss Sharpe.'

'May, please.'

'I'd be glad to, May... Might take my mind off...' He stopped, embarrassed.

'Was it very bad?' she asked gently. 'The war?'

He looked down at the floor, trying to block out the images that haunted his mind. 'It's nothing I ever want to see again. But I sure don't want to forget it, no sir...Lot of the guys, they've taken to drinking to blot it all out. But me. I want to remember everything, every last detail. So if anyone ever says we should fight a war again, I can remind 'em.' He looked up at her, shrugging off a tremor than ran through his body. 'Still that's all over. We're going back to make a new start. To build a new world... We sure deserve it. We gave enough for it...'

The knock on the door broke into his remembering.

CHAPTER THIRTY NINE

Eddie had answered the telephone in the hall, then gone into the lounge to fix himself a drink before going back to make his own call. Satisfied that things were in hand, he re-entered the lounge and saw the lights of May's car coming along the drive. He'd been mildly surprised and disappointed that she was not at home when he came back from the city. She had been to town earlier in the week to make preparations for Thanksgiving and had said nothing about making any other trips. More surprising was that she hadn't taken the dog with her. May never went anywhere without her damn dog.

He sat down in his chair by the log fire, which had been set by the maid in the morning and should have been burning brightly when he came home, except that May was out, and had neglected to light it herself. Lighting a taper with his gold cigarette lighter, he'd applied the flame to the kindling and had sat back to watch the flames rise, just as the phone rang. Now he was seated at ease again, looking forward to spending the evening with his young and beautiful wife. Life was good. Business was thriving. Success made him feel horny.

Mick was whining in the rear of the house where Eddie had put him out of the way. The animal always knew when his mistress was around. He adored her, but barely tolerated Eddie, sensing the man's disinterest, bordering on dislike. It was an instinct Eddie would have liked to have himself. A very useful tool in his line of work. Knowing what people really thought of you.

Minutes passed. The pine logs blazed in the hearth. Puzzled that he hadn't heard May get out of the car, he was about to get up to investigate when he heard the car door slam. Moments later, Mick's whining gave way to happy barking, and May's voice rang out as she greeted her pet.

'I'm in the lounge, princess!' he called. 'Wanna drink?'

There was no reply. She obviously hadn't heard above the dog's racket. He got up, went to the drinks cabinet, dropped three cubes into a crystal glass and poured a fine bourbon over the crackling ice. As May entered the room, clutching Mick to her, he held up the glass. She ignored him and went to stand facing the fire. He shrugged to himself. May could be moody at times, but the moods passed as quickly as they came, which was good. She was looking good enough to eat. He didn't want her in a mood this evening. 'It's sure cold out there,' he said. Moving to her side, he put an arm round her waist and held out the glass. 'This'll warm you up.'

When she turned, the fire in her eyes startled him. Tears were mingled with the flames. 'Hey,' he said, concerned. 'What's up, princess?'

Her voice, when she replied, was more sad than angry. 'How could you, Eddie? How could you lie to me?'

'Me, princess? Lie to you?'

'Don't make it worse, Eddie. You said you were through with strike-breaking.'

'And I am, doll,' he said easily, and raised his arms to hold her. 'I told you.'

She moved quickly away out of his reach, put Mick down on a chair and turned to face him stonily. 'Then why are you planning to murder Patrick Flaherty?'

Eddie blinked for a moment, taken aback. Then suddenly he flared like the flames behind him. 'Whose been talking to you! Who you been talking to? That rat Henry Rawl?'

'Never mind who told me!' Her tears were flowing freely now. 'What are you thinking of, Eddie..? Please, tell me it's a joke. Just bar talk. Tell me you never seriously meant to kill Patrick Flaherty!'

His face darkened with anger and frustration. May was stepping out of line. So far he had let her make the small decisions to make her happy and keep the peace, but she was treading into his territory now. She had to learn her place. 'Flaherty's a dirty lousy stinking commie, for Christ's sake! He's destroying our country! He's a traitor, May! In other countries they'd shoot him!'

'But not here, Eddie!' she cried. 'They wouldn't shoot him here! Not in America! That's called murder!'

'The guy's a frigging menace! D'you know how many of my guys he's had beaten up? He's gotta be stopped!'

May wiped away the tears with the back of her hand. She knew the mascara would be smearing her cheeks, but she didn't care what a mess she looked. 'You told me you were out of that, Eddie! You promised me!' she cried, brokenhearted. 'That's why I married you! You said you were out of it!'

Eddie's expression turned ugly and scornful. 'Out of it? Out of it! When are you going wise up and start living in the real world, May? When are you going to stop living in that dream world you had as a kid?' He swung his arms expansively at the room. 'How d'you think we got this place? What d'you think pays for your fancy car? The food, the booze. The dress you're standing up in, you dumb broad!'

May looked down at her dress. It was one of her favorites. A deep copper crepe de chine. Suddenly she hated it touching her flesh. 'This dress -!' she began, and started to rip at the material to tear it from her body.

'Hey, stop that!' Eddie yelled.

She ignored him, tearing the fabric from her shoulders. He rushed at her and grabbed her arms roughly.

'Stop it!'

May struggled in his grip. 'Let me go!' she cried.

'Stop it, you stupid Mick bitch!' He hit her hard on the cheek with the flat of his hand, sending her reeling backwards from the stinging blow. Mick leapt from the chair and hurled himself at Eddie, barking and snapping ferociously. Eddie kicked the dog away, but it came back at him wild-eyed, teeth bared. 'Bite me you fucking bastard!' Eddie snarled. Picking the dog up by its two front legs he rushed towards the French windows.

'No!!' May screamed.

She made a grab at Eddie, but he spun round like a hammer-thrower and hurled the yelping dog through the French windows in a flurry of splintering wood and glass. With an anguished scream May tore into Eddie. He warded off the flurry of blows with his arms, then floored her with a vicious left hook to the side of her face. She sprawled backwards onto the carpet, her head spinning. Before she could get up, Eddie straddled her and started to slap her face from side to side with the flat of both hands.

'I'll teach you, you fucking stupid Mick bitch!'

For a moment, May tried to defend herself from the attack, but he was far too strong. As the blows rained down she slumped back, semi-conscious. His anger finally spent, Eddie stopped and sat back on his heels, panting heavily. May lay softly moaning on her back, her dress hanging in rags from her shoulders. Her head was swimming in pain and disbelief. It all seemed like a terrible nightmare. She looked up at Eddie through glazed eyes, and saw him begin to tear at his belt and trouser buttons.

'No!!!' she yelled. In an instant she had a vision of her father astride her on the bed in the croft, about to enter her. 'NO!!!' she howled again, terrified.

But Eddie, possessed, unhearing, tore the remains of the dress from her body. May tried to fight him off, but the room was spinning wildly and she felt dazed and sick. As he thrust brutally into her, she cried out in pain and rage.

CHAPTER FORTY

The first streaks of day crept over the cold waters of the Sound. Screeching gulls began to wheel in the grey light, their cries splitting the still morning air. In the distance a lone fishing boat carved a silver path towards the place where the inland sea met the vast Atlantic Ocean. Overnight a blanket of virgin snow had covered the garden leading to the fine mansion overlooking the bay. Inside, May sat at the bedroom window cradling Mick in her arms, gazing out at the view, unseeing. The vivid bruises on her face were painless now. The pain was deep inside.

She had fled the house after the rape, stopping only to snatch her fur from the hall, against the icy night air. When he realized she had gone, Eddie had come out after her calling her name into the blackness.

'May! Princess! I'm sorry! Come back!' He repeated the same words over and over. 'I'm sorry! I was crazy! Please, I didn't mean to hurt you! I'll never, never hit you again! Never! I promise, princess!'

Crouched, shivering, in the deep shadow of a holly bush, May listened to the familiar words floating upwards towards the clouded sky. No stars nor moon shone. Away from the light shining from the house, the darkness was total. Eddie wandered the garden calling, 'Come back, princess! You'll freeze to death! Please, I won't hurt you! I promise. Angel, I will never hurt you again!'

She watched him go back to his car and rummage for something in the glove compartment. Slipping silently away over the cold grass down towards the shoreline, she ducked

228

behind a breakwater just as the long, bright torch-beam began to scour the empty shadows of the garden.

'Please, princess! I was crazy! I promise, I will never hurt you again!'

How many times had she heard those words? Lying frightened and cold in her little bed in the croft, she had listened to her father's tearful pleas for forgiveness from the next room, over and over again, as her mother cried in pain and despair. May shivered, but not from the cold. Eddie had not even been drunk.

After a quarter of an hour he gave up the search. 'Alright, princess, you win!' he called. 'I'm going to the club. I won't hurt you, but I know you don't want me near you, right now. But you have to come in. You'll freeze to death out there. So I'll go. I'll see you tomorrow, when you've calmed down. I'm going, so you can go back inside and get warm. D'you hear me, princess?'

She didn't reply. Holding her breath, she watched him get into his car. 'I'm going, princess! I love you! I really love you, you hear me!' he called, then closed the door. The car roared into life, and drove away down the long drive, its headlights turning the trees and bushes into fleeting white ghosts. Waiting until the sound of the engine had faded into silence, she emerged from her hiding place and ran back towards the house. As she neared it, she heard a painful whimper from the garden at the side of the house. It was only then that she remembered Mick.

The little dog was lying quite still on the lawn, picked out by the light from the shattered French windows, whimpering pitifully. Picking him up in her arms, she hurried in through the front door and into the dining room opposite the lounge. She never wanted to enter that room again.

It was clear that Mick was badly hurt. His body had been lacerated from head to tail by the glass, and his fur was matted with blood. He lay without moving on the table where she had put him, looking up at her with frightened, uncomprehending eyes.

'You stay there, sweetheart,' she said soothingly, gently stroking his head. 'I'll get help. You'll be okay.'

Mick whimpered and tried to raise his head as she went into the hall to call the local vet. She waited, anxiously, listening to the phone ringing. There was no reply. It was hopeless. At that time in the evening all surgeries would be closed.

Carrying Mick into the kitchen, she carefully washed the blood from his fur and bathed the wounds with iodine, all the time talking reassuringly to it. The dog lay prone, trembling slightly under her hands, tongue lolling from its mouth. It was unable to lap up the water from the bowl she placed near it, so she tried to dribble it into the dog's mouth with a spoon. But Mick was unable to swallow. Having done all she could think of, she wrapped herself and the dog in a woolen blanket and hunkered down in the large armchair in the corner of the master bedroom in the darkness, waiting for the new day to dawn.

'You remember when I first found you?' she asked softly, her lips close to Mick's ear. 'You were a sight then, weren't you? All muddy and starving to death. Like a drowned rat. I think someone had tried to drown you, hadn't they? Why would they do that to such a beautiful animal?

At first, her father had objected to keeping the stray. 'Just another mouth to feed,' he grumbled. But May had persuaded him that her new friend would earn its keep, keeping the rats and rabbits away from the vegetable patch. From that day on they were inseparable, roaming the bog land together in search of rabbits, which Mick would cleverly catch without making a bloody mess. She skinned them and made tasty stews. For his reward Mick got the carcass, covered with gravy she had kept back for him.

'It was your lucky day when you found me, wasn't it?' she whispered. 'And mine too...Haven't we seen some things together? We've crossed the big ocean. Lived in a big city. Been to Miami and swum in the sea. What an adventure! I'm sure not many dogs have done so much. And now...' She stopped. What now, she thought? Whatever happened, she knew her life had changed again, forever. 'But we'll still be together, won't we? We've still got each other.' She pressed her lips to the dog's warm cheek and closed her eyes.

Somehow, despite her racing mind, she must have fallen asleep, emotionally exhausted. It was the grandfather clock in the hall that woke her as it chimed three a.m. For a moment her brain struggled to register where she was. She was stiff and aching from being huddled in the chair, and the bruises on her face and body were throbbing painfully. Trying to move she became aware of a heavy object lying on her chest. Moving the cover aside, she felt the dog. Despite the warmth of the blanket, Mick was like ice.

Light snow was falling again as Joe drove out of New York towards the Sound. The relative warmth of the city had kept the snow from lying on the sidewalks, but as he drove through the empty streets of the suburbs and into the countryside the dark fields became more and more covered with a crisp, white blanket. The sun would not show itself for another hour and even then it would remain a pallid silver disc behind thin snow clouds all day. Blizzards were forecast for Thanksgiving.

He yawned. After the phone call from the precinct his disturbed night had become a busy early morning. Was it technically morning before the sun got up, he wondered? When did the night end and the day begin? He guessed it was different for different people. For cleaners and janitors, winter days began before sunrise. Midday was the start of the day for actors and hookers. For detectives day and night merged into one. Crime was a twenty-four hour experience.

His instinct led him to head out of town as soon as he had completed the formalities. As a precaution, he hadn't told his chief where he was going. Driving through the still, silent landscape, a thrill of anticipation at the prospect of finally seeing her home, mingled with his professional concerns. He hoped he'd arrive before they had risen. It was always better to catch people cold.

CHAPTER FORTY ONE

In the front room above the Blackbird club, Eddie stirred. His head was throbbing, which was not surprising considering the amount of booze he'd taken on board last night. Was he drowning his sorrows? His guilt? Whatever the reason, he'd got blasted. Even drunk he hadn't told the others why he was in town and not at home with his loving wife. And no one had asked. Just as it should be. A man could do whatever he wanted. No questions. That was his right. And he, Edward Theodore Young the Third, had more right than anyone. He had earned it by hard work from being a boy. Aged nine, running errands for the local hoods, he'd seen that if you were happy to be one of the crowd, you'd always be a punk. At ten he'd formed his own gang, petty thieving and robbery from old, frail people not able to defend themselves. In his two stretches in reformatory he'd learnt new skills from the older boys, which he put into practice as soon as he was free. As he left his teens behind, running girls had become his preferred source of income.

His growing feelings for May had taken him by surprise. In his line of work sex was freely available. He'd had two, three, four girls at a time, many times. It never ceased to excite him, but moving on to new flesh was always a necessity. For him, familiarity did breed contempt, or at least indifference. But not with May. Over the months they had been together, since the first time in Miami, he had never once strayed. There was no need. There was a particular quality about her that made every time a new experience. Wildness, tenderness, fire and laughter merged into one. She was unique and she was his.

But she had to learn her place. He'd had to show her that. Letting her dictate his actions would make him weak, and in this business weakness was not an option. In spite of that he felt very bad. He knew it wouldn't be easy to calm May's fiery temper and soothe her wounded pride. He had committed a terrible act which he would never repeat. He'd told her that, calling out to her in the darkness of the garden last night. She had heard his promise. In time she'd believe him. And forgive him. As soon as Tiffany's opened on Fifth Avenue he would buy her a very special present for Thanksgiving.

May stood in the middle of the rose garden, where the gardener had already pruned back the bushes in preparation for the long bitter winter. It was hard to believe that in a few months these short spiky sticks would be transformed with blossoms of a dozen different shades of pink, yellow, orange, crimson and white. Nature was a miracle, creating life from apparent death. In the snow at her feet, wrapped in a white linen table cloth, was Mick. With the tears flowing once more, she remembered the many times he had sat beside her as she dug the vegetable patch at the rear of the croft. After she had laid him in the hole, he too would become part of the rebirth, though she wouldn't be there to see it.

She looked up at the sound of an approaching car. A fist of fear gripped her stomach. But it didn't sound like Eddie's powerful roadster. Through the trees lining the drive she saw the black Model T and instantly recognized the driver. What was he doing here at this hour, with the invisible sun hardly over the horizon? She stood where she was, holding the spade in her cold fingers.

Joe saw her before he parked the car at the front door. She looked strange standing in the middle of the patch of earth wearing a fur coat over red silk pyjamas, with her feet engulfed in gumboots several sizes too big for her. As he walked across the snow-covered lawn towards her, he saw the cruel bruises that covered her cheeks. He'd seen domestic violence many times before, but he was shocked. Shocked and, instantly, very angry.

'Did he do that to you?' he blurted out.

She looked away. 'What do you want?' she replied in a flat, dead voice.

For the first time he saw the hole in the earth and the little white bundle at her feet. 'Your dog?' he asked in a gentler tone.

'If you don't mind,' she said wearily, 'I'd like to be on my own at this moment.'

'I'm sorry,' he said, genuinely. 'But I need to talk to your husband.'

'He's not here.'

'Do you know where I can find him?' He was resisting the urge to take May in his arms and magically make everything better for her. Ashen-faced, bruised and beaten, she looked more like a child than a woman.

'I don't know and I don't care,' she replied.

'I'm sorry. I know this is a bad time, but I need to ask you some questions.'

May looked at him, waiting without response, her face expressionless.

'Where was your husband around half past nine, ten o'clock last night?'

'He was here, giving me this facial.'

He noted the heavy irony with relief. It showed that somewhere inside the spirit was still alive. 'Was he here all night?'

She shook her head and said flatly. 'He left after he'd done raping me.'

Joe closed his eyes and gritted his teeth, trying to control the anger boiling in his blood. When he opened them again she was looking at him curiously. 'Do you want to make out a complaint?' he said, his voice struggling to remain calm.

Her laugh rang out in the frosty air, and died as suddenly as it had come. 'Is that all, detective?' she asked. 'If you don't mind, I'd like to bury my dog before I get frostbite.'

'Do you need any help?' he asked gently. 'I'd be glad to.'

'Why do you want to know where Eddie was last night?' she asked, pointedly ignoring his offer.

He watched her closely as he replied. 'They dragged Henry Rawl out the East River early this morning.' As her hand shot to her mouth, he saw she was genuinely surprised and shocked. 'Looks like an accident or suicide. He was full of booze.'

She stood stunned and silent, her fingers still gripping her mouth, as if holding it shut. Keeping its secrets.

'The guy should be strung up,' he said, his anger surfacing.

Her brow furrowed. 'What?'

'Have you seen a doctor?' She shook her head. 'I can take you.'

She shook her head again and looked away towards the grey water beyond the garden. Beneath the fur he could see her body was trembling.

'May-' he began.

'Just leave me alone!' she snapped, showing the first sign of her fire since he had arrived. 'Just-leave-me-alone,' she repeated more slowly, emphasizing every syllable.

Looking at her standing, incongruously dressed, in the mud of the rose garden there was so much he wanted to say. To help. But it wasn't the time. Maybe it never would be.

'I'm truly sorry about your dog,' he said.

With a brief nod, he turned and walked away, his boots crunching on the snow. She looked at the trail of his footprints.

His stride was long. But was it long enough to catch up with Eddie?

Harry, the proprietor of the Blackbird club, told Joe that Eddie had gone out early and hadn't said where he could be contacted. He confirmed that Eddie had arrived late last evening and stayed overnight.

'Do you know a guy called Henry Rawl?'

'Scrawny guy. Works for Eddie?'

'When did you last see him?'

Harry shook his head thoughtfully. 'Can't say. He never comes in here.'

Joe walked out of the club and back to his car. Eddie would now know he was looking for him and would probably guess what it was about. So he'd be prepared when Joe finally caught up with him. He had an alibi, but Joe was convinced Eddie was involved in Rawl's death. The timing was too much of a coincidence. Rawl had known something. He had something on Eddie and he was scared. But there had been no obvious marks of violence on the body, and the corpse reeked of booze. The verdict would be accidental death and Eddie would get away with murder. A murder that Joe had initiated by telling his chief about Rawl. But he could prove nothing.

She washed her hands and dried them on the towel in the kitchen. She would have to get dressed and put on some make-up before the maid arrived, though she knew no cosmetics could hide the swollen, discolored cheeks. Still wearing her fur she wandered into the hallway. The door to the lounge stood open. Inside the room were many of the mementoes of her life since her clandestine arrival in America. Her first photo with

Eddie, laughing together inside the Blackbird, the pair of them sun-bathing in Miami, the happy couple at the wedding reception, Eddie steering the boat, and May with Mick in her arms standing smiling before the Statue of Liberty. But those moments had been overshadowed, erased, by the event that took place in the middle of that room last night.

Going into the dining room where she had laid the fatally injured Mick, she went to the window and looked out at the grey seascape of the Sound, half obscured as the snow began to fall again in large, drifting flakes. America had first appeared to her like this, across grey mist and snow. As she gazed out across the water Henry's words came back to her.

'Ain't you never heard of the Statue of Liberty? Know what it says on it..? Give me your tired, your poor...Guess that's me... Not for long though. No, sir.'

It was almost three years since kind, innocent Henry Rawl had carried her down the gangplank in his kitbag to her new life. In that short time her world had been transformed. Now it was about to be turned upside down again.

Joe had just arrived back from the mortuary when the call came. It was put through to him at his desk.

'Perski?' he said into the mouthpiece. There was silence at the other end of the line. 'Hallo? This is Detective Joe Perski. Is anybody there?'

Finally she replied. ' It wasn't suicide...'

His heart began to race. 'May?' he began excitedly.

In reply her voice was flat, unemotional. ' Henry Rawl never drank.'

CHAPTER FORTY TWO

As forecast, the blizzard hit the North East on the morning of Thanksgiving. No one in their right mind would venture out unless they had to, but Patrick Flaherty had always been a hothead. He had promised his widowed Ma he would be there for her special turkey dinner and a little bit of snow wasn't going to stop him.

It was a nuisance that she had moved out of the city and into the sticks after his father had passed away, but he had the use of the union's truck and that would get him through. If the blizzard persisted he might be marooned out there for a while, but his Ma would be delighted at that. Since he had become a union activist, Patrick had seen little of his mother for months. That was a pity, because mother and son had always been very close, but he was living in exciting times. The One Big Union movement was locked in a deadly battle with the tyrants of industry. All over the world workers were demanding not only a fair deal, but control and ownership of the means of production. The dream he had fought for since surviving the war was in sight and, as his Medal of Honor testified, Patrick Flaherty was determined to be in the forefront of any battle. There would be time for his Ma and kid sister after the fight was won.

A solitary car passed him on the road, a big black limousine, its red tail-lights burning like hot coals through the falling snow. Moments later they had been swallowed up in the enveloping whiteness and he was alone again, his breath clouding the air inside the cab. Listening to the reassuring throbbing of the diesel engine, he thought of his Ma waiting in her little cabin, log fire blazing, and wished he was there.

The wipers were no match for the blizzard. Peering through the blurred windscreen he saw the diversion sign up ahead, attached to a wooden barrier straddling the road. 'Road Closed' it read, with an arrow pointing to a gap in the trees to the left. The track looked narrow, but the limo that had passed him was nowhere in sight. As he turned down the track a familiar feeling returned as his heart began to race in time to the beat of the pistons. His mouth ran dry. Stark trees crowded in on him from either side. Though it was still early in the day, the blizzard had turned the woods into night and his headlights could only pick out a thin white path in the gloom. A hundred yards from the main road, he pulled up as the track became an impenetrable wall of trees. Then the dark shapes of the men with guns appeared.

Waiting for Eddie to arrive home had not been easy. But, thankfully, he was much later than she had expected, and that had given her time to compose herself and put her swirling thoughts in order. She still felt guilty thinking of Henry Rawl, even though Joe had told her over the phone that Henry had died before Eddie had left for the city on that fateful evening. So it was not her questioning of Henry that had led to his death. That was a burden Joe would have to carry. For he was convinced that telling his chief Henry Rawl was about to crack had set the 'hit' in motion. Nevertheless, she had first introduced the honest, decent young soldier to Eddie's sleazy world. Without that he might still be alive.

After the lengthy, difficult phone call, she had taken a long bath and done her best to conceal the bruises with foundation before the maid arrived. As she pulled on a modest woolen dress, she was glad to hear the sound of the new Hoover downstairs. She didn't know what mood Eddie would be in and having a witness in the house when he arrived made her feel safer.

Steeling herself she went downstairs and entered the lounge. The over-turned furniture had been put straight, whether by Eddie, or the maid, she didn't know. The heavy drapes had been pulled across the shattered French windows, but an icy wind still filled the room. She would instruct the maid to lay the fire, knowing that Eddie had contacts who would have the windows repaired by the end of the day. Making the house feel normal again was essential.

As she stood looking down at the spot on the carpet where her dream had become a nightmare, she heard the throaty sound of the roadster approaching along the drive. Hurrying into the kitchen she found that the maid had already put on the coffee. She poured herself a cup and cradled it in her hands, waiting, as the front door opened.

When he put down the phone, to say that Joe was elated was the understatement to end them all. The thing he had been hoping, even praying for, for so long had finally happened. Something had urged him, even when it seemed absurd, crazy, a figment of his own over-heated emotions, something had told him that deep down May Sharpe was an honest and decent human being. Sure she had tricked him, humiliated him, got him temporarily demoted to traffic. But it had never felt malicious, just girlish high-spirits at having so much power over a man. He loved that in her, even when he was the butt of her jokes. He understood how she had fallen under Eddie's spell. She was young, alone and friendless in a strange new world. And handsome, charming Eddie Young had offered her shelter, protection, a job, and an exciting way of life, even if it was immoral. Joe knew there were far worse things than fleecing a few gullible men with their brains in their dicks. When you thought about it, who really got hurt? Maybe it even did some good if the guys were taught a lesson. Much better that the girl came out on top rather than wind up like so many he had seen. So many abused, scarred, wasted young women. So many, like Alice.

It had taken a tragedy to bring May to the brink. A tragedy that he was indirectly responsible for. He'd have to live with that. But if it saved May maybe poor Henry Rawl would be happy, wherever he was. Happy, as he was, that May, like a ship tossed in a storm, had regained her moral compass. He looked around the busy detective's office, feeling like shouting it from the rooftops, but knew he had to keep the precious moment close to his chest. Everything depended on it. May's life depended on it.

'Princess!' Eddie called. 'Princess!'

She listened to his footsteps echoing on the Maplewood floor of the hall. When he entered the kitchen, she hid the tremor of fear and hatred that ran through her body. He looked tired, hung-over, and probably was. He went down on his knees in the doorway, arms outstretched like a kneeling Christ.

'Babe. Princess,' he said softly. His familiar shrug was heavy with remorse. 'What can I say..? I know, I can't say nothing...' He lowered his arms towards her like a supplicant. 'Hit me. Beat me up. I deserve it.'

It was hard to move her lips to form the words, but that made it all the more convincing. 'I don't want to hit you,' she managed to say.

'Please, Princess,' he begged. 'Slug me. Beat me up. I deserve it. It'll make me feel better.'

'Get up, Eddie, please,' she said quietly.

'You forgive me?' He sounded genuinely surprised and relieved.

Unable to respond she gave a slight shrug of her shoulders.

'I know, I don't deserve it...Look at you. What I done to you. I can see you tried to hide it, but I know.' He got to his feet, but made no move to approach her. She was grateful for that. Over the years she had become adept at faking emotion but, in this situation, she knew she wasn't that good an actress.

'I didn't think you'd be here. I thought you'd have split...'

'You wanna a coffee?' She wanted to avoid the questions, the postmortem. Dragging over the incident that still gnawed like a bitter fruit in her gut.

'Hey -' he began affectionately.

She stopped his move towards her with a raised hand. 'Please, Eddie...I need time.'

He nodded his head and stepped back, holding up his hands again, palms towards her. 'Sure, princess. Sure. You got all the time you need...I'm just so grateful you're still here.'

For the moment she had managed to convince Eddie that all was well. That she was the contrite little wife who understood that what had happened had been her own doing. Almost for her own good, if she had learnt her place from the unpleasant episode they tacitly agreed not to talk about. He had given her the Tiffany diamond necklace with a great flourish, less as an abject apology than a celebration of their new understanding. Wearing it made her skin crawl.

Over the next few days he accepted her wish that physical contact between them should be delayed, even allowing her to sleep in one of the guest bedrooms alone and unmolested. He knew how she felt, he said.

'I've had a good kicking myself in the past,' he confessed. 'It takes time to get over it. It's cool. Just say when you're ready, princess.'

That she would never be ready again with him, she was certain. Just the thought of his hands on her body and him thrusting like an animal inside her made her physically sick. But she could feel his rising irritation. Eddie was a man used to getting what he wanted when he wanted, and she knew it wouldn't be long before the lock on the bedroom door would be unable to keep him from taking her again, willing or not. She sensed that having got a taste for the brutal act, he may want to repeat it. And despite her arrangement with Joe, she knew when that time came she would use the knife she kept hidden beneath her pillow.

Joe waited for the call every day, with anxiety churning his insides. He felt helpless and stupid. Helpless because he couldn't risk phoning, and stupid that he had talked her into it. She hadn't wanted to know at first. All she wanted was to unburden herself to someone about Henry. His murder had hit her hard and no matter what Joe said to convince her, she still blamed herself for getting the young soldier involved with Eddie. To make amends, and ease her conscience, she had done her duty as a decent, honest citizen and told him about Patrick Flaherty. Now all she wanted was to get as far away as she could. He could understand that, he told her.

'Listen,' he said urgently. 'I know this guy is nothing to you. Not like Henry. But he's got a mother, a kid sister. He got a Medal of Honor. He may be trying to turn the country commie, I don't know. But does he deserve to die for that?'

He could hear the nervousness in her voice. 'I'm scared. You've no idea...You're asking too much of me. It's not my fight.'

'I know that. What I'm asking, I shouldn't ask. I know. It's wrong of me. Very wrong. And you may hate me for it for the rest of your life, but that's a chance I have to take...Believe me,' he added, his voice growing husky. 'I'm not taking that risk lightly.' He paused to let that confession and his declaration sink in. 'But I wouldn't ask if I didn't know you can do it.'

She was genuinely curious. 'Why do you think you know so much about me?'

'Am I wrong?'

Through the long pause at the other end of the line he could hear her soft breathing. He cradled the receiver to his ear. He felt he had never been so close.

It was two days before Thanksgiving when the call came.

CHAPTER FORTY THREE

The man in the middle of the three yelled above the howl of the blizzard. 'Get out the truck, Flaherty!' Eddie called, leveling the Thompson machine gun at the windscreen. The two men either side of him were holding snub-nosed handguns. Patrick hit the floor of the cab, heart pounding, adrenalin pumping. He shifted the pistol in his belt into his right hand.

'Drag him out, boys,' instructed Eddie. 'You've led your last strike, you commie motherfucker!'

As the two men made their way to the truck through the driving snow, the front canvas above the cab of the vehicle dropped down and a piercing searchlight swamped the dim glow of the headlights, picking out Eddie and his two henchmen like actors on a brilliant-white stage. Joe's voice rang out through a bullhorn.

'Police! Drop your guns and put up your hands!'

One of the men raised his gun and began to shoot wildly towards the blinding light. A hail of bullets cut him down. He fell, his blood splattering a widening pattern on the fallen snow. Eddie dropped to the ground like a stone. 'Don't shoot! Don't shoot!' he cried.

The third man let his gun fall and raised his hands. 'Keep 'em covered, boys,' Joe instructed and jumped down from the back of the truck, followed by two other armed men. Joe walked over to Eddie, still lying face down in the snow. He nodded to the two men who hauled Eddie roughly to his feet. In the glare of the searchlight Eddie stared at Joe venomously.

'You!' he began. 'How the hell -?' He stopped as another, slighter, figure stepped into the fringe of the light. Eddie turned and squinted to make out the features, shadowed by the fur around her face. His face hardened into a murderous mask. 'You lying, cheating, dirty Mick bitch!' he yelled at May. 'You're dead! You hear? Dead!'

A surge of hot blood raced through Joe's body. When he swung his fist all the long months of pent-up frustration were behind it. Eddie flew backwards with a loud cry and landed heavily in the snow, out cold. 'You've had that coming a long while,' Joe said, elatedly. Then he looked at May's expression and saw that her ordeal was only just beginning.

She had wanted to see his face. Joe had protested as hard as he could, but in the end there was no way he could stop May being there. It was he who had pressed her to remain in the house with Eddie when all her instincts were to run away as fast and as far as she could. He had persuaded her to risk acting as a spy in her own home to find out the details of the hit on Flaherty. If Eddie had discovered her eavesdropping on his phone calls, she could have been the next corpse floating in the East River. Joe understood all that, so when she had insisted on being in on the action he had reluctantly agreed. After all, she said, without her there would be no ambush, no potential arrest. Without her there would just have been another murder. So he guessed she deserved it. Deserved seeing the expression on Eddie's face when the game was finally up. Except that, instead of the shocked defeat she had expected, what she had seen was pure vengeful hatred.

On the way back to the city Joe and May rode in the cab. Eddie, cuffed and manacled, was guarded in the back of the truck by the strikers who had formed Joe's ambush team. Despite the noise of the engine and the sound of the tires drumming on the road, Eddie's yelled threats could be heard loud and clear.

'You're dead, you fucking Mick whore! You ain't got a prayer of making it to the trial! You're never going live to testify against me!'

Joe stopped the truck and had Eddie gagged with a scarf. But the threats still hung in the air. After the clandestine planning over the telephone and the nervous excitement of the ambush, the reality of her situation had come back to her. There had been no murder. She had prevented that. Now the trial would rest on her word that Eddie's intention was to kill Flaherty, not just to scare and intimidate him. Even if the jury believed her, Eddie would escape the chair. He could get a lengthy sentence, but from now on she would always be looking over her shoulder.

The blizzard had gone as soon as it had begun. By the time Joe dropped May back at the mansion to collect her things the afternoon sun was shining brightly into their eyes as it dipped to the horizon. All around the crisp snow was turning golden-pink in the dying light. Joe stopped the car at the front door and put on the handbrake. He looked at May seated snugly in her fur alongside.

'Are you all packed?' he asked.

'Do I need to go to a hotel? I'd prefer a hot bath and a stiff drink.'

'As soon as Eddie gets word out, they'll come looking for you. You're the star witness.'

'Thanks for reminding me,' she said ironically.

He'd found her a small unfashionable hotel in a quiet residential area on the West Side. Wearing a dark wig May checked in and followed Joe as he carried her case to the room. He closed the drapes to shut out the night and then turned on the light. May took off the wig, shook out her curls and dropped her fur onto the bed.

Joe was acutely aware that they were alone together for the first time since she had tricked him out of his uniform and made a fool of him. She was looking at him expectantly. His heart was pounding. He put his hand to his face, it felt flushed. 'I, er...want to thank you,' he began. 'I know how hard this has been for you.'

'Can you order me something from room service? I'm starving.'

'They don't have room service here,' he said sheepishly.

'Jesus! Happy Thanksgiving.'

While Joe was out looking for food she hung the few clothes she had packed in the tiny closet, then stretched out on the bed to try to relax, sipping a shot of bourbon from the bottle she had brought along. Her heart was racing. It had been a nerve-racking few days and her body was in overdrive. Her life had been turned upside down and she had no idea where she was going to go from here.

She had some money of her own and could sell off the jewelry Eddie had bought her, but that wouldn't last forever and, after that what? First of all, she knew she would have to leave New York. Even in prison, Eddie would have influence, and there were a lot of people in town who would be happy and willing to do him a favor. Thankfully, America was a big place in which to hide, for she was under no illusion that was what she would have to do, for the rest of her life. The hatred in

Eddie's eyes, the violence of his threats, brought it home to her that he would never rest until she was dead. In a way she couldn't blame him. He was a proud self-made man who had never put his full trust in anyone, until he met her. May was sure that his feelings for her were genuine in his own way. He'd told her many times that she was the only one he'd ever truly loved. Now she had betrayed that love and trust. And, though she knew she had done the right thing, it still hurt.

Starting afresh in another city in the only profession she knew would be dangerous. In the underworld word got around. If she made a success of her new life, Eddie would find out. She needed to disappear, as completely as if she was dead. But where to? South America, Europe? As she lay thinking through the events of the past few days, the tears began to flow. It was Thanksgiving, yet she had little to give thanks for. The future looked lonely, difficult and dangerous. She was on the run again.

CHAPTER FORTY FOUR

Joe had brought back hot coffee and a selection of sandwiches, which they ate on their laps sitting on the bed. She was subdued, he was tongue-tied. He could tell she had been crying and desperately wanted to hug her, but didn't think that was appropriate and couldn't face the expected rejection. Looking at him sitting meekly on the opposite side of the bed, with his back to her, May's eyes traced the line of his broad shoulders. He was her sole protector now. What would it feel like to have his strong arms around her? She knew that Joe was besotted with her. It was in his eyes whenever he plucked up the nerve to look into hers. He was a kind, gentle man, who had devoted himself to saving her. Ironically, by trying to save her he had put her into mortal danger. She badly needed a hug, but he was a New York cop and she would have to leave the city as soon as she had given her evidence at the trial. She didn't want to start something else that could have no future. Not again. She was too raw.

'Whatcha you gonna do afterwards?' he asked as he stood in the doorway, about to leave. They had talked little, both still affected by the ambush and its aftermath. Swamped by the memory of Eddie's virulent hatred.

'Go to bed and try to sleep.' The loneliness was already creeping over her, but she resisted the urge to ask him to stay.

'I mean after the trial.'

She shrugged. 'Leave New York. Go back to doing what I know, someplace else, I guess.'

Joe shook his head. 'No.'

'I don't have no education, detective, and I have to eat.'

He hesitated for a moment, poised on the threshold, then stumbled into the words that had been forming all evening in his head. 'May...if I can help...You know...Well, what I mean is-'

Sensing his impending declaration, May put her hand on his sleeve. 'Hey, don't go getting any ideas,' she said, pasting on the grin he loved, even when it was at his expense. 'A cop's pay wouldn't keep me in silk stockings.'

He smiled a sad smile. She raised up on tiptoe and placed the lightest of kisses on his cheek. 'Night, detective' she said and closed the door.

With Eddie's arraignment set for the following Monday, May prepared to spend the whole weekend cooped up in her hotel room. New York was a big place, but she knew a lot of people and it only needed one to see her to spell danger. Joe came the next day with food and needed no further encouragement when she asked him to stay and talk, to keep her company and her mind off the coming trial. He talked of his early childhood with affection, then of the sadness of watching his parent's marriage end in acrimonious rows which he was forced to listen to from his bedroom. In return May told him a little of her own life, the happy times with her mother before, like him, she had to watch the marriage being torn apart. As she spoke his eyes watched intently every little movement of her body, every expression on her face. She became self-conscious under his tender gaze.

'Listen to us both,' she said, suddenly brightening. 'Aren't we a couple of sad boobies? Moping and feeling sorry for ourselves. Tell me some of the funny stories you told me when you came to see me in prison.'

'But you've heard them already,' he said, a little surprised.

She smiled. 'Yes, but this time I'll be able to laugh.'

The next day, Saturday, along with the food, Joe brought a brown paper parcel, which he handed to her a little sheepishly.

'A present, for me?'

'It's nothing fancy like you're used to.'

Intrigued, she tore open the package. Inside was a bundle of newspaper comic strips called 'The Thimble Theatre.' She had seen some of the crowd at the Blackbird chuckling over them on Sundays when the paper came out. He saw her looking down at the simple drawings and the unfamiliar words with a frown.

'You like funny stories,' he explained.

'But, Joe,' she said, 'I can't read.'

'If you like, I'll read them to you,' he said. 'And maybe, if you want, you can learn.'

'Okay.' She propped herself up on the bed with a pillow behind her head. 'Fire away.'

He stood awkwardly, holding the comics in his hand. 'You have to look at the pictures as well.'

May patted the bed beside her. 'Make yourself comfortable, detective, and read me some stories.'

Joe approached the bed diffidently and sat on the side.

'I can't see them from there,' she said.

Shifting himself further onto the bed, he leant his back against the headboard, still keeping his feet hanging over the side.

'That doesn't look very comfortable. Put your feet up.'

Obediently, he lifted his legs onto the bed so that they were seated alongside each other, close but not touching. He was conscious of how light she felt alongside him, seeming almost to float on the surface of the bed, unlike the heavy depression his body made. The tiny nails of her naked toes, protruding from her richly patterned silk housecoat, were painted bright red. He forced himself to look away from her snow-white, smoothly-sculpted feet, so like the images of the marble goddesses he'd admired in the Metropolitan Museum on Central Park's East Side. He would like to take her there. To share with her the amazing art objects from around the world, which he was sure she would love as much as he did. Selecting a comic he cleared his throat and began to read about the absurd exploits of Olive Oyl, her brother Castor and their friend Ham Gravy.

As he gradually got used to his proximity to her, he started to relax and read with more expression, giving each of the characters their own unique, silly voice. May watched his handsome profile as she listened and laughed at the nonsense stories. When he had finished them all, she asked him to read them again. After he'd read them a second time, with her peering intently over his shoulder at his finger tracing the words, May picked up one of the comics lying on the bedspread.

'Let me try, 'she said and began to recite the simple story from memory. Joe watched, fascinated, correcting her on words when her memory occasionally let her down. At the end she laid down the comic with a flourish. 'I can read!' she exclaimed triumphantly. 'Go get us another coffee and I'll read the rest to you.'

As he mounted the steps of the courthouse, Joe's head was still full of the magical weekend he had just experienced. He'd spent three days alone with May and, as he became more at ease in her company, he'd been able to relax into being the funny, lively companion his friends always claimed him to be. She had laughed a lot, both at his jokes and the comics. When they tired of repeating the comic strips they began to make up stories for themselves, laughing uproariously, for a brief while forgetting the circumstances that had brought them together and the grim threat hanging over May.

For his part, the more time he spent with May the more he realized how right his first instinct about her had been, that day at the dockside. May Sharpe hadn't a bad, unkind bone in her beautiful young body. And with a photographic memory like hers, she would be able to read in no time. Coupled with her sharp wit and natural intelligence that new skill would open up many opportunities for her. For them both he began to allow himself to believe.

Not knowing which of Eddie's seedy, and potentially dangerous, companions would be in court, he had persuaded May not to attend Eddie's arraignment for her own safety. Sitting at the front of the courtroom he watched as Eddie was brought in, shackled, alongside his sober-suited, distinguished looking lawyer. Eddie was looking immaculate in an expensive double-breasted suit, his silk cravat held in place with a diamond pin. As their eyes met, Joe suddenly had an uncomfortable feeling. There was something about Eddie's nonchalant expression that set the hairs tingling at the back of his neck.

When the usher made his announcement and Judge Bennett Palmer entered the court Joe's heart sank. He now knew the reason for Eddie's relaxed manner.

May was angry and scared at the same time. 'Bail!' she cried. 'How the hell did he get bail!'

'It wasn't supposed to be Bennett Palmer,' Joe said, feeling wretched at having to bring her the bad news. 'Eddie must have put the fix in at the last minute.'

'I didn't know he had that kind of muscle,' she replied, in a stunned tone.

'He's working with the big boys now. They protect their own.'

'Now you tell me!' She flopped down on the bed like a rag doll, shaking her head in disbelief.

'It's okay. We'll find you a safe place, until the trial.'

'Safe?' she exclaimed sarcastically. 'If he can fix the judge on an attempted murder rap, he can find me! You said yourself, I'm the star witness. Without me Eddie could walk.'

'May, listen,' he said, trying to sound reassuring, and not show that he was as worried as she. 'I'll take care of you.'

She looked up at him with haunted eyes. 'Twenty four hours a day till the trial..?' She shook her head. 'I know Eddie. He'll take the city apart brick by brick until he finds me...No, Detective Perski, I'm a dead woman.'

CHAPTER FORTY FIVE

Over the next few weeks, Joe Perki never felt so alone in his life. Not even on the day when he was told of his father's murder, which left him effectively orphaned at age fifteen. His mother couldn't be traced and so didn't attend the funeral, even if she had wanted to, which he doubted. As a young boy, Joe idolized his father and a bond grew between the two which his mother came to resent. It was a male thing and she felt excluded. The relationship between mother and son became increasingly strained, and she had no regrets about leaving the difficult boy with his doting father, when she escaped with the household goods salesman who had started to make frequent visits to the family's apartment while she was alone and feeling abandoned.

At the funeral, where they formed a solemn and dignified guard of honor, and afterwards, Joe had the solid support of his father's police colleagues. They encouraged him to join the force as soon as he was eligible and, as a man, took him under their wing when he became a rookie cop. Off duty he was never stuck for companions, older men happy to share their life experience with the personable young man. For his eighteenth birthday party they provided an attractive, mature stripper who was happy to stay on after all the other guests had left to initiate the handsome innocent into the adult world of sex. Though he seemed to be living a charmed life, on reflection Joe wondered if the attention they lavished on him was brought about through a sense of guilt. A shared, uneasy secret about the real events of his father's death. Whatever the truth, Joe knew that there was no-one in the force he could trust with May's life, especially not his chief, who he was now convinced was on Eddie's payroll.

He had been grilled by the chief, who was furious that he had not been told about the ambush until after Eddie's arrest.

'You used those striking bastards as deputies instead of our own men?' he growled. 'I should have you suspended!'

'I had to, chief.' Joe countered, feeling like he was walking on eggshells. 'I don't to like to say this, but I think we got a stoolie in the precinct.'

Seeing the chief's face darken, Joe hurried on. 'I don't know who, I wish I did, and I can't even be certain, but I couldn't take the risk. If word had got back to Eddie he would have called it off and hit Flaherty another time.'

The chief scowled, knowing his threat to suspend Joe was a bluff. How did you suspend a cop who had just become the darling of the press for preventing a potentially dangerous, political murder? Flaherty's death could have sparked union riots in a year when his own promotion was being reviewed and the resulting publicity would have reflected badly on his office. Beneath his desk, he clenched his ham-like fist in frustration. This kid standing in front of him was just like his fucking interfering father. He wanted rid of him, but he would have to bide his time. 'So what about the broad?' he enquired too nonchalantly. 'The one who stitched up Eddie Young. Whereabouts is she holed up?'

Joe looked the chief straight in the eyes, feeling the sweat beginning to soak his shirt under the armpits. 'I don't know, chief,' he lied. 'I swear, she just vanished. Must be scared as hell, poor bitch.'

The chief looked at Joe steadily, searching for a sign. Maybe the sweat was it. It was freezing cold outside. 'Yeah, she has right to be. If she testifies against him her life won't be worth a dime.'

On his way out of the office, the chief called out to him. 'If you should happen to bump into that broad bring her in. Tell her we'll take good care of her.'

Was that supposed to sound like a threat? With a nod, Joe opened the door and walked out, closing the half-glazed door behind him. For the moment he was feeling relieved, but he knew that from now on he was on his own. May's life depended on him not making a single mistake.

A detective's salary wasn't able to support two homes, but by pawning some of May's jewelry Joe had been able to rent her a quiet apartment in New Jersey. Though the trip to see her took a chunk out of his day, and he could only make it occasionally in the week rather than every day, on the longer journey it was easier to spot if the chief had put a tail on him. Each trip he would start out in a different direction, north, south, east or west, changing transport at irregular intervals, and not heading for the right route until he was sure no one was following. It never took less than two hours and, sometimes, when his instinct told him he was not alone, it could take much longer. On one occasion, shortly before Christmas week, he had to abandon the journey completely, convinced he was leading them straight to her door.

She was waiting for him impatiently when he next arrived. 'Where the hell have you been?' she yelled at him, as soon as he closed the door.

'I'm sorry -' he began.

But she was too wound up to let him finish. 'Fuck sorry! I've been cooped up in here waiting for days, wondering if they'd got to you. If they'd found out about me. Do you know what it's been like for me? I haven't slept, I've been awake every minute of every day, frightened at every footstep outside, waiting for a knock at the door, terrified out my fucking skin, you bastard! I'm gonna get the fuck out of here and fuck your trial!'

He felt as hurt as if she had slapped him in the face. 'What do you think it's been like for me!' he retaliated. 'Looking over my shoulder all the time, lying to everybody, even my friends, trying to get away to see you, expecting to get caught at any moment and beaten senseless to tell them where you are! It's been no fucking picnic for me, you ungrateful little bitch! So get the hell out if you want to, you'll be doing me a favor!'

There was a sudden deafening silence in the room. In the seconds that followed, they could hear each other breathing heavily. His hands trembled as he put down the bag of provisions he'd bought on the occasional table by the door. He noticed that her face was growing gaunt under the strain. Contritely, he said. 'I couldn't shake off the tail.'

She looked hard at him before replying. There was fear in her eyes when she asked, 'You're sure they're onto you?'

He shook his head. 'No, I'm not sure,' he lied. 'They're probably not. It just makes sense to keep a look out, that's all. And I couldn't be sure that day, I'm sorry.' He looked at her tenderly. 'I have to be sure.'

Though she was trying hard to control her emotions, there were tears in her eyes. 'It's so lonely, Joe. On my own here all day. Not able to go out. Not knowing...I'm lonely and scared.'

She was standing by the window, looking like a lost child, arms folded around herself protectively. Crossing the room, he put his arms around her. It was something he'd wanted do since the first time he saw her, but this was instinctive, without thought. He felt suddenly nervous, that he had crossed a threshold without being invited. To his relief, she didn't pull away, but leant against his chest breathing erratically. Closing his eyes, he drank in the smell of her hair and the warmth of her body against his.

As she rested in his arms, May was conscious of trying to stop herself from falling completely to pieces in front of him. That wouldn't be fair. She had been so wrapped up in her own fear she hadn't thought that he must be going through the same pressure every day, feeling all eyes were on him, unable to confide in any one, just as scared and lonely as she was. He didn't need any more problems at the moment. Worrying about her state of mind might make him careless and that would be the end for them both. For though she was the main target, she had no illusions that when Joe had led them to her, he would have outlived his usefulness to Eddie. Slowly, her breathing became calm and regular and she pulled away with an embarrassed smile.

'Thank you, Joe,' she said quietly. 'I'm sorry I yelled. I'm okay now. Just needed to let the lid off, that's all.'

He nodded and smiled in return. 'We'll be okay. It's gonna be okay.'

The rest of his stay that day was awkward, the conversation stilted. The news he brought of Eddie was the same. He spent most of his time at The Blackbird with his cronies, seemingly unperturbed by his impending trial. But, though it was unspoken between them, there was no doubt in their minds that his hit squad was combing the city, hunting for her. To lighten the mood, Joe took out the latest copy of 'The Thimble Theatre' from his pocket. May was becoming an able reader, capable of deciphering unfamiliar words and not just memorizing, but today she didn't read it aloud to him as she usually did. It was as if there was an invisible force between them, both drawing them together and pulling them apart. When he left she hesitated momentarily before giving him her usual goodbye peck on the cheek. After their earlier outburst and subsequent embrace it suddenly felt too intimate, a declaration which could lead them into turbulent waters, when they both needed to keep their heads to survive.

CHAPTER FORTY SIX

He knew he was taking a risk. If they saw him buying it they would know he had been lying all along and they would make their move somehow. But he felt it was necessary, crucial. And, despite the danger, he was thrilled to be doing it. The bright Christmas lights decorating the avenues, and the dazzling window displays, lent a bizarre touch to his furtive journey. Weaving along the busy sidewalks, he wished the circumstances could have been different. He had thought about times like this often in the past year or so. In his imaginings, they were always carefree and joyous like the season promised. God willing, there would be many other times, better times, for such moments.

The thronging Christmas shoppers provided him with good cover and he was pretty certain he had evaded the tail when he reached his destination, tucked in a small street on the Lower East Side, away from the bustling, festive avenues. This kind of purchase was unfamiliar territory for him and finding what he was looking for had involved a lot of research. But finally he had found the perfect thing. After paying for the item, he tucked the box under his arm and set off on his circuitous route out of the city. After three blocks he had lost the tail that in his excitement he hadn't seen.

Eddie enjoyed the run-up to Christmas. Even this year, with a trial hanging over his head in the spring, he was looking forward to the celebrations, which were always riotous at The Blackbird. And this year they would be something very special.

He had arranged for that. There would be the finest booze to be had, the best music from Harlem, the best food from Little Italy, and the raunchiest strippers in town. It was important to show the world that he was still on top. Just as important, they would help blank out the memories that still hurt deep inside. Moments and feelings he kept to himself for the times when he was alone in the dark corners of his mind. For that's where he had confined them, the wonderful times he and she had shared together. The days and nights when he had felt more complete than ever before in the company of the beautiful girl he had fallen in love with. The girl who had betrayed him and who was going to pay with her life.

Thanks to her, whose name wasn't allowed to be mentioned in his presence anymore, Thanksgiving had been a bummer. A hideous night spent in a cold police cell with drunks, bums and vomit for company. It had been a long, unpleasant weekend, which had fueled even more the ball of anger and bitterness that was growing inside his guts like an odious, deformed fetus.

Initially, he had been shaken by the events of that day. He was amazed he hadn't seen it coming, but she had been so contrite and forgiving, so convincing in every way. And, of course, feeling guilty, he had wanted to believe. Then as the surprise faded and the rage ignited, he had put his contacts to work.

After Bennett Palmer had come up trumps again and granted him bail, he felt a tinge of embarrassment the first time he re-entered The Blackbird to greet his jubilant buddies. How had he, Edward Theodore Young the Third, King of the Conmen, been fooled so completely? And by a young, ignorant peasant girl from the bogs of Ireland! He had taught her too well, his cronies said. That was all there was too it. He should be proud of himself. The master tutor had created a monster. Well, like the responsible citizen he was, it was his duty to destroy the monster before it did any more damage. And the man who had just entered the club was about to give him his chance.

It was stressful not knowing what time, or even if, Joe would arrive. The last visit was the first time he had let her down, or so she thought at the time. It was only after she had blasted him with both barrels that she learnt he had been thinking solely of her safety. She had thought a lot about him since that day. The strength of his arms around her, the musky, masculine smell of his body, and his diffidence around her, so different to what she had known with Eddie. Looking back over their many meetings it seemed that Joe had never wavered in his opinion of her, an absolute belief in her inner goodness that she had not felt from anyone in her life, except her mother and poor Henry Rawl.

She had gone to Henry's funeral, only days before the ambush on her ex-lover that had changed her world forever. Eddie had no objection, though he made the excuse that he was too busy to attend himself. 'Go pay your respects, princess,' he said, 'and say one for me. It's a pity. Henry was a good guy.'

The hypocrisy turned her stomach. She wondered at how her feelings for Eddie had changed so dramatically in such a short space of time. Had she really loved him? Or had she just been dazzled by his polished charm, the glamour of his world and the gratitude she felt for being chosen to reign alongside him? For that was how it had felt to a young, unsophisticated girl from a poor peasant life. She had felt like a queen, equal at least, if not better, than the ladies on horseback she had so wished to ride alongside.

Henry's mother was at the ceremony. Having received the heart-breaking telegram on the Friday, she had traveled all weekend to see her only child buried alongside his father, her dear husband. Unknown to Eddie, May had arranged and paid for the body to be taken to the family plot in Connecticut. She made the journey herself by train, arriving at the tiny cemetery on the outskirts of the little farming town just as the coffin was about to be lowered into the grave. The small funeral party turned to look as she stepped from the cab, elegant in fur. She suddenly felt conspicuous, a freak amongst the plainly dressed mourners, and wished that she had stayed away.

A sharp sting of rain was falling. The priest intoned his words as quickly as he decently could, and then hurried away to get back to the warm and dry. May remained at the graveside as the tiny group dispersed. The mother approached her, a frail grey woman in a shabby woolen coat. 'Thank you,' she said. 'Henry spoke a lot of you. He said you were kindest, most decent person he'd ever met.'

The words had cut her like a knife. When everyone had gone, May stood alone and said her own words over the mound of freshly-dug earth. 'I'm truly, truly sorry, Henry, for getting you mixed up in my dirty world. Please believe me, I did it for the best. And I promise you one thing. I will do everything in my power to get you justice. The justice you never got in this life.'

Joe arrived carrying the cardboard box under his arm. As he handed it to her, she noticed there were holes cut in the sides. 'I can't be here on Christmas Day,' he explained, 'so I brought you some company.'

As soon as she unfastened the knot holding the top flaps, the little brown puppy jumped out excitedly. May squealed in delight. It was a reincarnation of Mick, in miniature. She held the tiny animal up, her eyes sparkling, as it squirmed in her hands, licking her cheeks with its wet pink tongue. Joe looked on grinning, knowing it was the best present he could have given. That it meant much more than diamonds to her.

'I'm going to call it Micky,' she announced. 'Cos it's like a little Mick.' Her smile bathed him a warm glow. 'Thank you, Joe. I haven't been able to get you a present, but I can make you a proper Christmas dinner.'

May was as good as her word. She had saved up some of the provisions he had bought her for just such an occasion and, while Joe played with the puppy, she prepared a boiled ham with vegetables, which they ate at the small table by the window.

'Where did you learn to cook this well?' he asked. If he bothered to cook for himself it was basic. Fried eggs his specialty.

'I had to cook for me Da, didn't I? Everyday, after me mammy died.'

'What was he like, your father?'

Her expression clouded. 'Don't ask. We're having a good time, aren't we?'

After the meal, Joe helped May with the dishes, their fingers occasionally touching with a spark of electricity as she passed him the cutlery. Then they both played with Micky, until the excited puppy was worn out, flopping exhausted and soon snoring on May's lap. Joe checked his watch and stood up. 'I have to go or I'll miss my train,' he said regretfully.

She looked up at him with shining eyes. 'It's been a lovely day, Joe. Thank you for such a wonderful present.'

'Happy Christmas,' he said, and leant down to plant a tender kiss on her forehead.

On the long journey back through the dark city, Joe heart was bursting. It still felt unbelievable, but he now knew that his feelings for May were beginning to be returned. That what he had wished for so passionately was, like a miracle, coming true.

He bounded up the stairs to his apartment two at a time, not caring if he disturbed the neighbors who liked to take to their beds early.

He froze as he reached his door. It was gaping wide open. Even from the corridor, he could see that the place had been completely ransacked. Inside the apartment nothing had been left untouched in the search for what Eddie was looking for. Her address.

CHAPTER FORTY SEVEN

The garage on East 171st Street was a convenient place for the meeting. If anyone saw him go in, he was just having his wife's car checked out. He drove into the cold, grey, unloved space, littered with abandoned vehicle parts, oily rags and scattered tools. Incongruously, among the automotive detritus, a gleaming Harley-Davidson Sport motorbike stood in one corner, the proud possession of the lone mechanic who, at the moment, had his head submerged in the bowels of a huge truck. He didn't bother to look up as the man got out of the car and hauled himself up the short flight of steps to the back office where Eddie was waiting alone.

'Well?' he asked.

Eddie shook his head. 'They took the place apart. Nothing.'

The chief took the only seat in the tiny room, squeezing his fat haunches between the two spindly wooden arms. 'Didn't think you'd find anything. He's smart.'

'Not that smart or he wouldn't have bought her the dog,' Eddie replied grouchily.

'So what next?'

Eddie shrugged. 'The guy leaves us no option. We haul him in and beat it out of him.'

'Hold on, hold on,' the chief said, holding up a podgy hand, fingers spread. 'He's a cop. You can't just go around beating the crap out of my men.'

'He won't rat about it,' Eddie grinned. 'We'll dump him in the river when we've done.'

The chief's booming voice shook the room and rang out into the echoing space of the garage beyond. 'Whoa! Hold your horses there, mister! Wind it back! Waaa-yyy back!' He lowered his voice to a hiss. 'You're talking murder one. You're talking the chair.'

'Only if somebody finds out. Right now, if that bitch testifies, I'm looking at ten to twelve for conspiracy, remember.'

The chief shook his head. This was too close to home. Father and son cops both murdered in mysterious circumstances? The press would have a field day, rooting through the old files. He didn't want anyone reopening the long buried case of Officer Joe Perski, Senior.

'No, I'm gonna tell you what you do. You step up the tails. Round the clock.'

Eddie heaved an exasperated sigh. 'We done that already.'

'Then do it some more!' he snapped. He levered his frame out of the chair. 'Perski's only human. The trial's months away. He can't keep it going that long. He'll make a mistake. Believe me, he'll lead you right to her door.'

As he watched the chief waddle away to his car, Eddie scowled. Waiting had never been his bag.

As nothing had been stolen, Joe didn't bother to report the ransacking of his apartment. He knew they hadn't found anything, because what they wanted was only in his head. He'd made sure there was nothing to lead them to May at his place, as he half expected an unwelcome visit sooner or later. But he was very concerned. Eddie was getting bolder. Would he push all the way and try to wring the information out of him by force? Joe wasn't worried for himself. He knew there was nothing they could do to make him tell them where May was hiding. But Eddie was a natural killer. When he couldn't get what he wanted, would they dump what was left of him in the river, or the concrete foundations of one of the new blocks that were springing up all over the city? And if he was dead, what would happen to May?

The knock on the door startled her. At first she froze in fear, believing they had finally found her. Then she heard his voice through the door, calling her name. She rushed to open it, surprised, but delighted, to see him. 'I thought you couldn't make it today!'

He picked up Micky, who was yapping excitedly at his feet. 'Eddie's got a big party at The Blackbird. Even if he's got a tail on me, there's so little traffic today, I could spot them easily.'

'You came by car?'

Joe grinned. 'Courtesy of the NYPD.' He lifted the net at the window to show her the unmarked Ford Model T standing below in the deserted street. 'I'm supposed to be on duty.'

'That's great,' she said. 'Now we can spend Christmas Day together.'

When he had played with the puppy till it had quieted down, and she had made him coffee, black and sweet the way he liked it, he told her about the raid on his apartment. She was alarmed. 'There was nothing to find,' he said reassuringly. 'I promise you.'

'I'm scared, Joe. Scared for us both.'

He shook his head and sighed. 'I should have let him kill Flaherty.'

'What!?' she exclaimed in shocked disbelief.

'If I'd let him Eddie kill Flaherty, we'd have nailed him. Murder One. Even Bennett Palmer couldn't have gotten him bail. Eddie would be headed straight for the chair and you wouldn't have to hide away afraid for the rest of your life.'

Her voice was quiet and calm. 'I don't believe you're saying this. Patrick Flaherty is a human being, Joe.'

'He's a troublemaker trying to screw up this country,' he said testily.

'Haven't we plenty of those back in Ireland? But they're only fighting for what they think is right, Joe. No matter. Patrick Flaherty doesn't deserve to be murdered. That's why I told you about Eddie, because I knew you'd understand. Because you're a good person. Though it took me long enough to work that out,' she added with a guilty smile.

He nodded, already feeling ashamed. The thought had been turning round and round in his brain since the ambush. It would have been so easy to make it look like a tragic mistake. The press loved reporting when the cops screwed up, and the public took it for granted. But if he'd let a man die, to save the girl he loved, would he have been able to live with himself?

She could sense his embarrassment and felt sorry for him. What he'd said was in the heat of the moment, merely an expression of his love and concern for her. He didn't really mean it, of that she was certain. They were seated together on the sofa, later, when she asked,

'Have you ever killed a man?'

'Not yet,' he said.

'I almost did,' she confessed. 'And even though, at the minute, I thought he deserved it, sure it was a terrible feeling,' she said, remembering.

CHAPTER FORTY EIGHT

It was her sixteenth birthday. The day had begun with her gathering peat from the hut by the side of the croft, shivering in the rain as usual. Faithful Mick waited for her at the doorstep, having more sense than to go out in the wet. After she had made the fire, which was never easy in the wintertime when the peat was sodden, it was time to wake her father and make his breakfast. Fried potato and onions that she had dug from the field the day before. She took the kettle from above the fire and poured out his mug of tea.

'Can I not go with you, Da?'

Her father's face assumed its usual scowl. 'The market's no place for young girls. Getting ideas.'

'But it's me birthday,' she pleaded. 'Can I not go as a treat?'

'Shut yer whining, 'fore I take me belt to you.'

She shut up abruptly. Her father seemed to take pleasure in administering his leather belt to her back, and she had learned to avoid giving him an excuse. When he had finished his breakfast and drunk his third mug of tea, her father set out for the market warning her not to sit dreaming while he was gone. Dreaming, as if.

All her days merged into one. After first pulling water from the well, she would scrub the table and mop the floor, while waiting for the rest of the water to boil in the pot above the fire. With the hot water she would do the laundry. Between them father and daughter had so few clothes washing them was a perpetual chore. Usually, after treating herself to a cup of tea, she would dig the vegetable patch behind the croft, planting in season, and pulling up for the evening's meal. In winter the days were often so gloomy it was hard to tell day from dusk, and the rain fell continually, so it was impossible to go out for a walk, which was what she liked to do. So she would sit by the sputtering fire, wrapped in a blanket, mending clothes and darning socks, with Mick at her feet.

On that particular day she was disturbed by a strange sound coming from her bedroom. Opening the door she saw with dismay the raindrops forming a puddle on the earth floor as they dripped from a hole in the roof. Fetching the wooden pail from the hearth, she put it beneath the hole to catch the drips. By the time she retired to her icy cold bed, swathed in a cotton nightgown, an old jumper and socks, the rain had stopped, so the raindrops didn't keep her awake. As usual Mick snuggled onto the bed beside her.

It was pitch black in her room when she heard the front door crash open and her father's voice calling out, drunkenly.

'Mary! Mary!'

She had been called Mary after the Virgin Mother, but her mother preferred to call her May, because the child's sunny nature reminded her of that month, the beginning of spring.

'Mary! Wake up!' he shouted. She could hear him stumbling against the wall outside her room. 'I got you something. Open up. I brung you a present!'

She didn't want to get up in the freezing cold darkness and open the door to her drunken father. But he was hammering on it by now, and she was terrified that his mood would turn to the brutal fury she had witnessed so often with her mother. Lighting a candle, she slipped out of bed and reluctantly slid back the iron bolt. Her father pushed open the door roughly and stood swaying, waving a bottle in his hand which he thrust towards May.

'Happy birthday!' he roared, stumbling into the room.

'Where's me present, Da?'

In reply he waved the bottle in her face. 'Here! Here y'are! Have a little drink!'

'No, Da,' she cried, trying to ease him out of the door. But he was a big, heavyset man and even in his drunken state, easily resisted her.

'Come on, drink up! See, I've another present for you,' he said fumbling at his leather trouser belt and tearing open his flies.

A cold bolt of fear shot through her body. 'No, Da! No!' she screamed, cowering back against the wall and letting the candle fall from her fingers.

'Ah, come on now! Be a good girl,' he said, lust overriding his drunkenness. 'It's your birthday.' Groping towards her in the dark, he wheedled, 'Come on now, Mary. Haven't I respected the priest's word all these years? I've not touched you at all in that way. But you're a grown woman now.' He lunged for her, his trousers falling around his ankles.

'No, Da! No! Leave me be!' she screamed.

But he had hold of her now and she fell backwards onto the bed with his heavy body crushing down on top of her. She cried out and fought with her fingers clawing at his face as he fumbled to pull up her nightgown. Yapping wildly Mick leapt up at the man, teeth bared. He kicked out at the dog with his boot, sending it crashing into the stone wall.

'Away, animal!' he roared.

'No, Da, no! It's a mortal sin!'

Ignoring her protests he ripped her nightgown away from her stomach. She hit out at him wildly, but he grasped both her wrists in one large hand, and sat astride her. 'Lie still, or I'll brain you, you filthy young bitch!'

She lay frozen in terror as he forced open her thighs and reared up, preparing to thrust into her. In desperation her hand sought out the handle of the wooden bucket beside the bed. As he lunged brutally forward, she swung the bucket with all her strength against the side of his skull. With a cry, he crashed against the stone wall and collapsed face down on the bed. She scrambled up, clutching her torn nightgown to her. Mick, recovered from the blow against the wall, began to bark, as much in panic as in anger.

'That'll teach you, you filthy dirty pig!' she screamed at her prostrate father.

She stood in the dark, hearing her own rasping gasps as she tried to catch her breath. She wanted to run, but where to? Her father lay very still. Shivering with cold and panic, she fumbled around in the dark, found the candle and lit it. Mick continued to bark. 'Shut yer row, Mick!' she snapped. Leaning forward she saw the blood trickling from his hair and down his cheek. 'Da?' she whispered. 'Da?' There was no response. Tentatively she reached out and shook his arm. 'Da?' she repeated, fearfully. He lay still and quiet. She forced herself to lean closer, but she could hear no sound of breathing. She drew back, hand to her mouth. 'Oh, Mary, Mother of God, I've killed him!' Mick barked at her voice, the sound echoing harshly in the silence. She snapped, 'Will yer shut it! If I've killed him, they'll hang me for certain.' As she stood trembling in fear, her father suddenly gave a loud grunt and began to snore. Relief flooded over her. 'Ah, yer old bastard!' she snarled. Then blind panic took hold. If he wasn't dead, when he woke he would take terrible revenge on her. She had seen it with her mother, who had never once dared stand up to him. How much worse would it be for the daughter who had fought him off and nearly killed him?

She went into the main room and crouched beside the dying embers of the fire, her mind racing with crazy, frightened thoughts. The priests would not protect her. They would never believe her word against her father. Most of the local villagers were as frightened of her father as she was, so she would get no help or protection from them. She was on her own, and she had to get away.

Removing a stone from the wall near the hearth she drew out a small tin box. It was locked. She crept back into her room. Her father was still lying on his face, snoring heavily into the mattress. Holding her breath she gingerly searched the pockets of his trousers hanging at his ankles. The key wasn't there. Terrified of waking him, she slipped her hand into his jacket pocket. Her father suddenly turned and snorted. She froze with her fingers trapped inside the pocket. He snoring began again. In the dead of night it was an ugly, frightening sound. Not daring to breathe, she slowly slid her hand out, holding the tiny key.

'He'd hidden enough money in there to pay for my passage and a nice suit of clothes,' she told Joe. 'And all the while we were living like paupers,' she added indignantly.

Joe was both gripped and shocked by her story. He understood very clearly now why the life Eddie had offered seemed so magical to her. A little crime in return for such luxury. Riches she could never have dreamed of as that frightened little girl. A life she had now chosen to turn her back on, when it would have been so easy to look the other way. Darkness had fallen as he listened. He stood up to draw the curtains and turn on the lamp.

'Don't,' she said softly.

He looked at May, her face lit only by the glow of the lamps from the street outside.

'I grew up in the dark,' she said. 'You could go outside on a cloudy night and not be able to see a hand in front of your face.' She smiled, 'When I got my first apartment, I'd spend hours just turning the lamp on and off, on and off. Like it was magic...Now the dark seems safe.'

Joe shrugged. 'New York always seemed safe to me. Guess 'cos my dad was a cop. I thought he could protect me from anything. Till they found him in an alley with a bullet in his brain.'

'I'm sorry...Do you ever see your mother?'

He shook his head ruefully. 'Not after she lit out...I don't think Dad cared about much after that. Sort of gave up. Even stopped talking to me. Just lost himself in his work. Trying to clean up New York on his own...Some people said he didn't care if he got shot.' He gave an embarrassed little laugh. 'Never knew it was possible to care that much about someone until...' He stopped, and shifted his feet, awkwardly.

She rose, went to him and took his hand. Her voice was soft and light, like a breath. 'Stay with me tonight.'

Their bodies were touching in the darkness. He could feel his beginning to tremble and felt foolish, like a clumsy child. 'You don't have to be afraid, May,' he began, 'they don't know-'

She stopped him with gentle fingertips on his lips. Again, he felt the soft sweet breath caressing his cheeks. 'I'm not afraid, Joe.' Taking his face in her hands, she drew him down to her. Her full lips met his breathless mouth.

CHAPTER FORTY NINE

His chief was glaring fiercely at him from behind his maple wood desk. Joe had agonized all day and night about whether to make his confession. In the end he'd decided he had nothing to lose.

'I'm sorry, chief, I had to lie to protect her,' he explained, his hands outstretched in apology. 'Eddie's goons were crawling all over town looking for her. And without her evidence his sleaze ball lawyers will drive a truck through the prosecution.'

'So where is she now?'

Joe shook his head helplessly. 'I swear to god, I don't know. She was holed up in a place in Jersey. I used to go see her every week. Take her food and stuff, y'know. Two days ago she was gone. No word, no nothing.'

'Did she say anything before she split?'

'About leaving? No. She was scared though. I could see that.'

The chief scrutinized the young detective's face. Thirty years in the force had made him pretty good at reading liars. He'd known that Joe had lied to him about May the first time, which was why he'd warned Eddie to watch him round the clock. Now, something about Joe's expression, a pained, boyish bewilderment, persuaded him that Perski was telling the truth. So the frightened little bird had flown. If she stayed away Eddie could relax. There was no need to keep a tail on Joe now.

'You think that's it?' he asked. 'Think she'll duck the trial?'

Joe shrugged despondently. 'That's my guess.' The truth was he didn't know.

Even in his wildest imaginings he'd not dreamt of anything so wonderful. How could he? It was the jazz age. Women had got the vote and with it came a new sense of social and sexual freedom. So he'd had his share of liaisons, some torrid one-night stands and two affairs that seemed like 'it' at the time, but he had never experienced anything like the thrill of making love to her. He had lived a lifetime in a night, lost in the magic of their bodies and souls fused in complete harmony. As the first light of dawn crept in through the window, he looked at May, sleeping cradled in his arms, and his heart felt like it would burst with joy. Then, in an instant, fear gripped his body like ice. The fear that he could not protect her forever. And now, even more, it was vital that he did. Now he could see the future he had mapped out for them so many times in his mind, no longer as some poor obsessive's fantasy, but as real, tangible. They could live their lives together just as he'd hoped and dreamed, almost from the day he met her. But only if he could keep her alive. The sense of her, of them being together, was so overpowering that he wondered if he was capable anymore of performing the task he'd set himself. From now on, he knew he would have to be a hundred times more careful than he had already been, and that thought scared him. When she woke he must be careful not to show his fear to her.

She had given him a key so he could let himself in. Not that she had ever left the apartment in the weeks she had been in hiding there. But today there was no answer to his knocking and, as he turned the key in the lock, he had a deep sense of dread. It didn't take him a moment to realize that she was not in the tiny apartment, nor was Micky. Panic overtook him. He looked around the room. There were no signs of a struggle. Surely, if they had come for her, she would have put up a fight? Perhaps she had become bolder, or grown so bored by her surroundings that she had taken Micky out for a walk? He was about to leave the apartment to search for her when he saw the letter lying on the table. He picked it up and read the brief note with shaking hands.

'My darling Joe,' her unformed handwriting began, 'I have to go away. I have to think. I'm scared. Scared for both of us. I know you are scared too. Scared for me. I felt it. If we never meet again, please forgive me. All my love always, May.'

He sat down, the paper hanging limply from his fingers. An hour later, he was still there, staring into space.

In the early 1920's California's year round sunshine, cheap building land, and the glamour of the new movie industry made Los Angeles the fastest growing, most exciting city in America. Every wish, every dream seemed possible here. New lives could begin and blossom like the crimson and purple bougainvillea framing the wooden arch of her terrace. She had traveled the length and breadth of the country since leaving New York at Christmas and she had seen nothing to compare with her new home. Renting a single-storey clapboard house on one of the fashionable Venice canals, her daily routine consisted of taking the short walk to the vast sandy expanse of Venice Beach to bathe in the sparkling waves of the Pacific Ocean, followed by a leisurely lunch made from the succulent fruit and salads of the region, then a lazy afternoon basking in the warm shadow of the terrace, indulging in her new passion of reading. She devoured stories and novels, living vicariously through the comic adventures of Tom Sawyer, the horrors endured by the unnamed narrator of The Pit and The Pendulum, and feeling deeply the shame and humiliation of Hawthorne's heroine of The Scarlet Letter. At the moment living vicariously was all she could do, for she was in limbo.

For weeks she had been turning the decision round and round in her mind. The money from the sale of her last few pieces of jewelry would not last her forever. But she had choices now. Now she could read and write, there were many exciting jobs for the asking in the rapidly expanding city. A beautiful, intelligent and resourceful young woman could become almost anything she wanted to be in this brave new world. She could assume a new identity, become successful in another walk of life, and forget the fact that without her evidence Eddie would walk away from his trial laughing. She could. But, when not lost in the magical words of the great American writers, she missed him every single waking minute.

She could close her eyes and see Joe's handsome, gentle face, trace his smoothly muscled chest beneath her fingertips, smell the exotic musk of his skin and feel the heat of him deep inside her. The few short hours they had spent together as lovers were the crowning glory of her life. An almost overwhelming fusion of body and spirit. A sublime passion she doubted would ever be surpassed. Now, she was at a crossroads and if she took one path those special moments they had shared would never be repeated. She had been keeping track of the news through the New York papers, which she bought every morning from the store on the main street leading to the pier. The time was near when she would have to make her decision. A decision that could mean the difference between her life or death.

CHAPTER FIFTY

Joe sat staring blankly out of the third storey window of the
District Attorney's office, as the prosecutor leafed glumly
through the trial documents on his desk. He didn't know what
he would do when the trial was over. All he knew was that he
no longer wanted to be a cop. His dad had died trying to uphold
the honor of the badge, but Joe knew that the corruption went
far too deep for one man to stand against. And he wasn't
prepared to give his life for that. The prosecutor grunted. He
was a year or two older than Joe and very ambitious. After five
years studying Law at Harvard and another three working his
way up the ladder, this was his first big case, and he was
profoundly depressed. He closed the file and shook his head.

'With a fair wind we'll get conspiracy. But with his
lawyers...' He didn't need to finish. They both knew that Eddie
had employed one of the most skillful team of attorneys in the
country. Despite Joe's presence at the alleged crime scene there
were technical loopholes experienced lawyers could, and
would, exploit to the full. 'You haven't heard anything at all
from her?'

Joe shook his head. 'Not a word in months.' The truth was
he didn't know whether to be glad or sad. He had missed her
every moment since the day he had read her little note. After
experiencing the joy of being with her so completely, he felt he
couldn't live without that intense feeling. Now he knew what
his father had felt. An emptiness that nothing could fill. A deep
sadness on waking every day and remembering that she was not
there in his life. Every day he would ask the janitor at his
apartment block if there were any messages. There never had

283

been. And, as the weeks grew into months, he began to believe there never would be. That she was gone out of his life forever. He wondered daily where she was. What she was doing. Whether she had started a new life and had found someone else to take his place. Though that thought hurt him more deeply than he could give words to, in another way he was grateful that, at least, she was safe. The glimmer of hope he clung to was that she had written that she needed time to think. With the trial due to start in two days, the time for thinking was over.

Despite his stellar defense team, Eddie knew there was the possibility that he could be spending some time behind bars after his trial. So he had decided to have one last fling to tide him over until he was free to indulge himself again. He had hired a boat with full crew to take himself, some of his closest companions and a dozen girls out to the Sound for a long, and totally dissolute, weekend. Booze and cocaine were flowing and being snorted freely. In the warm spring sunshine the girls had been persuaded to strip off all their garments both on deck and below in the sumptuous cabins. Surrounded by naked, nubile flesh day and night he had forgotten about her until Charlie, one of his drunken companions, lurched on deck from below and asked, 'Sure you didn't rub her out, Eddie?'

'Say what?' He was lounging in the stern wearing shorts, having oil rubbed over his belly by a heavy-bosomed brunette, whose prominent nipples were brushing his thighs as she worked.

'Me and the boys, we's taking bets on whether you rubbed the broad out. To stop her squealing.'

'Me? Hurt a broad?' Eddie replied in mock offense.

Charlie's deep laugh boomed across the water. 'So why ain't she around no more?'

'Guess she'd rather stay alive than testify,' said Eddie, brusquely.

Looking unconvinced, but feeling unwelcome, Charlie went back inside. Taking hold of the girl's smooth shoulders, Eddie gently eased her away. 'Later, doll,' he said. He pushed himself up and stood holding the rail looking out across the water, irritated at Charlie for breaking the mood of the day. Thinking about May always brought back bad memories. They had both been so happy together on the same stretch of water, on the day that he had shown her their new home. Was it only less than a year ago? Thankfully, she'd seen sense and split. He hoped she was holed up in some godforsaken place, scared of every footstep and regretting she had ever ratted on him.

That she had made the choice to turn her back on a life of easy luxury had shocked him at first, but, later, reflecting on May's feisty, spirited personality, he realized he shouldn't have been surprised. Hadn't she tracked him through the freezing night to the Blackbird, to demand the return of a purse containing a few worthless Mick notes? Money that would have scarcely bought her a bagel and a soda. The warning signs had been there from the start. The feistiness was what had drawn him to her. Well, if that same spirit drew her to try and make her revenge stand up against him in court, he had people waiting.

Along with the headlines that Babe Ruth was returning to the New York Giants after his suspension, and the announcement of the construction of a new baseball venue to be named the Yankee Stadium, he had noticed her picture under the words 'Star Trial Witness Still Missing.' The photograph had been taken by Eddie on their honeymoon, though the man didn't know that. What he saw was that she was smiling prettily and looked very happy. No doubt she looked different now, especially as she wouldn't want to be recognized because some people in town were undoubtedly looking to kill her. But beneath the hat brim, the dark wig and the sun-cheaters, the smile was just the same.

He'd been about to go off duty for the evening when she arrived in the lobby. 'Can I help you, miss?' he asked.

She was plainly dressed in a grey suit and flat shoes, with no accessories, though in a better outfit she would clearly be a looker.

'I hope so. I'm looking for Joe Perski,' she replied. Her voice had the slow, easy cadence of the West Coast. Looking closer he saw that her face had a healthy glow that wasn't the effect of cosmetics.

'He ain't in right now.' He'd seen Joe go out in the morning, looking grim, and he knew he hadn't come back yet, as he always stopped by his room to ask if there were any messages on his return.

Her face fell. 'Oh. He said he'd be here. But he said if he was delayed the janitor would let me into his apartment.'

'He didn't mention it when he went out.'

'It must have slipped his mind.' She smiled sweetly at him. A smile that must be the envy of many women. 'Could you, please? I guess it's against regulations, but... '

'S'okay. He should be back pretty soon. I'll show you up.'

As he showed the woman up to Joe's apartment and let her in with his passkey his heart was pounding. Again she flashed him the dazzling smile, as she closed the door. 'Thank you so much,' she said.

He was sweating on his way down to the lobby, not from the effort of climbing the stairs, but from anxiety. His mind was racing. He'd never really expected he'd be put in this situation. Now that he was, he had a terrible choice to make.

CHAPTER FIFTY ONE

The idea came to her in Los Angeles, while she was watching 'The Man From Beyond', an action movie starring the world-famous, illusionist Harry Houdini. At first it had formed in her mind like a fantasy, the childish wish-fulfillment of the kind she used to have back in her tiny, damp bedroom in Ireland. Something deeply desired, but hopelessly unattainable. But gradually, as she reclined on her terrace in the balmy afternoon air, the pieces began to fit into place like a jigsaw puzzle, and the plan grew from a dream into a potential reality. All the elements were there. Looking back it was almost as if everything that had gone before had been leading to this moment.

That it was crazy she knew. Just thinking about it brought her out in a sweat. But desperate situations sometimes required desperate remedies, and as crazy solutions went, this was the mother of them all. If it worked she would be free. Maybe for the first time in her life truly free. If it didn't, well, she would be free in another way. It was a gamble. A gamble with her life, but it was one that she had to take. She had gambled on her escape to America and found a new life. She had lived her dream, but it had turned into a hideous nightmare. Over the past few weeks she had come to know how, and where, she wanted to live her life. And she was determined. If she couldn't live it her way, why bother to live it at all? Now all she needed to do was to convince him.

Joe sat in the unmarked car, alone. In the NYPD working without a partner wasn't the norm, but since the ambush and arrest of Eddie, he'd been able to make a convincing case to pursue the case on his own terms. Across the street Eddie was holding court in the Blackbird. A creature of habit, he'd arrived in the late afternoon, which was what they had planned for. But Joe was uneasy. No, uneasy was inadequate. Terrified was closer to the mark. Not for himself, but for May.

He had arrived home from the D.A.'s office, feeling despondent. When the night duty janitor told him he had a female visitor, who the day janitor had let into his apartment, he was intrigued. As he mounted the stairs his heart began to race. What if? What if by some miracle it was May? What if she had finally decided to testify? To risk everything to bring Eddie to justice? By the time he reached his apartment door he had dismissed those thoughts as a fantasy. He had to face the fact that in forty eight hours they were due to begin prosecuting Eddie without their star witness. Opening the door he saw her, sitting nervously on the sofa.

'May!' he gasped, disbelievingly. He closed his eyes tightly and opened them again.

She smiled, that smile. 'Yes, I'm still here.' Jumping up, she rushed into his outstretched arms. They stood wrapped together silently, for a long time, their eyes closed, feeling the painful days, weeks and months of waiting ebb away. Their minds were racing. There was so much to say. Where to begin? Opening her eyes, she explored his face with a tender look. 'Joe, I -' she began at last.

He stopped her words with a kiss. Still with his lips on hers, he lifted her up and carried her into the bedroom.

After the debauched weekend on the Sound, Eddie was feeling unusually fragile. He was in The Blackbird, nursing Harry's patent pick-me-up in his private booth, when the call came. At first he was stunned, and grilled the caller urgently, asking him to repeat every detail over again. When he put the phone down, his head was spinning, but now not only from the booze. There seemed to be no doubt. She was back. And there could only be one reason for her return.

He ordered a double bourbon on the rocks from Harry behind the bar and picked up the telephone. After he had given his orders down the line, he replaced the receiver and sat in grim silence, cursing himself for relaxing his guard by spending the weekend out of contact on the water. He shook his head ruefully. He had really believed that May had gone for good. She was intelligent and knew if she gave evidence against him, she was a marked woman. That somewhere down the line he would get to her. But he should have learnt by now that May was a law unto herself and you could never predict what she would do next. Maybe that fink detective had planned it? Spiriting May out of town and lying through his teeth that he didn't know where she was. He should have ignored the chief and had his boys beat it out of him. It was too late now. She was back and would have to be dealt with. It was a pity. He'd rather she'd stayed away, and kept her mouth shut for good. Well, he would just have to do it for her.

It was the first time it had happened to him and he felt deeply embarrassed. She stroked his naked chest tenderly. 'Don't worry about it,' she said gently. 'It's all too much for me as well.'

'Really?' He felt reassured. The shock and emotion at seeing her again had overwhelmed him, being even more powerful because it was so completely unexpected. Over the past few weeks he had gradually resigned himself to the fact that he would probably never see May again. Every day, like a cancerous worm, that thought bored deeper into his soul until he felt he could bear it no longer. So when he saw her sitting on the sofa his sense of joy was indescribable. But quickly coupled with his joy came alarm. The knowledge that he would have to protect her for the next forty-eight hours until the trial. And then, realistically for the rest of her life, because even after she had told the court she had overheard the plan to kill Flaherty, it was unlikely Eddie would get the chair.

He would have to get her to the prosecutor to be taken through her evidence. The thought filled him with dread, because then the word would be out. The chief would be told May was in town and then Eddie would know. Panic gripped him. Perhaps he already knew? The janitor had seen her and what did he know about him? Eddie was thorough and resourceful, which is why they had never been able to pin a rap on him until Joe's ambush sting on Thanksgiving. It wasn't beyond Eddie's reach to bribe a lowly janitor for a few welcome bucks. He shot up in the bed.

May was startled. 'What's the matter?'

He was already out of the bed, scrambling into his clothes. 'Get up! Get dressed!' He was almost yelling.

She was concerned, hugging the bed sheet to her breast. 'Joe, what's the matter? What's wrong?'

'We've got to get you out of here. We've got to keep you safe so you can give your evidence at the trial.'

She was still sitting upright in the bed, holding the sheet to her chin. Her next words stunned him. 'But, Joe,' she said calmly, 'I'm not going to give evidence at the trial.'

CHAPTER FIFTY TWO

The two men searched the empty room, as the janitor watched nervously from the doorway.

'She was here last night.' His voice sounded cracked and dry. 'Herb said they left mid-evening. Seemed like they were in a hurry.'

The taller of the two men turned to him. He had the broad, flat face of an ex-boxer, one who had been in many fights, and lost quite a few of them. 'Who's Herb?' he grunted.

'The night duty guy. I go off at six.' He hurried on in explanation. 'Got to get home to my wife. She's sick.'

'Sorry to hear that,' said the other man flatly. He had cold, expressionless eyes that made the janitor feel uneasy.

'Medicine's such a price. Them damn swindling doctors.' He shifted uncomfortably, cleared his throat and said, 'Eddie said there was a couple of C notes in it for me.'

The two men looked at each other and then back at the old janitor. His face was sallow beneath his thinning, grey hair. He had the scrawny, weary-looking body of someone who had worked hard all his life for very little reward. An attempt at a wheedling smile twitched at the corners of his mouth.

'Sure,' said the ex-fighter, and put his right hand inside the left breast of his jacket. When it came out it was holding a gun.

The evening traffic was building outside The Blackbird. Inside the car, around the corner from the club, Joe shifted stiffly in his seat and looked at his watch. It was ten minutes before seven. They had arranged she would make the call at seven on the dot. He wiped his sweaty palms on his handkerchief and put it back in his jacket pocket. The previous evening, after he had found her a safe hotel for the night, she had outlined her plan to him. He had listened, stunned and dismayed, unable to believe what he was hearing. It had taken her almost the whole night of explaining and pleading to persuade him. He had argued till they risked coming to blows, but in the end he had agreed. He still didn't like it. In fact he hated it, but he couldn't fault her damned logic. She was right. There would never be any peace for her unless her plan worked.

Emotionally exhausted, they had not made love that night. The air was too fraught with danger. Instead they had lain together, fully clothed, holding each other tightly as if frightened the other would float away. In the morning they had made love, gently, tearfully, as if for the last time, which it could well be, if things went wrong. His life too was hanging by a thread. She had come back to him, and now only hours later, he risked losing her again, forever. If that happened he had already decided he would follow her, wherever she was going, in the hope that they would meet again, in spirit if not in body.

Absorbed in his own morbid thoughts, when a nearby taxi horn bellowed at the snarled traffic ahead, he didn't hear the rear door of the car open. The first thing he felt was the cold, hard muzzle of a pistol pressing against the base of his skull.

Eddie pushed away the plate of spaghetti untouched. The news of May's return had spoiled his appetite. He had dispatched his guys to do what had to be done, and he was confident they would deliver, but it didn't give him any pleasure. Of course he bore May a grudge. After what she had done, any normal guy would. Yet she was a beautiful young woman with all her life ahead of her. It was such a waste, and so unnecessary. He blamed the damn government for giving broads the vote. What did broads know about business? How the world really worked? Their place was in the home, in the kitchen or in the sack. Maybe the fellas were right. He had trained May too well. Now she wanted to take over. Still, it was a sad waste and he needed another bourbon to take away the bad taste in his mouth.

Harry had just put the cut-glass tumbler down in front of him and returned to the bar when the call came. Eddie looked up edgily as the shrill bell tone jangled.

'It's for you,' Harry called. There was an extension in Eddie's private booth. His hand hovered over the shiny black receiver. He was expecting them to call when the job was done. They had been quick. Taking a slug from his drink, he took a deep breath and picked up the phone.

'Yeah?'

The woman's voice surprised him. For a moment he didn't recognize her.

'Eddie..? Eddie?'

He was puzzled. She was still alive, and calling him? 'May? Is that you?'

Her voice sounded urgent, a little hesitant. 'We need to talk. I need to talk to you. Can we meet?'

'Sure, princess. Sure. Whenever you say.'

'Now. We need to talk now.'

She gave him instructions to a place across town. 'Why there?' he asked.

'It's quiet there. We need to be private...And Eddie..?'

His pulse was racing now, he couldn't believe what was happening. 'Yeah, princess?'

'Come alone. If there's anyone with you, you won't see me.'

As he was leaving the club, George, his chauffeur stood up. Eddie waved a hand at him to sit back down. Outside he got into his car, started the engine and eased the limo into the steady stream of traffic. He checked the gun in his shoulder holster. If it was a trap he was pretty sure he could take care of himself. The place she had picked was open ground with good sight lines all around. There was no way anyone could hide or sneak up on him. And there was no way that she could escape.

When the two men arrived at the garage with Joe, they told the mechanic to get lost for an hour. He had been polishing the chrome-work on his Harley and wasn't too happy to be disturbed, but knew better than to protest. They had tied Joe's hands behind his back and as soon as the mechanic left the garage, they started on their victim, pummeling him to the body and the head. The ex-prizefighter had quizzed him on the way over in the car, but he had retaliated, telling them they were in big trouble for kidnapping a detective. It was a capital offence, he told them. They would get the chair. It was obvious he was worried though. Very worried.

The one with the boxer's face was clearly the boss. 'Where's the broad?' he demanded.

Joe looked at him defiantly, but there was panic in his eyes. 'You better let me go, you jerk!'

A blow to the head sent him sprawling into a stack of discarded vehicle parts piled in the corner. As he fell he felt the sharp edge of a twisted fender cut into his back, and the moist warmth on his shirt as blood began to flow. They began to lash out at him with their shoes, which, judging from the pain they inflicted, had steel toecaps. Joe curled himself up into a ball, trying to protect his head. He had to keep a clear head and somehow get out of this. May was depending on him. And by now, Eddie would be on his way to meet her with murder on his mind.

CHAPTER FIFTY THREE

The journey across town had taken longer than he had expected. The mayor had closed a bunch of uptown streets to allow work to start on the new Yankee Stadium and the knock-on effect was causing traffic chaos all over the city. The sun was sinking as he drove onto the wharf past the silent, grey warehouses, each one locked securely for the night. Towards the end of the last century the pier had been built a long way out into the river to create a deep water berth for the larger merchant ships. At the moment the berth was empty and the pier deserted. He drove along the wooden structure, his tires drumming over the planks.

Stopping the car a little way from the end, he got out and looked around. The wide river stretched away to the East. To the West the city hummed quietly in the distance. A passing seagull's cry startled the tranquility of the scene. As the cry faded on the still evening air he heard the engine. Squinting into the setting sun he saw the Model T turn from the wharf and head towards him along the pier. He hefted his gun from his holster and stuck it into his belt within easy reach. As the car drew near, he recognized her curls, silhouetted against a bright orange sky framed in the car's rear window. His heart was pounding now. She was alone.

May stopped the car ten yards away. He watched warily as she opened the door and climbed out with some difficulty. Despite the warm spring weather she was wearing a full-length fur which bulged out at the front. Eddie frowned, surprised. She looked heavily pregnant.

'Hi, Eddie,' she called, walking clumsily towards where he was standing at the end of the pier. 'Surprise, huh?'

He shook his head. 'Are you nuts, or what?'

'We need to talk. Please?'

'I'll say this for you, May. You sure got some nerve.'

She smiled. 'Isn't that why you fell for me, Eddie?'

'You know, May, I never thought you was crazy, 'til now.'

'I was crazy before. I'm not now.' She opened her fur. She was wearing a plain blue cotton dress buttoned to the neck. Her breasts and stomach were thickly swelled. 'I wasn't going to come back. I wanted to. I wanted to so much, but I knew I couldn't. I knew I'd crossed the line.' She put her hands on her swollen belly. 'And then this came along...It's okay, Eddie. I'm not going to testify against my baby's father.'

The two men were growing tired of kicking Joe. They had concentrated their kicks on his legs, back and buttocks, as the last thing they wanted was to knock him unconscious so he couldn't answer their questions. But Joe had remained tight-lipped throughout the brutal attack. The ex-boxer stood back, panting.

'Leave him,' he instructed. 'I'll call Eddie. He won't want to miss out on the fun.'

Joe raised his head and watched as the man stomped away towards the office. His companion leant back against the side of a Buick whose hood was wide open awaiting repairs. He took out a packet of Camels, shook one out and stuck it between his lips. Joe could feel the sharp edge of the broken fender pressing into his back. He waited until the man was distracted lighting his cigarette then carefully shifted his position so the rope binding his wrists was against the knife-like edge of the fender. Keeping his eyes fixed firmly on the man, he worked at the rope behind his back. His aching body was wet with sweat. If this didn't work both he and May were dead.

Within moments he felt the strands shredding one by one. With a sharp tug he tore his hands free. The man turned at the sudden movement. His hand shot to the holster inside his jacket. Still on the ground, Joe grasped the end of the fender and hurled it at his assailant. The twisted metal cart-wheeled through the air and smashed into the man's face. Before he could recover Joe was on him. Ramming the man's head down into the open engine space of the car, Joe slammed the hood down on his neck repeatedly, until he felt him go limp. He turned at a sound from the office. The other man was lunging out of the door reaching for his gun. Yanking the unconscious man upright Joe groped inside the hoodlum's jacket for the gun nestling in the holster.

The sound of the gunshot in the confined space rang like the inside of a gigantic bell. Joe felt the impact of the bullet as it tore into the chest of the man he was holding up against him. Squeezing on the trigger Joe emptied the clip in the direction of the ex-fighter and saw blood spurt from the ruptured jugular in the man's neck. He let the dead man he was holding fall at his feet. In the sudden deafening silence Joe's ears were ringing from the echoing gunshots. His whole body slumped. He was free. But he felt no elation. There was no way he could drive across town to the pier in time. He was late. Much too late.

Standing near the edge of the pier, May was deeply worried. She had been trying to sweet-talk Eddie, to stall him, but he was growing impatient. Patience had never been his thing. She looked anxiously down the long pier towards the wharf. It was empty.

'Take me back, Eddie,' she pleaded. 'Please. I was crazy. I don't know what came over me. I guess it was Henry and poor

Mick. I'd had Mick since he was a puppy. He was my only friend for years. When he died in my arms, whimpering, and all broken and bloody, I just went crazy...I'm sorry. Give me another chance, Eddie, please.'

'They'll subpoena you, May. The D.A.s boys will work you over real good.'

'I can handle it, Eddie. You know me.'

'Do I..?'

She tried not to flinch as his took hold of her shoulders. She faked a smile and looked into his ice blue eyes. 'You and me, Eddie. Just like it used to be. It'll be better. I'll make it much better.'

His expression set hard. 'Sorry, doll.'

'Eddie!' she screamed, as she felt him try to push her off the pier. She grasped his hands and struggled to get free. 'Eddie, no!'

'Sorry, princess. I can't take that chance.'

May broke free and stumbled away along the edge of the pier. 'Eddie, please! Believe me! I'm carrying your baby!'

Eddie shrugged. 'Yeah, we never did talk about that, did we? Whadda'ya know? I hate brats.' He pulled the gun from his waistband. 'Sorry, doll.'

Joe was unfamiliar with a Harley-Davidson, but he'd ridden motorbikes before, though never one as powerful as this. He cut through the stalled traffic, weaving this way and that. At the intersection a huge truck loomed into his path, horn blaring. Gunning the screaming engine Joe hurtled the bike at full throttle across the front of the towering truck and found himself headed straight for the wall of traffic on the other side of the road. He mounted the sidewalk and tore along, scattering pedestrians in his wake. His mind was racing to find the quickest route across town. Then he remembered. Mayor Hylan had closed a whole section of the city around the scheduled new Yankee Stadium. The roads there were clear, traffic free. When he reached the cordoned area he saw a flimsy wooden barrier across the first closed street. Opening the throttle wide he smashed through it and roared down the empty tarmac. A policeman on the sidewalk blew his whistle. Joe didn't stop. He cleared his mind and focused on the road ahead.

Eddie leveled the gun and took aim. At the end of the pier May held out her hands pleading. 'Eddie, please God, no! I'll get rid of it! I promise! It'll be just you and me!'

'Sorry, doll. It's too late.'

It was all going wrong. Something had happened and her plan was falling apart. Then she heard it. The roar of a motorbike. She saw flashes of the gleaming chrome between the warehouses, and heard the tires squeal as the machine spun onto the pier. She knew if she was going to finish Eddie it had to be now. It was either her or him. And the last throw of the dice was up to her. She gritted her teeth and then spat out the words. 'Well kill me then, you bastard, or I'll take you down!'

The bullet hit her before she heard the gunshot. Falling backwards with a loud cry, she spiraled down towards the murky water below and plunged into the depths.

Eddie turned at the sound of the roaring engine, too absorbed to register it before. Man and bike were bearing down on him. He raised the gun again as Joe flung the heavy machine into a skid, sending himself and the bike barreling into Eddie. Both men were hurled, tumbling, along the pier. The gun spun along the wooden decking and flipped over the edge into the water. Eddie was first on his feet and kicked out at Joe lying winded on the boards. Twisting his body Joe grabbed the foot and pulled Eddie to the ground. Locked together both men rolled over and over towards the edge. As he rolled on top Joe's fist smashed into Eddie's face and he felt him go limp. Scrambling to his feet, Joe grabbed Eddie by the collar of his jacket and dragged him to the edge where May had fallen in. Joe's eyes frantically searched the water. The last ripples from May's fall had already faded into the wide river. The dark water below was empty.

'May!' His yell, echoing over the calm water, mingled with the siren of an approaching police car. Joe hauled Eddie up roughly by the lapels and glared savagely into his face. 'You dirty, murdering scum!'

CHAPTER FIFTY FOUR

That summer was unbearable. The temperature rose and the vast stone and concrete hothouse that was New York radiated the stored heat of the sun, morning, noon and night. Though the air-conditioning in the courthouse made it tolerable, in the street the humidity was nearing one hundred percent. So, when the usher announced to the huge waiting crowd outside that the jury was about to return to give their verdict, Joe was relieved to be able to file back into the relative cool of the courtroom along with everyone else. He found a place, standing at the back of the room, leaning against the wall which felt moist and sticky through the thin cotton of his shirt. He was tense. After the long weeks of waiting his ordeal was about to reach its conclusion.

For twenty four hours after the shooting, the police had searched the river and then gave up. At that time of the year especially, as the snows in the mountains finally melted and the water rushed downstream, the currents were unpredictable. A body could be taken anywhere, even all the way out to the ocean. Some were never found, and so it proved with May.

Despite that, the D.A.'s office was convinced Joe's evidence would be more than enough to get a conviction. As a serving NYPD detective, he had witnessed the murder at first hand, tragically arriving just too late to prevent it. In addition, the two dead men in the garage, who had kidnapped Joe to get to May, were known to be on Eddie Young's payroll. So, with Eddie behind bars with no chance of bail, the decision was taken to drop the conspiracy charge relating to Patrick Flaherty and go straight for murder one for the shooting of May.

Though no-one knew the true extent of his relationship with the murdered young woman, people suspected it had become more than just professional and everyone around Joe was sympathetic, treating him with kid gloves. In the weeks leading to the trial, he kept pretty much to himself, confiding in no one and just going about his work. On his rest days, despite many invitations from colleagues to barbecues and picnics in the park, he would take himself off out of town, to get away from it all, he said. Now the trial was over. He had sat in the witness box giving his evidence opposite May's alleged killer, facing down the efforts of the slick, high-profile defense team to discredit him. He had stood firm. Without a body, it was basically his word against Eddie's. Who would the jury believe? He was about to find out.

The jury had reached their decision quickly, having been out for a little over an hour. From experience Joe knew that could be either good or bad. With juries you could never tell. As the court rose, he could see the back of Eddie's well-groomed head standing at the front. The judge entered and took his seat, looking down, magisterially, on the packed courtroom. He was new to the circuit and had handled the trial well, dealing calmly and firmly with Eddie's frequent outbursts. As soon as everyone had resumed their seats, the all male jury entered and filed solemnly back to their places. The watching gallery was hushed as the judge addressed them.

'Gentlemen of the jury, have you reached your verdict?'

The foreman, a middle-aged, balding man with a pencil-thin moustache and an air of self-importance, rose to answer. 'We have, your honor.'

The usher took the sheet of paper from his hand and, crossing the room, handed it up to the judge, who glanced cursorily at it before continuing. 'On the charge of murder in the first degree, how do you find the defendant, Edward Theodore Youngman?'

The foreman cleared his throat and, after a theatrical pause, pronounced the verdict, 'Guilty.'

Cheering broke out among the onlookers. The judge banged his gavel vigorously and shouted, 'Order! Order in court!'

As the noise subsided Eddie sprang to his feet, shouting angrily, 'They never found no body! Where's the body? They never found no body!'

A week after the trial the mortuary called him. He went straight over and then made arrangements to bring Eddie from his cell on Riker's Island. Joe had known the superintendant of the mortuary since the day he had arrived, as a fifteen year old, to see his dead father lying on a slab. Since then, through his work, the two men had met several times and had become good drinking buddies, sharing beers and stories until the Volstead Act and prohibition put a stop to such heinous activities. As Joe and the superintendant waited in the grey stone doorway, the spiraling heat of the day at last gave way to the thunderstorm that had been threatening all morning. A brilliant lightning flash illuminated the prison van as it drove up to the door in the pouring rain. Joe and the superintendant exchanged a glance as Eddie, manacled at wrist and ankles, was hustled from the rear of the van by two prison guards to the accompaniment of a rolling peal of thunder.

The superintendant led the way, along the tiled corridor and into the bleak, neon-lit room. Watched over by an attendant, the metal trolley stood in the centre, the body entirely covered by a white sheet. Joe stood alongside Eddie as the superintendant gave a brief nod. The attendant pulled back the sheet covering the head and shoulders of the young woman. The body was badly bloated and discolored from lying so long in the water. Some hungry fish, or perhaps a passing boat's propeller, had rendered the features unrecognizable. It could have been May, or any other unfortunate girl whose young life had gone tragically wrong.

Eddie glanced down at the gruesome remains impassively. He turned to Joe, 'So?'

Joe reached under the sheet and lifted up the arm. 'Recognize this?' Almost enveloped by the bloated, blackened flesh of the finger was the brilliant-cut diamond ring May had made from the one stone she had kept back from the Chicago robbery.

Eddie looked away guiltily. 'Take me back,' he muttered to the guards.

Not a soul from the Blackbird Club attended the funeral. The general conclusion was that May had got what she deserved. That she had thrown away a chance others would sell their grandmother for. Deprived of his club's best customer, 'An ungrateful, stupid Mick bitch,' was Harry's verdict. So Joe stood alone in the veil of warm rain as the priest intoned the service. When he had finished he shook Joe's hand and walked away leaving Joe looking down at the coffin lying at the bottom of the soggy grave. Taking his gold badge from his overcoat pocket he tossed it into the grave, then turned and walked heavily away.

In his tiny room Joe packed the last of his belongings, the ones he wanted to take, into his suitcase. Apart from a few clothes, they were mostly memories. Photographs of his parents in happier times, a wax crayon portrait of his mother he had drawn as a six year old which she hadn't taken with her to new life, his father's badge, his citation's and medal's for bravery and public service, the well-worn baseball mitt father and son had played with on the wasteland behind their tenement building. And finally, the only photograph he had of her, smiling that smile, holding Mick in front of the Statue of Liberty.

The chief had seemed very relieved to see him go. Joe guessed it had to do with his father, who had been the chief's partner all those years ago. The man behind him on the day he met his death in the alley. Joe wondered about that. But, whatever the truth, it was too late now. There were some wrongs you couldn't right, some battles you couldn't fight on your own. Like everything else he regretted, he had to let it go.

The businessman got on the train at Chicago and struck up a conversation with the handsome young man sitting over a club soda in the restaurant car.

'I used to be a New York cop,' the young man told him, 'but I got out. It's a dirty business.'

'So where're you headed now?'

'California. Always wanted to live in the sunshine.'

'You got work out there?'

'I plan to set up a detective agency in Los Angeles.' He grinned. 'Going to clean up the city.'

The businessman grinned in return. 'Single-handed?'

'Oh, I'm not alone.' As he spoke there was a yapping sound and a small brown dog bounced up to Joe and licked his hand. He picked it up. 'This is Micky.'

The businessman patted the little dog's head. Then they both turned as another passenger entered the dining car. She was a beautiful young woman, slim and elegant, with a crop of dark brown curls. Joe rose as she approached their table. He looked down at his companion and smiled. 'May I introduce my wife, Mrs Mary Perski?'

The businessman rose and shook the woman's small, but surprisingly strong, hand. 'Glad to know you.'

The woman gave him a radiant smile. She had the most amazing emerald green eyes. 'Likewise.'

The man looked at her more closely. 'Say, don't I know you?'

'It's not likely.'

'No, you're famous. I saw your picture in the paper.'

The woman laughed prettily. 'You're thinking of Chicago May. People say we could have been twins.'

'Yeah, that's it. Chicago May. The con-woman. She was murdered, wasn't she? Poor kid. May she rest in peace.'

May grinned and took Joe's arm. 'Somehow I don't think she will.'

The speeding train headed west towards the sparkling ocean, far away over the horizon.

Lightning Source UK Ltd.
Milton Keynes UK
173561UK00001B/1/P